Taming the Lyon

by

Loretta C. Rogers

Taming the Lyon

Cover Art by *Debbie Taylor*

The Wild Rose Press, Inc.
PO Box 708
Adams Basin, NY 14410-0708
Visit us at www.thewildrosepress.com

Publishing History
First Vintage Rose Edition, 2017
Print ISBN 978-1-5092-1609-3
Digital ISBN 978-1-5092-1610-9

Published in the United States of America

Margaret unbuckled the straps on her leather satchel and removed her journal, pen, and ink bottle. Sitting on the edge of the cot, she realized she was holding her breath. Using meticulous care, she uncorked the bottle of ink and dipped her pen.

Mombasa

December 1909

No one prepared me for Africa's beauty and dangers. No one prepared me for Jeremiah Lyon. Great White Hunter. Dangerous. He is arrogant, terrifying, and oh, so magnificent. It shakes me to the very core that he instills unsettling emotions inside me.

Pen poised, she listened to the voices. She wondered what had caused Lyon's gusty laughter, and prickled at the thought of being the subject of the men's conversation. She ran her tongue around her lower lip. Realizing guiltily the direction her thoughts were taking, she focused on memories of Seamus. She sighed. He had once dubbed her the "iron maiden." She was too brusque, too angry, too closed off when dealing with people. Not great qualities for a doctor. Seamus had later explained that he'd meant it as a compliment, that she was in control, and that is what he admired about her.

Other books by Loretta C. Rogers
available from The Wild Rose Press, Inc.

Murder in the Mist
Shadowed Reunion
Cloud Woman's Spirit
Lady Adel's Captain
The Witching Moon
Forbidden Son
Bannon's Brides
McKenna's Woman
Isabelle and the Outlaw

Dedication

To my friend Margaret Boynton
who has never been to Africa
but is bold enough to create her own adventures,
and
to Kay, who tamed the real Lyon

Dear Readers,

My love for the jungle and the animals that inhabit it was instilled at a young age when the Tarzan movies were popular on the big screen and then television. It has always been my dream to take my camera and go on an African safari.

In *Taming the Lyon*, which is set in early 1900s East Africa, I have done my best to bring to you the feel and flavor of the Dark Continent. I have made a special effort to portray some of the cultural diversity of the area through the use of names, dialects, words, phrases, and customs. A glossary of these words and phrases can be found at the back of the book.

For book clubs, I have included a list of general questions that will help you lead a discussion for a fiction romance novel.

Of the many dialects in Africa, Swahili is the most common. Most words can be found in a Swahili-to-English dictionary. The rest are unique to the vernacular, words and phrases that evolved out of necessity to fit the environment and the people in it.

In a world where we are increasingly pressured to conform and homogenize, ethnic diversity is a precious gift. My thanks to the people of Africa and the world who strive to protect Africa's national parks and the wildlife that is rapidly becoming endangered species.

Asante
Loretta C. Rogers

Part I

"To say goodbye is to die a little."
~Raymond Chandler

Chapter 1

York, England, 1909

Margaret Ashton Boynton wanted to feel the cold. She wanted it to leach into her bones, to freeze the anguish gnawing at her heart. She wanted to stitch the vicar's lips together, to shut out his droning words. She wanted to lie between the two gaping holes, close her eyes, and wait for the gravediggers to shovel the wintery, rain-sodden dirt over her face.

The cadence of splatters against a sea of black umbrellas thrummed in Margaret's ears and grated against her fragile nerves. Just when she was certain the pallid scarecrow's shrill voice would send her into a fit of screaming hysteria, he said, "Amen."

"Father," she whispered to the man standing next to her, "escort me to the house. I fear I will embarrass you by fainting."

He spoke low and firm. "Can you not endure a few more minutes? Protocol, you know."

She placed the lace hankie to her lips to catch the sob. "Then bloody damn these pompous fools. I cannot bear to watch my beautiful son and gentle husband placed in icy dark graves. I don't give a fig about your *protocol*."

Oblivious to the rain and without an umbrella, Margaret pivoted on her heel and strode toward the estate house.

"Margaret!" Her father called from beneath his umbrella.

Lifting her heavy woolen skirt, she hastened her steps.

"Margaret Mary!" Thunder swallowed his voice as he yelled again. She paid little heed to the sharp edges of his command as she pushed through the curtain of heavy mist. A root snagged the heel of her high-buttoned black leather boots. Her hands and arms flailed outward as she sprawled forward. The impact whooshed the breath from her.

Strong arms lifted her from the muddy mire. "Beg pardon, milady. I mean no familiarity, but me missus would ne'er forgive me if I 'lowed ye to catch yer death."

Margaret wasn't sure if her chest hurt from the fall or from the grief that threatened to steal away her breath. "Thank you, Finley."

Rain lashed her face, the streaming rivulets on her cheeks blending with her tears to puddle in a salty pool in the cleft above her upper lip. A soppy hank of auburn hair dangled in her eyes. Her vision blurred so that she could no longer clearly see the graves. Not that it mattered. The downpour had made fast work of flattening the freshly mounded dirt.

She didn't speak another word. And when he carried her up the steps of the manor house, she simply looked at the staff lined against the wall like soldiers standing at attention. She didn't nod and neither did they. They just looked at her, their eyes silent with obvious grief.

Weary to the bone, she allowed Finley to carry her

up the stairs. He opened the door to her bedroom and gently laid her upon the large four-poster bed. The bed she had shared with Seamus. She didn't cry. She kept thinking she should—kept feeling like she needed to.

"She be sodden through and through, Agatha."

Finley's wife clapped her hands together, her voice sharp as a peal of thunder when she commanded the young chambermaids. "Don't stand there gawping wid yer mouths 'angin' open. 'Ot water and lots o' it." She offered her husband a slight turn of a smile. "Ye done good. Fer shame on that stone-'earted ole totter, makin' our Margaret stand in the storm like she was born wid ne'er feelin's."

"Watch yer words, wife. The walls 'ave ears and blatherin' tongues."

The elderly woman answered with a sharp nod. "Go mind yer business whilst we take care of our Margaret a'fore she catches a chill."

The words mingled like gibberish inside Margaret's head. She conjured a vision of her favorite childhood rag doll.

Rag doll. That was how she felt as the wet clothing was stripped from her body, her hair toweled dry, her arms and legs bathed with soothing hot water, and a flannel gown pulled over her head, arms guided through the sleeves, and then a quilt pulled to her chin. She barely heard the words spoken to her, or the closing of the bedchamber door.

She could only stare at the bed's maroon-and-gold brocade canopy. Odd that she focused on a wayward strand of dust clinging like a thread of gray string. What must it have been like for her beloved husband and son in those final moments? Had they clung to life as desperately as this strand of gray?

She didn't remember succumbing to sleep until a voice intruded into her silent sanctuary. Margaret placed her hands over her eyes to shield them from the sun.

"Good morning, milady. 'Tis good to see ye're awake. We worried that you 'ad slipped into a permanent malaise."

"How long have I slept, Agatha?"

"Nigh on three days. Do you plan to go down for breakfast, or shall I bring you a tray?"

The maid's perky voice irritated Margaret. Had the dunderheaded woman no respect?

"Tea and toast in my room will do."

Margaret wobbled as she stood, and grasped the bed post to steady herself. The room seemed to spin out of control, and she collapsed against the bed.

"Beggin' your pardon, milady, but ye be needin' mor'n tea and toast. I'll have cook make ye a plate of sausage and eggs, clotted cream and crisp bread with jam."

The maid turned back. "A new medical journal come fer ye. 'Tis there on your readin' desk."

Silver streams of sunlight shone through the window and fell across Margaret's bed. Before long, her mind somersaulted with the events of the funeral. Restless, she scooted to prop against the pillows and pulled her knees to her chin. A feeling of total failure washed over her as she stared pensively at the portrait of husband and son. Her sole purpose for living had died when the gravediggers had tossed the last shovel of dirt on the soggy mound. She slapped a fist against the palm of her hand. *I should have been with them. I should have died, too.* She prayed the men responsible for her loved ones' deaths would rot in hell.

She buried her hands in her face. What was it the constable had said…a shot had spooked the horses, and rounding a bend in the road the carriage had overturned, crushing her precious son, and a bullet had ended her already wounded husband's life.

A shroud of doom wrapped its mystic arms around her, and she sobbed long, gulping sobs.

By the time she opened her eyes, dusk had fallen. A lighted lamp cast eerie shadows against the wall. Margaret concluded the maid had slipped in and out of the room without disturbing her sleep.

Sliding barefoot from the bed, Margaret padded to the mahogany rolltop desk and picked up the medical journal. The last thing on her mind was medicine and treating patients. Her emotions were still too raw. Within the darkness of her refuge she idly flipped through the pages.

Bold black letters drew her attention. *Africa.* Barely realizing the maid had entered the room with a tray of food, Margaret scanned the article, and then reread it word for word, line for line.

A kernel of an idea formulated as she read. She lifted the gold-rimmed demitasse cup and drank deeply, as if to reinforce her decision.

Later in the evening, and without knocking, she walked into her father's study. "I'm going to Africa, Father."

She almost laughed out loud when the pen fell from his fingers, leaving a dark moist stain on the stack of papers in front of him. "The devil you say! Have you lost your mind?"

Loretta C. Rogers

"On the contrary, Father. I quite believe I've found it."

He harrumphed. "Margaret, you have always been a wayward girl. I indulged your whims to become a doctor, when a respectable woman would have settled for becoming a nurse. Why couldn't you be more like your sisters? You even married beneath your social status, to that ne'er-do-well Irishman."

Margaret leaned forward to place her hands firmly on the desk. She spoke between clenched teeth. "My sisters are simpering twits who married the idiots you picked out for them, and why? To add more wealth to your already burgeoning coffers." Her eyes squinted, revealing the anger that seethed inside her. "Although you considered him otherwise, Seamus was from the upper gentry. I know how you hated him, but he was a gifted artist, a gentle soul, and a wonderful father. Much more than I can say for you."

"Watch your tongue, daughter, or I'll…"

Anger flushed her cheeks. "Or you'll what, Father? Disinherit me? Banish me? Well, fret yourself no more. I have already sent Finley to post my letter of interest for the position."

Hiram Douglas Ashton scrubbed his hands over his face. "If you insist on pretending you are a doctor, then why not stay in York? You know nothing of Africa. It is disease-ridden, rife with dangerous animals, and the people are even more dangerous. They don't call it the Dark Continent for nothing, you know."

Margaret sighed. "I *am* a doctor, Father. You should know. After all, you paid for my education."

"Nonetheless, I'll get you a commission at the hospital in London, I'll buy you a seat on the medical board." He cast his hands wide. "Make me understand why you want to traipse about some god-awful land filled with savages."

Straightening to her full height, she was thoughtful for a moment, weighing her words, not certain why she felt compelled to leave England. The words clawed at her throat when she finally rasped, "My husband and child are dead. I am no longer a wife, and no longer a mother, and a hospital in London would only remind me of all I have lost. I don't know who I am or what my purpose in life is. I honestly don't think I've ever known who I am." She walked to the large window and gazed beyond the manicured yard to the family gravesite. She swallowed a building sob. "Perhaps in Africa, if I can heal the sick, I can find a purpose to continue living."

Anguish burst inside of her as she folded her hands against her chest and faced him. "How can you not understand, Father?"

He had never been a man to show affection, so as she watched the stoicism fade from his face, surprise overtook her when he pushed from his chair, rounded the desk, and folded her into his arms. "I know a little something of your anguish, my child. I don't think I've ever fully recovered from your mother's tragic death. So young and beautiful. You were but eight years old, and yet you continually remind me of her. You are also just as strong willed." A great sigh heaved from his chest. "Go with my blessings, Margaret, and when you find yourself, I hope you will return home."

Chapter 2

Margaret reclined against the sun-blistered leather chair, gripping the brim of her pith helmet to keep the breeze from toppling it from her head. The tails of the white silk scarf bound around the crown fluttered in the wind. She gave a deep contented sigh. A welling of excitement filled her as she gazed at the vast land that was to be her new home. The shooshing of the boat's bow slicing the dark waters like a knife, the grunts of hippos, blended with the shrill cacophony of water birds and the ka-chug-a-chug of the riverboat's motor, all created its own rhythmic music as the captain guided them down the Congo River.

Captain Buchmeir was squat and plump, and though he had come highly recommended for his skill on the river, she considered him of dubious character. The African sun had parched his skin to the hue of a prime russet apple. She now questioned her decision against disembarking at Léopoldville and instead opting to continue upriver rather than waiting a month for the guide her father had hired to escort her to Angel of Mercy Medical Compound. Against his better judgment, he had contacted an old Army friend with connections in Africa to make contact with a hunter who led safaris and captured animals to sell to European and Russian circuses.

She had leaned over the side to catch a spray of

water when the captain's voice scolded her. "*Nein, nein, Frau* Doctor." He pointed to the shore. "They are particularly fond of English meat." And then he laughed at his own joke.

Margaret chose to ignore the man's crude witticism as she the peered more carefully at the logs lining the riverbank. She shaded her eyes against the white glare. "What are *they*?"

"Crocodiles, *Frau*." He slowed the boat to a stop and then spoke in a language she didn't understand. One well-muscled man grabbed a spear attached to a coil of hemp rope. He drew back and with a quick thrust sent it spiraling into the water. He grinned widely as he brought up a fish and held it as if it were a trophy. His teeth shone in contrast against his ebony skin as he removed the flopping body from the prongs and tossed it into the water. The logs lining the shores came alive, rapidly slithering from the banks, and within minutes surrounded the boat.

Margaret gasped and took a step backward. Fear and repulsion were replaced by temper as the captain guffawed. "Crocs are especially fond of humans."

She shot him a glare that caused his tanned face to redden. "You are a disgusting, vulgar man, Captain. May I remind you that it is my money paying passage on this decrepit heap you call a boat, and it is my father's influence that can ruin your reputation. How much longer before we arrive at Ngomo landing?"

A sneer replaced the smirk on his bewhiskered face as he turned back to the wheel. "One hour, *Frau* Doctor."

She glanced at the watch that resembled a brooch, and marked the time. Two hours later, the captain sounded three loud blasts as the boat rounded a bend in the river.

Margaret gathered her skirts and black leather satchel. She watched the bearers lift crate after crate of medical supplies and then her personal steamer trunks onto broad dark shoulders that glistened with sweat as they made their way down the gangplank into waist-deep murky water.

"Captain Buchmeir, surely you do not expect me to swim ashore? I was assured an escort to the Angel of Mercy Medical Compound in Mombasa."

Her skirt billowed, buffeted by the wind, and strands of copper-red hair escaped from her neat chignon to tickle the nape of her neck. She stared at the land that was to be her home for an interminable amount of time. She loosed a shuddering sigh and allowed the sadness to sweep over her as she thought about Seamus and how much he would have loved such an adventure to live among the native people, to write about them, to capture their images in his art journal.

The captain's gravelly voice intruded on her privacy. "Look there, Doctor. He has arrived. The Lyon."

Following the captain's gaze, she said, "What is this hunter's name?"

"As I said, he is the Lyon."

"Surely you don't mean as in the animal?"

The captain pulled the chewed stogie from his mouth, hawked a wad, and spat in the water. "*Bwana* Lyon. Spelled with a 'y' but just as dangerous as the jungle cat. I will pray for your safety." He emulated a throaty growl as he formed his beefy hands into talons and clawed at the air.

Revulsion coiled in her abdomen, sending chills to prickle her arms. According to her research, lions had been known to enter villages and drag people out of their homes. Could this man who was to guide her to the hospital be as fierce as the captain implied?

She squinted as she lifted a hand to shade her eyes from the sun's brilliant white glare.

Beyond the shoreline loomed a lush green jungle. Even from where she stood, a variety of colored flowers, thick vines, and numerous unidentifiable flora and fauna greeted her. Hippos' grunting mingled with the chittering of birds. Everything gave the impression of being cool and thick, and dangerous.

Bwana Lyon stood taller than any man she had ever met, including her Seamus. Her first impression was that of a scowling baboon. Of course, she'd only seen drawings of such animals.

A hundred thoughts, a hundred concerns, rushed through her mind. A sting of apprehension caused her a moment's distress.

"What is he waiting for, Captain?"

"For the bearers to get ashore with your many crates, *Frau* Doctor."

A blush tinted her cheeks. "Oh, for pity's sake. Why can't you move this barge closer, or why isn't there a pier for civilized folk to disembark without getting wet?"

The captain's condescending smile and cocked eyebrow further evoked her temper. "*Frau* Doctor, this is Africa, not London. The water is not deep enough to get closer to the beach." The intensity of his German accent rose. "Und the *Wilhelmina* ain't no barge. She ist a first class riverboat."

Margaret blinked, then leaned against the rail. She stood silent for a long moment. Watching. Watching the man called Lyon emerge from the shadows, stealthily as a cat, a large rifle cradled in the crook of his arm. A revolver hung from his waist.

The man stalking toward her seemed to take stock of her character. As he neared, her eyes went to the necklace around his neck. A necklace of large yellowed teeth. Her gaze meandered to his face. Handsome. Chisled. Flawed. Old scars that resembled deep gouges. Perhaps from the claws of a big cat.

A natural masculine confidence emanated from him. She was acutely aware that his dark piercing gaze was assessing her. The enigmatic eyes of this tall, broad-shouldered stranger held no adoration or humility. She looked away in confusion.

****

Jeremiah Lyon stood in the shadows, studying the woman. Not counting Mother Superior and the Sisters at St. Dominic's Cathedral, and the mulatto whores at the Crystal Palace, how long had it been since he'd seen a white woman? He discounted the safari six months ago with the Duke and Duchess of Hamburg. At the age of sixty, the dour-faced duchess was no beauty and well past her prime. Perhaps last year, when he'd escorted a shipment of baboons to Léopoldville? Ah, yes, the magistrate's wife. Skin the color of cream, tawny hair, and eyes as blue as the sky and as hungry as a lioness in heat. He shifted to ease the discomfort in his groin as he swallowed back the memory of her unexpected visit to his room.

Lyon studied the woman doctor for a long moment. He was overcome by the sudden urge to unclasp her hands and loosen her shoulders so that she didn't appear so…knotted up. He mused at the way she toyed with the buttons on her suit. She looked like a princess. A very nervous princess. He noted the high color on her cheeks. By the square of her shoulders and the tilt of her chin, she seemed strong, resilient—but she would not be hardy enough to survive the jungle.

He drew up an eyebrow and heightened his scowl. He had backed men down with his glare. The beautiful woman doctor didn't so much as flinch. This goaded his temper. Why would a woman of obvious wealth and social standing give up a life of luxury to live in a land where danger lurked around every bush?

Disgruntled because he had a great deal of work to do before he left for the Okavanga Delta to hunt a rogue lion, he let his frown deepen.

"*Bwana*, why you tink dis one mama, she hab so many crates?"

Lyon shrugged. "Don't know much 'bout white women, and can't say I know anything 'bout a woman doctor."

"I tink dis mama daktor, she bring bad *juju*."

"Bad luck? Why?"

"Her hair. It bleeds like the sun. Bad *juju*."

"M'pika, you think too much."

Buchmeir's voice bellowed, "Lyon, tide's going out. Light a fire under your boys. Otherwise I'll be stuck here for a week."

Lyon stepped from his shady spot and allowed long strides to carry him toward the river bank. He offered a smug salute to the captain. Cupping his hands to his mouth to amplify his command, he bellowed, "*Harakisha!* Hurry up! Get those crates ashore."

He handed his rifle to M'pika. "Settle the boys while I go get her highness."

Without thought, he waded into the dark waters made murkier by the trail of men shouldering their heavy burdens ashore.

With hands on hips nearly submerged, he stared speculatively up at her for several seconds. "Hmm," he finally grunted. "So you're one of those."

"I'm certain I don't understand your meaning. One of those?" she demanded.

He gave no direct answer and instead held out his arms and ordered, "Jump."

"What?"

"Listen, Princess. I don't have all day. Either jump into my arms or jump into the water and wade ashore. Your choice."

She clutched her medical bag, then gathered her skirts and drew in a deep breath. "Oh, for pity sake. You are a despicable cad."

As she sailed into the waiting arms, Captain Buchmeir called out, "See ya in a month, Lyon."

Ignoring the boatman's raucous laughter, Lyon cradled Margaret against his chest and waded past the last bearer, who struggled with an apparently extra-heavy trunk.

Lyon inhaled her delicate scent. It smelled of cleanliness, fresh air, and something more elusive but nice. He didn't want to let her go. This emotion agitated him as he stood her on the edge of the shore. Water lapped across her expensive, hand-tooled boots. She let out a shrill scream as a long dark body slithered across the toes of her feet. "S-snake!"

Her shrill scream startled the man carrying the

heavy chest, and he lost his balance. The cumbersome box slid from his brawny shoulder to land on his foot. He let out a pained yelp.

Lyon reached forward and scooped up the black water snake. He thrust it toward her. "Lucky for you this one is harmless. Better learn the difference, Princess. Africa is home to a dozen or more whose bite is poisonous enough to kill you before you can say, 'Don't.' " He tossed the reptile into the water and watched it swim away.

She snatched her medical bag from his grip. "My name isn't Princess. It's Doctor. Doctor Margaret Boynton, and you will address me by my proper title."

****

At that moment, Margaret would have liked to kick Lyon in the shins, but she knew her safe travel to the hospital depended upon him and decided not to incur his wrath.

She squatted next to the moaning man and gently lifted his foot. Wild-eyed, he jerked away and mumbled unintelligible words. Looking over her shoulder at the white hunter, she commanded, "Tell him I won't hurt him."

Voices all around her seemed to open fire in loud angry volleys; bare feet stamped the ground, and fingers pointed. Lyon shouted in Swahili, "Settle down. Respect that she is *wajinga* of the jungle." His authority silenced the rumblings as he spoke. He nodded for her to proceed.

"How bad is it, Princ…" The forbidden word trailed off. "Can he travel, Doctor?"

She probed the black flesh. "No broken bones. A bad bruise. He'll limp for a few days." She reached into her bag and drew out a round tin. "What is his name?"

"Y'ro."

"Tell him this is salve. It will take the soreness away."

Lyon translated. "I told him it was magic. These people are born and live with all kinds of superstitions." The tone of his voice shifted to sarcasm. "Several crates are stamped 'Bourbon.' While I enjoy a couple of evening nips, I don't abide drunkenness. Makes a person careless, and careless gets you dead. You a heavy drinker, *Doctor*?"

Margaret recapped the tin of balm and stowed it inside her medical bag. She opened a bottle of witch hazel to cleanse her hands. She stood up straight. "Whether I imbibe or not is none of your business. However, to satisfy your perverse curiosity, Dr. Williams ordered the spirits. Alcohol has many medicinal properties and can be substituted for some modern medicine, items I could not bring with me." Without giving him a chance to respond, she hurried on. "Why do you dislike me, Mr. Lyon? Do I make you feel inferior?"

He gazed beyond her as if searching for something he'd lost. "Why did you come to Africa?"

"First, I'm a physician, and second, Dr. Williams sent a letter to the hospital board in London requesting medical supplies and an assistant." At the great sound of the riverboat weighing anchor, she swallowed back the doubt clouding her decision to leave England. "My reasons for answering the call are personal. However, I believe I can make a difference in bringing updated medical techniques, equipment, and newer medicines to my colleague."

He was blunt. "You're not the first middle-aged woman who has thought she had the health and vigor"—he cleared his throat—"and mental flexibility to make a life for herself in a hostile environment."

She gasped. It was the first time anyone had ever referred to her as middle-aged. Thirty wasn't old by any standards. She felt every nerve in her body tightening. Even to her own ears, her words sounded brittle. "I don't know that I came to Africa to make a life for myself."

He looked at her hard and long. "Other than bringing medical supplies to the hospital, then, why did you come?"

He'd asked a simple question. She expected to see a sneer on his lips, to hear sarcasm in the words, but there were neither. The question put her on the defensive, yet she was aware that, in spite of anything and everything, she respected this man. Respected that like herself, he harbored inner wounds that needed healing.

"We're at an impasse, Mr. Lyon. You didn't answer my question—do I make you feel inferior?"

"There's no mister in front of my name. It's Lyon. Nothing more. As for feeling inferior to you—" He didn't finish his sentence nor answer her question. Instead he pierced her with a sneer she would never forget.

As the sun turned orange and went sliding down toward the horizon, Lyon issued an order. "Time's wasting. One hour of daylight left, at best. M'pika, get the boys moving."

"Why do you call them boys when they're grown men? Isn't that rather insulting?"

Lyon laughed like an impish child. "You have a lot to learn, Doctor. In Africa, all males are called boys, whether they are *totos* from ages six to twelve or white-haired grandfathers of sixty or more. It's no different than in England, where you have servants." He cocked an eyebrow that seemed to offer a challenge.

Margaret felt her cheeks heat. She shot him a look of disgust. "Surely these men are not slaves."

"No, ma'am. Slaves are free labor. *You* have already paid the wages of these workers."

M'pika barked orders at the boys, who hefted crates onto their shoulders. Single file, they wound their way along a narrow path parallel to the river.

Lyon took up the rear position, his heavy elephant gun propped against his shoulder. "Try to keep up, Doctor."

Margaret raised a crumpled handkerchief to her face and blotted away the sweat that ran down her forehead. The day had turned into a steam bath. Her white shirt was soaked through. Her linen jacket hung on her like damp wallpaper. She wanted desperately to take a cool soak in a bathtub. Determined not to lag behind, she hardly broke stride as she followed behind Y'ro, the limping man.

Chapter 3

She thought this day would never end. Her new boots pinched her feet, and her legs ached from the long hour of walking. Hot and sticky and tired, Margaret soon learned that tropical Africa had no twilight. The sun sank below the horizon with a rosy afterglow which quickly shaded into purple, and then unexpectedly the stars twinkled away as if tangled in the branches of the tall jungle trees.

She wiped perspiration from her face with a lace handkerchief. In England, she never perspired. Ladies in polite society didn't sweat. Resolute not to complain, she dropped wearily into a canvas chair.

When the camp was made and the tents set up, the boys went about their own settling in. They cooked their suppers, no two using the same campfire, but no two campfires more than a few feet in distance from each other.

"Mr. Lyon, why do these men call you *bwana* if they are not slaves and you are not their master?" She was proud of knowing one African word.

"Some people might interpret it as that." His words were noncommittal, but something in his tone caused her to look at him.

"Has it another meaning?"

"It can also mean 'brother,' if the brother is older or well-beloved." He hesitated a second and then went on. "You notice that M'pika calls you 'Mama Daktor'?"

"Yes, I wondered about that."

"Many will call you 'Mama,' and perhaps even '*bwana*.' Only respect will be meant. Do not insult the people by rejecting the title."

She acknowledged this information with a slight tilt of her head, pride warring for control of her expression.

"You've asked me a great many questions. I have one for you, Doctor."

"Of course. I have no secrets."

"We all have secrets. Some more than others, but we'll save that for another time. Why is it a woman of your position does not have a female companion or a maid traveling with you?"

She took her time to weigh the answer. "In my father's house, there are many servants. Most of them are up in age and not fit for rigorous travel. My personal maid is a mother. I could not ask her to leave her children for an unknown amount of time." She hesitated as if collecting her thoughts. She peered into the darkness before she continued. "I suppose I need to prove to myself that I am an independent woman and can take care of my own needs. What better place to prove that than the wilds of Africa."

Lyon made a face that was a cross between a smile and a frown. "The jungle consumes everything. It preys on the old, the sick, the wounded. It preys on the weak. Go home, madam. Go back to England."

Searching for a suitable answer, she stared at him. "I am a doctor. I came to bring my knowledge of medicine and healing to the patients at the hospital, and to any who need me. Know this, Mr. Lyon—I am not old or sick or wounded, or weak, and for the last time, I will not return to England."

His mouth was set in sterner lines. He looked tough and dangerous, like a predator, and she couldn't help second-guessing her judgment in following him out here. Then he smiled, teeth flashing bright in the gloom, dimples cutting into his cheeks, and the world seemed to tilt on its axis beneath her feet.

After a meager supper of fried potatoes and canned beans heated over hot coals, Margaret relaxed in a folding chair, a cup of coffee in her hand. "Why do the men crowd so close together?"

"Protection."

Margaret stiffened as she scanned the perimeter of the encampment. "From what?"

"Hear that?"

In spite of the heat, the deep throaty bellows chilled her. "Strange gruntings."

"Exactly." His calm voice did not temper the danger. "Hippos. They are feisty critters."

"But we're on land. Surely we aren't in danger from them?"

Lyon leaned forward. He braced his elbows against his knees and rolled the tin cup between his hands. He skewed a look toward her. "Do you know how to shoot a rifle?"

"Yes, I'm a fair shot. I often hunted on my father's game preserve."

His voice was low and smooth. "This is not England, and you won't be shooting pheasant. The river has many hippos. They are big, dangerous, and on land can outrun a man, and they feed mainly at night. It's not uncommon for a hippo to leave the river and charge a camp."

Heaving an indignant sigh, Margaret quipped, "A target that large would certainly be difficult to miss. However, since you are the expert, where do you suggest I might aim my rifle?"

"Hippos have very small brains. For a quick kill, between the eyes is your best target. If you miss, or your rifle jams, run like hell for the nearest tree."

She tensed, then forced herself to relax. "Are you always so crass, Mr. Lyon?"

He continued to pierce her with his stare. "They eat meat, Doctor."

She stood abruptly, causing the chair to tip over. "If you're trying to frighten me…you are…well…" She tossed the remainder of the coffee into the fire, sending a shower of red winking sparks into the air. "Goodnight, Mr. Lyon."

The echo of his laughter followed her as she strode to her tent. "Welcome to the Dark Continent, Doctor."

Once inside her tent, Margaret huffed about the small enclosure. She rarely cried, which made the tears that burned behind her eyes that much more frustrating. She unbuckled the straps on her leather satchel and removed her journal, pen, and ink bottle. Sitting on the edge of the cot, she realized she was holding her breath. Using meticulous care, she uncorked the bottle of ink and dipped her pen.

Mombasa
December 1909

No one prepared me for Africa's beauty and dangers. No one prepared me for Jeremiah Lyon. Great White Hunter. Dangerous. He is arrogant, terrifying, and oh, so magnificent. It shakes me to the very core that he instills unsettling emotions inside me.

Pen poised, she listened to the voices. She wondered what had caused Lyon's gusty laughter, and prickled at the thought of being the subject of the men's conversation. She ran her tongue around her lower lip. Realizing guiltily the direction her thoughts were taking, she focused on memories of Seamus. She sighed. He had once dubbed her the "iron maiden." She was too brusque, too angry, too closed off when dealing with people. Not great qualities for a doctor. Seamus had later explained that he'd meant it as a compliment, that she was in control, and that is what he admired about her.

Exhaustion taking its toll, she stored her writing materials in the satchel.

Margaret undressed down to her chemise and, as Lyon had instructed, turned her boots upside down on the knobs at the end of the cot to keep out scorpions and other unwanted creatures. She crawled between the sheets, sat up, and untied the lacings that held the mosquito netting out of the way. The cascade of gauzy material reminded her of a gigantic bassinet. An overwhelming sadness gripped her as she thought of her son. She squeezed her eyes shut to conjure an image of Jonathan's beaming smile and blue eyes. All she saw was his lifeless, mud-splattered body. Tears welled, and she stifled a sob.

She rolled to her side and listened to the fearsome night sounds just outside the canvas walls of her tent. Hippos splashed and grunted up and down the river…*URRnnt, UUrrrnnnt*…so loudly she pulled the pillow over her head to shut out the noise. She reached beneath the netting and touched the rifle for reassurance. Africa, the Dark Continent, had sounded so romantic. Why had she believed coming here would erase her grief, would make her feel whole again? Self-doubt crowded her thoughts, and she questioned her judgment in coming here. Surely tomorrow would be a better day. She hoped.

She loosed a ragged sigh. The urge to cry grew stronger, and she blinked. Feeling oddly numb, she stared at nothing. She tried to assemble the past few months into a meaningful whole so she could grasp exactly where she was and where she was headed. Africa was not as romantic as she had imagined. It truly was as Lyon had said—the Dark Continent. She felt dizzy, as if the cot were spinning and at any moment she would tumble to the ground. All the things she had ever counted on had been snatched away: her life as a wife and mother and her future as a doctor. How could she heal others when she couldn't heal her own emotional hurts?

A lion's roar lofted through the air. Margaret raised her head and listened. Like fingers of ice, fear rippled up her spine. Her eyes filled with fresh tears as she gripped the edges of the thin blanket and pulled it to her chin. She didn't like the direction of her thoughts and gave herself a stringent mental shake.

On the fringes of netherland, she felt more than saw a giant staring down at her. She wished desperately that she were any place other than in a tent along the Congo River. Venturing to open one eye to a narrow slit, she nearly shrieked. Lyon stood there, staring, his fists clenched. A feeling of panic filled her. It didn't take a genius to figure out why he was here. She heard him give an exasperated sigh, and then he bent almost double, carefully tucking the filmy netting material in all around her. Then as if satisfied that not even the most persistent mosquito could reach her, he turned and in one long stride was outside the door.

His unexpected show of tenderness rattled her senses. This occurrence would make an interesting entry in her diary. In her world, strange men simply did not tuck women into bed, even if their own wives were sleeping in the same room.

****

Lyon had not tried to hide his satisfied smirk as Margaret swept past him and strode toward her tent. He stretched his long legs toward the campfire, his thoughts as restless as the flickering flames. What was it about this woman that made him want to antagonize her and protect her both at the same time? It was an oxymoron, and he knew it.

"You do not like the mama daktor, brother." It was more of an observation than a question from M'pika as he offered to refill Lyon's cup with bitter coffee.

Lyon waved away the pot. He harrumphed. "I don't *anything* the doctor."

"Yasss, brother, and the butterfly does not *anyting* a flower, either, but sooner or later desires to taste its nectar."

Lyon frowned at his blood brother. "Go to bed, M'pika. I don't need you philosophizing over me."

The Bantu tribesman inclined his head to acknowledge the dismissal, and then laughed when the hunter winked at him before rising from his own chair.

Lyon stood and stretched his full length to relieve his tired muscles. Margaret's shadowy silhouette drew his attention. She obviously was not aware that the lantern light illuminated her every movement. Watching her undress was a detriment to any man, no matter his ethnic origin.

"M'pika…"

"Say no more. I take care."

The Bantu sprinted forward. He stopped a short distance from the tent. "*Jambo*, Mama Daktor. It is I, M'pika, who wishes to speak."

Margaret quickly clasped the front of her unbuttoned blouse. She peeked through the opening slit. "Yes?"

M'pika lowered his voice and looked at his feet. "In de dark, de lantern light makes pictures for all seeing eyes to admire."

"I'm afraid I don't understand."

M'pika released a heavy sigh. "If you please, I will show." He motioned her outside, and then entered her tent and walked about making motions with his hands. Once again, he stepped outside, then stood before Margaret, his eyes downcast.

Margaret had gasped. "Oh, my." She touched his arm. "I had no idea."

Lyon's loud guffaws caused her to spin around. She waggled a finger toward him. "You are a vulgar man." And then she said, "Thank you, M'pika. I shall be more cautious. G'night."

An hour later, Lyon sat on the edge of his cot, nursing a brandy, not at all certain of the emotions warring inside his head. New feelings. Confusing feelings. He downed the last dram of the delicate brown spirit. The warmth of it slithered through his belly to tease his manhood. Damn M'pika and his philosophy about butterflies tasting nectar.

He left the tent intending to let the warm sultry air cool his thoughts. He had every intention of avoiding the haughty Doctor Margaret Boynton's abode, until a feral urge gripped him. With the stealth of a lion, he eased inside her quarters. Like the king of the jungle, he wanted to sniff her, to taste her, to mount her. Instead, he tucked the haphazardly placed mosquito netting tightly around her body. Without a backward glance, he returned to his own bed.

After several moments of controlled breathing to quell the desire-ridden tremors in his hands, he rummaged around in his rucksack and removed a small bag made of blue velvet, now faded from the years. He gently unfastened the drawstrings and dumped the contents into his palm. He lovingly caressed the rose gold vintage locket adorned with a sparrow and a pearl droplet. He opened the clasp and looked at the photographs—a woman with a man, and a baby boy. And then, as if angry, he snapped the pendant shut, dropped it into the pouch, drew the gold-threaded strings tight, and placed it inside his canvas bag.

Damn the woman doctor for evoking memories that he wanted to keep buried.

Chapter 4

Rhythmic throbbing of drums startled Margaret awake. The noisy banging competed with a chorus of grunting hippos. She sat up straight in the cot, still half-asleep. It took a few minutes to gain her bearings.

The sun had barely weaned itself from its night's sleep, yet a clammy warmth already stole into her tent. With the nearly unbearable heat and humidity, Margaret considered her chance of getting a few more moments of sleep impossible. Through most of the hours of darkness, she had tossed in restless anticipation of the morrow.

The idea of lingering in bed didn't appeal to her. She had perspired enough to dampen her cotton chemise. It clung to her with a maddening persistence until she was driven to pluck the garment away from her bosom and fan herself with it, creating a billowing motion that forced a light current of cooling air over her moist skin. It brought instant relief, but that, at best, would last no longer than her efforts.

Her lengthy yawn bordered on a recalcitrant groan as she crawled from beneath the mosquito netting and tottered drowsily toward the wash stand. There she poured water into the porcelain basin and cupped the liquid to her face.

A disconcerted sigh escaped as she donned a fresh chemise, blouse, and skirt. Next came the long cotton stockings, and then the leather boots. She lifted one and shook it upside down, in case a scorpion or spider had managed to crawl inside it despite her precautions. Satisfied it was insect free, she repeated the action with the second boot. Sitting on the edge of the cot, she placed her feet inside the knee-high boots and laced them to the top.

Making no attempt to stifle another yawn, Margaret lifted her long, copper-red tresses off her neck. In the African climate, her hair had proven as heavy and warm as wool, and in view of the heat yet to come, which only promised to worsen with the coming months, she could only foresee added discomfort unless she started braiding the thick mass before retiring at night.

Only two months ago her personal maid had coifed her hair in a sedate yet charming motif befitting a woman physician. That was then. Now she had to care for the unruly mane herself, making her fully conscious of how arduous the task of just keeping her hair clean and reasonably subdued in a chignon was. Merely combing out the tangles after every washing was an ordeal, one of which led her to consider the benefits of reducing its length by at least half.

As she placed the last hairpin to secure the bun, a scratching sound caused her to look toward the tent's tied door. Her heart stilled. Surely if it were an animal someone would have raised an alarm. She grabbed the rifle. The scratch came again, followed by a voice. "*Jambo,* Mama Daktor."

She laid the rifle on the cot and with swift fingers loosened the ties and swept back the tent flaps. She looked at the man who stood on one foot, the other, badly swollen, supported against his inner knee. "*Jambo*, Y'ro. Go sit over there." She pointed. He gave her a quizzical look as he followed where she indicated.

"Sit."

He did not respond. She again pointed to the cot, then gave it a series of pats. She hoped he would understand. Instead, he shook his head and pointed to his foot.

Margaret realized the first handicap she needed to overcome was the language barrier. How could she care for people if she couldn't understand what they were saying?

"*Jambo,* Mama Daktor." M'pika stood at the opened flaps and greeted her with a toothy smile. "Niunga is the camp cook. He asks if you like tea or coffee with your morning meal."

She offered a smile. "*Jambo*, M'pika. A nice cup of hot tea would be wonderful. Do you mind asking Niunga to boil a pot of water and bring it to me? I need it to tend Y'ro's foot. And please tell Y'ro to go sit in that chair."

He nodded his understanding but did not speak to Y'ro.

As he turned to leave, she called him back. "M'pika, why do those drums keep beating?"

A dark eyebrow angled upward as the onyx eyes gleamed back at her. "They are talking drums. It is how the people communicate."

"What do the drums say?"

He listened. "They say, 'She comes. The white witch doctor.' "

Margaret gasped. "Why do they call me a witch?"

When he cast his glance to the ground, she urged,

30

"What else do the drums say? Tell me, M'pika."

He scuffed a sandaled foot against the dirt, sending up tufts of dust. "They say, 'She bring bad *juju*.' "

Margaret had no idea what '*juju*' meant, only that the word caused a stabbing concern in the pit of her stomach. "What does '*juju*' mean?"

Lyon's deep baritone voice spoke from behind her. "Go see that Niunga brings breakfast. I'll explain to the doctor."

The relief that washed over the Bantu man's face was obvious. "Yass, *bwana*, and hot water, too."

Margaret waved a hand toward the waiting man. "You can explain while I examine Y'ro's foot."

Lyon followed as she went toward where the bearer squatted while he waited.

"Tell him to sit in the chair."

Lyon spoke a series of what seemed unintelligible words. Y'ro obeyed. Margaret knelt and lifted his badly swollen foot to her lap. She used gentle fingers to probe, and reaffirmed her original diagnosis that there were no broken bones. "He has a very bad bone bruise. The weight he carried yesterday, with the pressure he put on his foot during the long trek, has aggravated the bruising."

For lack of a bandage, she reached under her skirt and tore a strip of petticoat. When M'pika arrived with the bucket of hot water, she asked if they had salt. M'pika sprinted toward the cook tent and soon returned with a small sack.

Margaret dumped a goodly portion of salt into the steaming water. She asked Lyon to instruct Y'ro to gradually put his foot in the hot water and to let it soak until the water completely cooled. "Tell him that after breakfast I will wrap his foot, and that he is to keep the bandage on until I say to remove it."

With the native bearer's foot soaking, she followed Lyon to the cook tent. Niunga promptly brought her a cup of steaming tea.

While they waited for breakfast, Margaret queried, "Well, are you going to tell me why the drums say I'm a witch and explain what '*juju*' means?"

Setting his cup on the table, Lyon began, " '*Juju*' means medicine or luck. As for the witch doctor, you have to understand that you are probably the only white woman any of the tribesmen have ever seen. They've seen plenty of white men—hunters, poachers, soldiers—but white women are rare to none. Plus you have hair the color of fire, the sign of the devil. Put it all together—white woman with red hair, and who calls herself a doctor."

"But I—"

He held up his hand to silence her. "You are dealing with people who are born, raised, live, and die with countless superstitions. It's their cycle of life."

The way his eyes flicked over her in a sweeping glance left Margaret feeling as if she had been stripped from head to toe. She arched her brow. "Please enlighten me. The more I learn about the natives' customs, the more beneficial to me."

He stabbed a fried potato and held it on the fork as if examining it before popping it into his mouth. "If a pregnant woman eats eggs, the people believe she will give birth to a snake. When a child reaches the age of two without sitting, crawling or talking, that child is a spirit child who must be sent back to his spirit masters. And this one is especially interesting: if you see a white person in your dream, you have seen a witch." Lyon offered Margaret a lopsided grin. "Every witch doctor from here to Timbuktu will send up their own special *juju*, hoping you will fail."

He pointed to Y'ro. "You better damn well pray that his foot heals, and fast. If it doesn't, the drums will let the entire jungle know. And you better double damn well pray that the first tooth you have to pull doesn't get septic, or the first baby you deliver doesn't die." Lyon's eyebrows knitted together, and he seemed suddenly in distress. "Even if nothing goes wrong, you are still in danger. And if any of that happens, you better hope I'm close enough to save you."

The intensity of his words caused her to shudder, and the deep blue eyes grazed her in a way that left no doubt that his words were not exaggerated.

She forced her voice not to tremble when she spoke. "Why would they want to harm me? I-I'm only here to do good."

"Simply put, you are a woman—in their eyes, an inferior person. If you have the power to heal, then you must be a witch. Your powers will shame-face the *sangomas* or shamans and take away their respect."

"And the only way for them to keep their respect is to—" She didn't want to think about the kind of harm a *sangoma* might do to her.

As if he'd read her thoughts, Lyon's voice was quiet. "Yes, to kill you."

Her appetite diminished, she shoved the plate away. Margaret stood on wobbly legs. "Thank you for your honesty." She heaved a great sigh. "How many days until we reach the hospital?"

"A half-day trek to the village where we pick up

the *shimbecks*. With good weather and no incidents, we'll reach the hospital in a week."

"Y'ro shouldn't bear weight on his foot."

She watched Lyon consider her words. "He'll either carry the crate or leave it behind."

"No, those are medical supplies. We can't leave them."

"He's a strong fella. He can rest in the boat. It won't hurt his foot if he uses his arms to paddle, will it?"

"Your sarcasm is not appreciated, Mr. Lyon, and you'd better hope that I'm around to save you if you're attacked by a…by a…wild animal."

By the time the camp was taken down, with tents, tables, and chairs packed, and Lyon had called for the bearers to heft the crates onto their brawny shoulders, dawn had given way to a butter-yellow sun, a soft, indistinct ball on the far side of the morning haze.

Lyon whirled the long black whip over his head and snapped it. The loud crack echoed through the treetops and sent a flock of flamingos soaring from the river. "*Harakisha*. We need to make Tani village by noon."

Chapter 5

The first cluster of huts Margaret saw were dwarfed under a clump of tall palm trees. Their round, whitewashed walls gleamed in the sunshine, and the cone-shaped thatched roofs were so high-pitched that it looked as though they could easily pierce the clouds.

An assembly of men stood in the yard. Draped in leopard loin clothes and feathered headbands, the men looked fearsome. Behind them, in shifting, wide-eyed groups, was the entire village.

Lyon led the troupe of bearers into the compound and gave the command to rest.

With M'pika by his side, Lyon addressed the man who stood apart from the others, an impressive chap with an air of arrogance whom Margaret guessed was the village chief. There was a lot of pointing, and loud voices, and gestures, and mostly at her.

A man of striking appearance stood in the forefront of the throng. His piercing glare centered on Margaret, scorching her with eyes so hot the angry chocolate irises seemed to be melting into the white. He lifted his arm and pointed at her. "*N'Devli!*"

When he stalked off, the villagers made way for him. By the arrogant swing of his broad shoulders, Margaret guessed he was the shaman, and not a man anyone would want as an enemy.

The day already had been long for her, unused to

extended hours of walking. Lyon had suggested they stop for respite, but knowing how anxious he was to make it to the village, she had refused. He came to stand next to her now, and saw the lines of exhaustion drooping her face.

"Sometimes stubbornness works against you," he said. "I should have insisted we stop."

Margaret straightened, more steel in that narrow back than anyone who looked at her would have expected. "It was my choice." Her eyes flashed toward the assembly. "With all their fierce scowls and loud voices, I'm assuming we're not welcomed."

Lyon made every attempt keep the concern out of his voice. "The people expect a show. Most of the time that's all it is..." His voice trailed off. "You understood what the witch doctor said?"

"He called me a devil."

"In his world, you are. His name is Demissie, which means 'destroyer.' His magic is powerful, and he won't hesitate to use it if he thinks you mean to challenge him."

"Will he harm us?"

"Not us—you." Lyon patted his rifle and winked. "But my magic is deadly." In a more serious tone, he said, "For all our safety, we need to get on the river within the hour. Which crate has the payment for passage?"

She looked at the men resting on the ground, and pointed. "Him, the fourth man."

Lyon called instructions and motioned the man forward.

Lyon whispered to Margaret, "I hope what you brought pleases the chief and his elders. Our getting the canoes and boatmen depends on it."

She made a bold step forward. Lyon grabbed her arm and pulled her back. "Unless you value your life, you will not disrespect the chief or the witch doctor with a show of superiority. I'll handle this."

New fears congealed in Margaret's chest. She, too, hoped she had made practical but wise choices. She nodded her understanding.

With a show of authority, Lyon removed a broad-blade knife from the sheath at his waist. He used it to pry open the large crate's wooden lid. He continued to wear a frown as he scanned the neatly packed goods as he made his selections. In one hand he grabbed two large cook pots, and in the other hand two bolts of brightly colored fabric.

"Chief Zuberi"—Lyon turned and pointed toward Margaret—"Mama Daktor comes from a land across the big water. She brings new medicine to the Angel of Mercy Hospital. She has come not as an enemy but as a friend to the people of Africa." He swept his arms wide. "For payment to hire Chief Zuberi's boatmen, she brings gifts for all the wives and daughters, totos, and grandfathers of the Tani village."

The man that reminded Margaret of an overstuffed chicken stepped forward. "And what does the woman with hair like fire bring to honor the chief?" He touched a finger to his chest.

Without hesitation, Lyon selected a long slender blue box. A gold crown adorned the top. He opened the spring-hinged lid, and ensconced on a bed of blue velvet lay a dirk with a silver braided handle of the finest steel, with a blue sapphire stone embedded in the top of the hilt. The knife was the finest Lyon had ever seen. He almost envied the old man, nearly unwilling to give it to him. With the lid still open, he held it forward. "A weapon fit for a king."

Margaret held her breath and prayed.

The chief clasped the knife in one hand and the ornate box in the other and lifted them high. With a wide grin he repeatedly shouted, "*Hii ni nzuri.*"

Lyon commanded to M'pika, "Get the boys and the crates loaded in the canoes, and be quick about it."

Amid the laughter and shouts and singing from the villagers scrabbling for their share of the goods inside the crate, and their elation over their choices, Margaret found the noise almost deafening.

Lyon grabbed her by the arm. "Time to get the hell out of here."

"What is he shouting?"

"He's saying, 'This is good.' Now, c'mon, walk as fast as you can, without running, toward the river."

"I thought these were friendly people."

"Chief Zuberi is an honorable man, and the people are trustworthy. As I said before, the witch doctor is your enemy, and his magic is deadly. He possesses more power than the chief."

Lyon half carried, half dragged Margaret to the river's edge. It hadn't occurred to her that she was to ride in the *shimbeck* until she saw her boxes, crates, and miscellaneous luggage being tossed into the arms of the Tani rowers. Whether from exhaustion or fear, or both, for one awful moment she was terrified. Before she could blink twice, she was seized by the forearms and just above the knees by four brawny hands and tossed as lightly and almost as unceremoniously as one of her steamer trunks into two big, black, waiting arms. Then, very gently, as though she were something delicate and fragile, she was deposited upright on a bedding roll. A trickle of sweat plunged down one side of her nose. She removed her pith helmet and mopped her forehead.

More shouting. The boat swayed like willow branches. She feared it would capsize, but then they were gliding over the water like skaters on ice. Then, in the blink of an eye, the placid current turned into a raging beast.

Her stomach somersaulted as she stared up into a massive wave of green water and then soared as dizzily as though she were a bird, peering over the edge of the canoe into a frothing trough where the wall of water had been only a second before. If everything had not been so utterly new, she was certain she would have given way to hysteria. As it was, she was in the middle of a new world, and all she could do was pray she survived.

Lyon settled beside her, the butt of the rifle on the dugout's floor and resting between his knees. "Well, you made the first grade."

"What do you mean?" She shouted above the roar of the Tani River.

"You didn't squeal and kick and make a fool of yourself, and you've won the admiration of all the boys."

She looked out on the glassy waves rising beside them. "It makes one feel small, doesn't it?"

"Compared to the Congo, the Tani River is a mere trickle of water."

She clasped her hands together to keep them from trembling. "I was most happy to sail down the Congo aboard Captain Bachmeir's riverboat. At least I felt safer in a larger vessel than in this…floating log. I'm afraid I'm not much of a sailor."

Lyon offered a lopsided smile. "In the jungle you either walk or travel by water."

She didn't feel overly safe in the *shimbeck* as Lyon explained how the boats were made. The vessels were not more than thirty-five feet long and had been hollowed out by fire and obsidian adzes. Each was made out of a single tree trunk with a diameter of about five feet. Dried out by the fire and adz work, the shell was then plunged into a pool, weighted with stones, and left to soak up enough water to make it slightly pliable. The process was repeated until the finished boat was almost eight feet wide. She feared that with the weight and the swaying movements of the standing rowers, the vessel might capsize, but the skill of the boatmen seemed equal to their task.

She turned back to look at them in time to observe an unforgettable spectacle as they worked. Every oar left the water at the same instant. Then the oars were plunged into the depths, sending the long canoes forward. The boys rowed to the cadence of their chanting. The sound created a friendly feeling for the boys, but at the same time there was an air of the most primitive magic.

She marveled at the oarsmen's ability to labor for such long hours without resting, and without complaint. Her body ached from head to toe from sitting in a cramped position. If only she could stretch her legs. *So be it,* she thought with a heavy sigh. She leaned forward and rested her cheek on her knees, thinking of her husband and son. She couldn't help feeling a certain despair.

The heat increased with each passing hour as they traveled down the river. Heaving an impatient sigh, she prayed for the sun to go down and night to fall so she could get off this boat.

She let the magic of the river slip over her, hypnotically soothing, as was the gentle sluicing of the oars through water. Margaret didn't realize she had drifted off until she felt a hand on her shoulder. "Are we in danger?" she asked in alarm, rubbing her hands over her face, only to see Lyon smiling down at her.

"Nope. We're merely stopping for the night." Lyon stepped out of the canoe. "One of the boys will carry you ashore."

Rubbing her eyes with her knuckles, she was too tired to argue.

The first night they camped on the banks of the Tani. Margaret lay under a lean-to of bamboo and palm, only a blanket between her and the hard-packed dirt, and a handful of blazing logs to ward off those animals that hunted and came to the river to drink under the cover of night.

The ground beneath her throbbed in pulsating waves. "Good heavens. Am I having a heatstroke or suffering from a case of uncontrollable jitters?" she whispered under her breath. She was too unacquainted with Africa to recognize the vibrations of distant drums.

She hadn't realized she spoke aloud. The words were indistinct to her ears. She looked up in quick embarrassment. Lyon stood over her, smiling.

"Jungle telegraph. You'll get used to them. Sometimes there is no sound, only the vibrations."

"What are they saying?"

"Remember the last village we passed? They're

41

sending word to the hospital that we'll arrive in a couple of days."

"Did we pass a village? I didn't see it."

"You never see the river villages from the river itself. That would make them too easy to attack. They are always back a bit, hidden by the jungle. Tomorrow, if you look closely you can usually see a well-defined path leading away from the river. That means a village. The Africans have a saying that can be translated, 'Every path leads somewhere, but the broadest path leads to the king's table.' Remember that if you ever get lost in the jungle."

Margaret yawned. She lay down and tucked her hands under her chin, her eyes fluttering shut of their own will. "Thank you. I'll try to remember that."

She forced them open and glanced up at him. His face was a blank, unreadable mask, the scars on the side of his face almost silver under the moon's bright light. And then as silently as he'd come, he faded into the darkness.

****

Lyon tossed and turned most of the night, trying to make sense of his jumbled thoughts. Fully dressed, he shoved the thin blanket aside and laced his boots. He swung to his feet and left the campsite to stare out across the moonlit river.

Still and quiet, the expanse of dark water gave him serenity. He found a stillness of mind as he stood there, his thoughts drifting away into nothingness. And then his tranquility was broken.

M'pika's deep baritone voice was barely a whisper. "Brother, what troubles you?"

Lyon harrumphed. "I must be losing my keen

senses to let you sneak up on me like that."

"Yass, I, *namiri* the panther, sneak up on the Lyon." He gave a soft chuckle at the joke. "Is it the woman that troubles your thoughts?"

Lyon heaved a deep sigh. The ache in his chest intensified. "Yes, no, maybe. Her presence seems to have opened memories I'd like to forget."

"Yass, and the way you look at her is not the way a man looks upon his mother. You have too long been without a woman in your bed, my brother."

Lyon grimaced. "The haughty doctor is a woman with her own pain. It is written all over her. She is vulnerable, and I will not use her for personal pleasure, unless she invites me. As for my mother…it's an ugliness I wish to forget. Don't mention her again."

"We have been brothers, you and me, since we were small monkeys. I hurt when you hurt. We are no more than flesh and blood. We are men with our own set of flaws. You forget I was in that village, too. You are not the only one who lost a mother."

Lyon clasped his friend on the shoulder. He recalled when the two of them were at the orphanage and would have their quarrels, and how Mother Superior would make them apologize and then say an extra round of Hail Marys. "Perhaps we should both find our rosaries."

M'pika grinned. "Yass, brother, I tink that would make Mother Superior proud. Now come and rest. Lightning dances across the sky. It will rain tomorrow."

Chapter 6

It took until midmorning of the next day for the Dark Continent to show Margaret exactly why there was no other place on Earth like it. The day dawned wet and windy. By the time the small fleet of six *shimbecks* reached the depths of the river so the boys could make good time with their oars, sinister clouds seemed to become one with the river, leaving the impression that sky and water were inseparable. Dull thunder rolled like volleys of distant cannon fire from the Sagala hills back toward the canoes.

Two boats ahead, a reedy oarsman was a dark shadow in the gloom. He stood tall and yelled as he pointed. All around her, male voices rang out, punctuated by a cacophony of grunts from countless hippos.

Before embarking, Lyon had given Margaret a rifle and instructed that he would be riding in one of the other canoes. He had seemed more angry than usual—more detached. She searched her mind. She knew he didn't like her, didn't like having to escort her, didn't like being called away from his usual assignments, and, in general, considered her a nuisance. She wondered what else she had done to antagonize him.

With a growing sense of trepidation, she held the weapon tight against her chest. Her throat suddenly dry, she looked across to where Lyon stood, the rifle at his shoulder. She shouted, "What is he saying, Lyon?"

"Hippos. Hundreds of them. It's mating season, which makes the bulls more aggressive. It seems we've managed to navigate right into the midst of 'em. Whatever you do, Maggie, don't stand up. If you have to shoot, aim between the eyes. Only a brain shot will take 'em down."

A streak of vicious lightning splintered across the sky, and roll after roll of thunder snatched Lyon's voice away. The first raindrops fell, fat and warm, like heated bathwater. The rowers sat hunched forward, tense, picking their way through the gloom while trying to avoid bumping into any of the massive beasts.

An eerie silence shrouded the river. Only the rising and falling swish of the oars through the water broke the silence. What was it Lyon had said? *When the jungle is quiet, that means a predator is nearby.*

Margaret struggled with her fear, her gaze riveted on the dark depths.

Out of the gloom and so close she could smell its fetid breath, a massive head broke the water, its jaws wide, teeth as big around as her wrists, eyes ominous and seeming to stare right at her.

Lyon called, "Steady, Maggie. It's the ones you don't see that you need to fear."

She merely nodded. Again she recalled his words: *If a hippo capsizes a canoe and a man survives, he is extra lucky if the crocs don't get him before he is able to swim for shore.*

Even in this dire situation, she was mindful that he'd addressed her by a name no one had ever called her—*Maggie*. She didn't like his audacity in such over-familiarity. She had just turned to voice her objection when Lyon shouted, "Shoot, damn it, shoot! Hard to port!"

She looked about. "What?"

"Left, on your left!"

Forgetting his earlier warning, she stood to get a better look. Rain slashed her eyes and blurred her vision.

"Pull the trigger. Now!"

She fired. The rifle barked and bucked against her shoulder. She heard a *pffft!* Had she hit her target?

The bow of the boat reared up. Two oarsmen fell backward. Someone screamed. Was it her? She didn't know.

More shouts. Another scream.

The coppery scent of fresh blood.

Splashing. Rain. Thunder.

Pain knifed up her thigh. Rain pelted her even as she sank into the putrid collection of slime. She was certain that she hallucinated when she saw her husband's outstretched hands beckoning her. *Seamus, oh, Seamus, why did you leave me?*

A claustrophobic breathlessness came over her. Confusion followed in its wake.

****

Margaret was thoroughly spent both mentally and physically. Though she tried to remain alert, her eyelids sagged beneath the weight of her fatigue. She gave up her futile attempts to stay awake.

She roused briefly to a vague awareness that the rain had stopped. A breeze cooled her sweat-drenched body and evoked shivers. Someone pulled a sheet up to her chin. They soothed her brow and cheeks with a damp cloth. Shadows moved about the room, their words garbled. She tried to speak. Nothing came.

A hand lifted her head, and a bitter liquid was spooned between her lips. She found no energy to resist. As she drifted off again, she wondered distantly if Seamus and Jonathan were out riding, Jonathan on his pony and Seamus on his beloved stallion.

Much later, she awoke stiff, sore, and so completely exhausted that she was unable to differentiate between tensed muscles and utter fatigue. She was also very thirsty. She considered staying where she was, for it would only cost her more pain if she tried moving, but hunger, thirst, and the need to relieve her bladder were very strong incentives. Wincing, she tried to sit up. She felt positively wretched, to a degree she had never before experienced.

"Maggie?"

A disconcerted sigh escaped Margaret. The name, though foreign to her, nevertheless sounded familiar. She opened both eyes and swept her gaze beyond the canopy of mosquito netting. For a moment, it reminded her of Jonathan's baby bassinette.

"Lyon?"

The deep male voice emanated beyond the bed. "It's good to see you're awake. I was…that is…we were all worried about you."

"Where am I?"

"At the hospital."

"Angel of Mercy?"

"Yes."

Margaret gripped the sides of the bed. For a split-second she had the rising and falling sensation of being in a boat. "How long have I been here?"

"Three days."

She closed her eyes and pinched the bridge of her nose between her thumb and forefinger.

He waited a moment as if giving her time to collect her thoughts.

A roiling tide of nausea washed over her. "I remember everything. I remember that huge gaping mouth, the teeth, and the boat flipping over, and...and..." She buried her face in her hands and sobbed.

Lyon's voice was urgent when he called, "Sister Adah."

A middle-aged woman entered the room and lifted the mosquito netting. "Doctor Margaret, I am Sister Adah Luke." She touched a hand to Margaret's forehead. "It is good to see you awake, though I fear your fever has returned. I will bring something to help you rest."

Margaret offered the woman a wan smile before shifting her eyes toward the hunter. "Lyon, what about the others? I remember screams...awful screams...and the crates, the medicine—?"

A muscle along his jaw twitched. "Except for one of your steamer trunks, nothing was lost. It was an especially angry bull that up-ended your *shimbeck*. We thought you were a goner when he clamped onto your leg and pulled you under." Lyon flicked away a fly that landed on his knee. "Unfortunately, two of the Tani oarsmen were taken by crocs."

Her eyes brimmed with tears. In a taut voice, she whispered, "You were right. Africa is dark and ugly, and I was naive to think I could come here and make a difference." The tears pooled and spilled down her cheeks.

Silence descended by degrees. Like a stone tossed into a placid pond, ripples of muted pain leached through Margaret's brain.

He looked at her with unsympathetic eyes. "Maggie, it doesn't matter where we live—Africa, England, America—life roars by you like a herd of stampeding elephants, and you get up the nearest tree and pray it will hold you up." He rose and went to stand next to the bed. "Most people come here because they are either searching for something or running away from something. It's written all over you, Maggie. What are you running from?"

The question left her feeling as if the wind had been knocked out of her. Running? He thought she was running. Feeling oddly disoriented, Margaret reeled her thoughts back into line.

She tried to rise. "I have to…go…to relieve myself."

Lyon beckoned the Hausa woman forward. "Help me get her on the chamber pot."

"No!" Margaret protested. "It isn't proper."

The nurse implored, "Doctor Margaret, you have almost one hundred stitches in your left thigh. I cannot lift you, and Doctor Williams will have my head if you tear your wound open. Not to speak of possible infection." Sister Adah Luke presented her most fierce face as she, again, motioned Lyon forward.

Margaret gripped the sides of the bed. "No. Anyone but him. Where is Doctor Williams?"

"He is not available." It was clear the Hausa woman was provoked. "Lyon, will you please to bring Sister Aganza Mary, and then see that the torches are lit?"

Lyon smiled in that knowing way he had. "G'night, Maggie."

Moments later, the two women gripped Margaret under the armpits and helped her from the bed. She bit into the sides of her mouth to keep from crying out as she bore the pain in her thigh. The struggle to get her back into bed was even more agonizing.

It was apparent that Sister Adah Luke held the senior position as she directed the other woman to bring a bowl of soup for Margaret. After the woman made her exit, the Hausa nurse washed her hands. She picked up a small clay pot. "This is a balm made from a plant called Devil's Claw. It grows wild in the jungle. It will help with the pain, and the healing, too."

As the woman gently applied the salve, Margaret asked, "What are those markings on your face?"

"I am a Hausa woman. These are the markings of my people."

"How did you come to be a nun?"

When the woman did not immediately answer, Margaret feared she had offended her. "I'm sorry, I didn't mean any disrespect. In my country, we do not often see people of color. I'm merely curious."

"Of course. I take no offense." She offered a smile. "In my country we do not often see people with hair the color of fire."

Both women laughed.

" 'Sister' is a term of respect for a woman who prefers to not marry and bear children. When I was a child, the missionaries came to my village. I liked the school where they taught us to speak English, and I especially liked to read and hear the stories of how *Yesu* healed the people. I have learned all I know from the

Reverend Doctor Potterfield and his wife. Some I learned from the village witch doctor, also. When Mrs. Potterfield died, the doctor returned to England. I then came to Doctor Williams, as did Sister Aganza Mary. Like me, she is Hausa."

Aganza Mary entered with a bowl of steaming liquid. She placed the tray across Margaret's lap, then poured a cup of tea. "It is chamomile and will help you sleep. Eat."

The soup's aroma elicited a series of noisy growls from her stomach. All of the women laughed.

Aganza Mary said, "There is a man, Y'ro, who insists on sleeping outside the hospital door. He says he must make sure the torches do not go out."

The effects of the chamomile tea and the sheer effort of holding the cup had exhausted Margaret. "I don't plan to trek into the bush to relieve myself. I'll use the chamber pot."

Adah and Aganza exchanged rolling eye looks. Laconically, Adah Luke explained, "The torches are to scare away any leopards that might be lurking about."

Margaret glanced at the small square windows covered by thin muslin curtains. "Could we put some bars on the windows tomorrow?"

Adah Luke tsked. "Leopards are cunning, and have been known to rip bars out as though they were straw; and these walls are nothing but mud mixed with grass and dung. They have also been known to enter buildings and drag off their prey. Even as big as the hospital is and with all the people and many buildings here, only fire keeps the big cats away."

As Adah Luke turned to leave, Margaret asked, "What is wrong with Doctor Williams?"

The three words Adah Luke spoke chilled Margaret to the bone. "Black water fever."

Adah Luke's seriousness impressed Margaret. Yet even more dangers she had not expected caused her to again question her reasons for coming to this place.

Chapter 7

Margaret lay staring at the pressure lamp and for the first time in her life was truly afraid of the dark. At last, dazed by pain and uncertainty, she closed her eyes. And then she heard it, a soughing, scraping sound. She sat up in bed and scanned the room. Surely a leopard had not slipped past Y'ro. He would have sounded an alarm. Where was Lyon when she needed him? The thought shocked her. She didn't want to think of him in that way. No, she was still grieving for her husband. She merely needed Lyon for protection.

In the dim light, she scanned every nook and cranny of the small room and saw nothing except a cane-backed chair, a small table, and the fluttering of the muslin curtains. She lay back and stared up at the netting spread out like a tent over the bed to prevent spiders, scorpions, all sorts of vermin, and snakes from getting into bed with her.

The sound came again.

"Probably my imagination. Laudanum will do that," she reassured herself.

Again she sat up. Perhaps she should summon Y'ro. No, if she were to live in Africa, she had to be brave.

She drew the sheet snugly to her chin. A heavy bulge moved slowly along the edge of the muslin canopy. Margaret stared, hypnotized by what looked like a looped shadow as it oozed over the edge. The loop grew until it struck the edge of the pressure lamp. For a second it sparkled like a fold of jewel-encrusted cloth, and in that second she knew what had literally been sleeping above her head.

Even in her panic she was surprised at the volume of her scream.

There was a plop like a stone dropping in a mud puddle, and a python slid half on, half over the chair that Lyon had earlier occupied.

Still shrieking, she became entangled in the yards of mosquito netting, and fought against it as it imprisoned her.

A pair of strong arms folded around her. The next thing she remembered was looking into the faces of Lyon, the two Hausa nurses, Y'ro, and M'pika.

****

For a moment Lyon didn't know what to do with his hands. He curled his fingers loosely around the side of Margaret's neck, acutely aware of the throbbing pulse in her throat. He'd already had his fantasies about her, but he mustered enough willpower to resist pressing his face against her silken hair, embracing her. It was brief. Within a heartbeat she stiffened, and he loosened his hold so she could pull back a bit. She fastened frightened eyes on his. Cupping her chin in his hand, he grinned impishly. "You have nothing to fear from that snake."

Margaret glanced around at the smiling faces. "Did you kill it?"

Y'ro said in his best pidgin English, "Snake bery good. We make chop-chop, Mama Daktor."

She grimaced. "Please tell me you are not going to

eat it!"

Lyon laughed at the bewilderment on her face. "Why not?" he countered. "It is very good chop-chop."

She flashed him a stricken look, and her face flushed scarlet.

Sister Adah Luke smiled. Her eyes were kind and wise. "What a ting to happen to you. I have lived in Africa my entire life and have never seen a python. Alive, I mean."

Rising from the side of her bed, Lyon said, "I think what the mama doctor needs is a shot of brandy. Her ear-piercing scream scared ten years off my life. I could use a shot myself."

His words seemed to signal that the excitement was over. The Hausa nurses and the native men made their departure. Lyon pulled a flask from his back pocket. He unscrewed the top and wiped the small round neck with the tail of his shirt. He offered the container to Margaret. At her hesitation, he urged, "A couple of tots of ol' joe will help settle your nerves."

She lifted the flagon to her lips, held the sweet liquid fire in her mouth, and then allowed it to slide down her throat. She sucked in a breath when the brandy hit her stomach.

Lyon was impressed by Margaret's unparalleled beauty. The texture of her creamy fair skin was as lush and smooth as satin. The effects of the brandy heightened the rosy blush of her cheeks, brightening her aqua eyes until they seemed to glow. Her nose was pert and slender, her soft mouth winsomely curved and in much need of kissing.

Her nightgown had fallen away from the graceful column of her neck to rest against a bare shoulder. The vision set off a fiery torch of delectable sensations against his loin. Without conscious thought he stepped even closer, until his knees touched the edge of the bed.

It was no more than a light brush of his fingers against the netting that seemed to break his hypnotic hold on Margaret. A gasp escaped her lips as she quickly clapped a hand against her breast, barely catching the falling nightgown, and in doing so she thwarted Lyon's intent to lay bare all the delights hidden beneath the fabric.

Margaret's fine nose lifted to emulate an arrogant noblewoman. "Thank you for the brandy. Perhaps it is time for you to say goodnight."

His lips twisted into a derisive smirk. He offered a gentleman's bow, and without a word strode out of the room.

****

The next morning, Lyon perched on a chair and leaned slightly forward to study Margaret's face. Her mouth had settled into a resolute line that had become all too familiar to him. He swallowed the laughter building in his throat and made every effort to school his face into a studious awareness, lest he provoke her temper further.

"They used ants to suture the wound in my leg." She hesitated briefly before yelling, "Ants! Where in the bloody fig is Doctor Williams? Surely he would not approve of such a primitive practice. Why I've never heard of such a thing." When her protests had no apparent effect on the white hunter, she added, "And stop grinning like a drunken baboon."

Lyon laughed at her consternation. "Settle down, Maggie."

She slapped a fist against the rail-thin mattress. "Why do you call me that infernal name?"

He shrugged. "Margaret is formal and…elegant. With your fiery temperament, you act more like a Maggie…feisty…always ready for a fight. It suits you."

Her eyebrows knitted into a frown. "It sounds like *maggot*, and I don't like being called a larvae that eats rotting flesh."

He limited his mischievous amusement to his eyes as he dropped his gaze to her soft bosom.

"Don't be vulgar, Lyon. It shows a lack of breeding."

Merriment tugged at the corner of his lips. "Like I said, *Maggie*, it suits you."

The soft tread of feet entered through the hospital room's open door. A man with pasty skin, thin wispy gray hair, and shoulders that drooped forward walked to the bed. He acknowledged Lyon with a pleasant nod and said to Margaret, "Good morning, Doctor Boynton. I understand you have been asking for me."

Eyes aglitter with irritation, Margaret looked at the man clad in a white coat that matched his pallid complexion. "What kind of witchcraft medicine do you practice that you permit a patient to be virtually eaten by ants? Did you run out of catgut?"

The old man pulled at his chin as if considering his answer. "The ants are called driver ants or safari ants. Healers have used them since before the early Egyptians. Had I known you preferred your wound to be stitched with the intestines of sheep, I would have instructed Sister Adah Luke to use the catgut. As far as witchcraft medicine, Doctor Boynton, if you remain in Africa long enough, I can only hope you will come to appreciate the holistic techniques used by the native healers."

He was interrupted by a severe case of shivers. It was obvious the man was ill. When he wobbled, Lyon came to the elderly doctor's aid. A spasm of coughing overtook him, and he wilted like a thirsty flower. Lyon gathered the frail man into his arms before he collapsed to the floor.

"Accept my apology, Doctor Boynton. I am afraid I have not yet recouped enough to return to my duties."

****

Lyon cradled the elderly doctor as if he weighed no more than a child. The look he cast upon Margaret scorched her as if he had seared her with a hot coal.

Hours later, Sister Aganza Mary brought a plate of fresh fruit. With eyes downcast, she set the tray across Margaret's lap and then poured a cup of tea. As she made to leave, Margaret called the Hausa woman back. "If you will help me out of this bed, I will tend to Doctor Williams."

"No, Mama Daktor. You will do harm to your leg."

Margaret knew the sense in the woman's statement. "Then find Y'ro. He can carry me to the doctor's house."

"I cannot. It has been ordered."

"Ordered by whom?"

The woman peered around as if eyes were watching her. "The people whisper that you are N'Devli. Your words burn like the fire of your hair."

N'Devli…the devil. The word felt like a punch to the stomach.

"Sister Aganza Mary, you are an educated woman, a nurse. Surely you do not believe the superstitions that the color of one's hair determines whether they are good or evil."

When Aganza didn't answer, a voice from the doorway spoke. Sister Adah Luke stood there with a stack of white linens in her hands and replied, "Mama Daktor, it is true that we are learned in the ways of the *mzunga,* the white man's church, but we are also Hausa, and the old ways do not leave us. Is it not that way in your land?"

Margaret was reminded of how much her father hated Seamus. It was not her husband's nobility that was in question but rather that he was Irish, and that he was an artist who preferred beauty to politics, and her father, being a Protestant, considered him a heretic. To add more salt to the indignity, the social elite accepted Seamus only to please Margaret, which made her revile the members of polite society even more.

Suddenly, she fell victim to a chest-constricting emotion comparable to the grief she had suffered after the deaths of her husband and son. It seemed as if in an instant of time, with the purity of Sister Adah Luke's honesty, that she had become barren of human compassion.

She needed to find a way to win the confidence of the people and prove that she was truly Mama Daktor. *Mganga*—healer.

"Sister Adah Luke, how much longer before the safari ants can be removed? I am growing lazy idling in this bed."

The Hausa woman smiled. "Maybe in two days, with the aid of a crutch, you can walk a little."

"I have much to learn. Will you teach me?"

"Oh, yes, Mama Daktor. I will teach you all I

know. Now, if you will excuse me, I must see to our other patients."

Chapter 8

Margaret was tired of lying in bed, tired of being idle, and tired of her wayward thoughts. More often of late, she felt adrift in a sea of uncertainty. Part of her wanted to return to England to a comfortable bed, a kinder climate, a decent meal, and an environment where wild animals didn't lurk around every bush. The practical side of her brain said it was the sensible thing to do.

She had wanted a new life. A life where she made her own way, her own rules, and didn't need to combat the discrimination of being a woman in a man's profession. She laughed. It seemed the joke was on her. In England, the most affluent patients avoided her. Even the gutter whores were leery of a female physician. It was her father's money and influence that would have afforded her a seat on London's hospital board. Halfway across the world, the same prejudices were alive. Africa was no different. She was a woman doctor now having to compete with village witch doctors.

She had created this situation for herself, and it was up to her to come up with a solution. Stay or go. The decision was hers and hers alone.

"From the scowl on your face, I'm assuming you didn't sleep well last night. Either that or someone or something has ruffled your feathers." Lyon stood with a shoulder propped against the open doorway, a tray of food in his hands.

She had no wish to discuss the mental upheaval she was suffering. "I admit to not having rested well after nearly being attacked by a mammoth reptile."

Lyon laughed as he sauntered forward, setting the tray on a table. "I dare say you gave the poor creature as much a fright as it did you."

"I truly have my doubts about that." A shudder wracked over her. "I hate snakes."

His broad shoulders lifted casually. "Most women do."

She turned an apprehensive look toward the ceiling. "I suppose the wily creatures can slip through any crack when you're not looking."

Lyon tossed her a grin. "That they can. The trick is to learn the harmless ones from the poisonous."

Margaret pulled back her anxiety. "How will I know the difference?"

"Look at the eyes. Non-poisonous snakes usually have round eyes. That's all you need to remember."

Lyon's smoky blue eyes gazed at her. She couldn't even begin to guess his thoughts. Desiring to change the subject, she sniffed. "What is that delectable aroma?"

"Coffee. Africa grows some of the finest beans." He poured a cup and handed it to her.

The past few days the two of them had co-existed in polite but stilted congeniality, eating and conversing together.

She thought he looked travel worn. His taupe trousers and short-sleeved tan shirt were slightly wrinkled, his tawny hair in desperate need of a trim. She lifted the cup to her lips and tried not to notice how handsome he was. His shoulders were remarkably wide, his arms admirably wrought with lithe muscles. From her experience as a married woman, she knew that beneath those trousers his hips were narrow enough to be coveted by any woman. As a hunter who traversed all types of terrain on a daily basis, she guessed his muscles were well honed to a vital hardness.

His features were noble, his jaw sharply chiseled beneath burnished skin. His lean aquiline nose had a slight curve to the left that indicated it may have been broken at some point in the past, and deep dimples graced his cheeks. In London's society circles, his darkly translucent blue eyes and engaging smile would not fail to capture the attention of ladies both young and old.

The way his eyes flicked over her in a sweeping glance left Margaret feeling as if she had been stripped from head to toe. What was worse, it aroused in her a yearning that a wife would have for her husband. It was a well-worn path upon which her memories trod. She fervently wished she could banish the remembrance of last night's touch from Lyon. It was enough to bring a bright glow to her cheeks and leave her voice unsteady.

He'd shaved. He wasn't skilled with a razor. His very fine jaw was marred by a couple of nasty nicks from the blade.

She lifted the cup to her lips and was aware all the time that he watched her with minute care. "This is an excellent beverage. A little bitter for my taste. I suppose cream and sugar would be too much of a luxury."

"There's a fine nanny goat in the compound for milk, and the sisters grow mint in their kitchen garden. Next time I go on safari, I'll see if I can trade for a box of sugar cubes."

His smile melted Margaret's insides.

The silence settled again, prickly and obvious. Lyon appeared utterly at ease with the silence. She herself was digging for words, searching for a conversational subject that would sparkle with intrigue. And yet he always answered effortlessly, without any trace of the stultifying shyness that often afflicted those who preferred quiet.

"Have you always lived in Africa?"

Lyon arched a dark brow as he finished the last of his coffee. "Why do you ask?"

She shrugged. "No reason. Just making conversation."

"From my earliest remembrance, I have always lived in Africa."

In a split second the atmosphere changed from congenial to tense. Margaret noted the slight twist to Lyon's lips. What had she said that caused him to tense like a knotted cord?

He said nothing more. He wasn't smiling. Pain flashed through those midnight blue eyes of his, and he gazed at her with a fierce concentration.

For want of breaking the awkward silence, Margaret set the empty cup on the tray. She tilted her head. "As long as I'm laid up in this bed, I might as well read. Crate number eight is filled with medical books. There are two with information about diseases. Would you mind terribly bringing them to me? I have no knowledge of Black Water Fever or other African maladies."

"Sure, why not?" She couldn't read his expression. His mouth was relaxed, not smiling, not frowning. His next question surprised her: "Who are Seamus and Jonathan?"

Margaret struggled to subdue the sickening roil of her stomach. It seemed like yesterday that she had stood in the pouring rain and watched the gravediggers sling mud on two lonely caskets. She glanced around in hopes of finding an object that would draw her attention away from the dark recollection.

"How do you know about them?"

"In your delirium, you kept calling their names and repeating that you were sorry."

She released a quavering sigh, and took her time answering. "Seamus and Jonathan are my husband and son."

Almost the moment the words passed from her lips, she regretted saying them.

He looked startled at her answer. A sound came from his throat, a strange sharp bark of surprise. For a moment he did nothing but stare at her. Hard, in the eyes, with an intensity that robbed her ability to breathe.

To her abashment, she realized she had deliberately given Lyon a misleading answer. She had answered his question in the present tense—as if her husband and child were still alive. She mentally argued with her conscience. "Lyon, I—"

Whatever explanation she had planned to offer was cut off by the throbbing beat of the jungle telegraph. Lyon glanced aside as he heard the patter of brisk footfalls from M'pika, who hurried up the steps with another man by his side.

The Hausa hunter was rail thin and looked as if a strong wind might blow him away. He was a beautifully made man with almond-shaped Egyptian eyes, black and piercing. His face was a study of poise. He was loyal to Lyon, and had become a good friend to Margaret. He was an expert at woodcraft and cooking, and according to Lyon a crack shot and an expert tracker.

M'pika was panting as if he'd just run a hard race. "Lyon?"

"I hear them, M'pika. Get the boys ready. We'll travel light. No tents; only food, and ammo."

Margaret shifted her glance from man to man. "What is it? What's happening?"

Lyon spun on his heel, and without acknowledging her question nor giving her a backward glance, he left the hospital room.

Margaret implored, "M'pika, please, what are the drums saying?"

"Rogue *timbo* attacked Kikuyu village north." He extended his arm and pointed. "No time to talk now." Then, like a wisp of smoke, he disappeared.

From her hospital bed, Margaret watched the flurry of commotion in the compound. Her shoulders slumped. She cursed under her breath as Lyon moved out of her line of vision. It hurt so much, the thoughts in her head.

She looked at her leg. The safari ants were still intact, but the swelling had disappeared, and the stitched flesh itched, which signaled healing. She closed her eyes for a moment and then drew in a breath. She was dumbstruck when the realization hit that she was alone with strangers, and the decision to return to England was instant. What foolishness had made her think she could make a difference in this savage land?

A little over an hour later, Sister Adah Luke brought afternoon tea and biscuits. She examined Margaret's leg. With gentle fingers she touched several ants. More than half the dried heads fell away from the incision. She smiled. "See, Mama Daktor? You are healing just fine. When all the heads fall away, you can walk again."

"How soon, Sister Adah?"

"One, maybe two more days. I don't tink the scar will be bad."

"How does this work with the ants?"

"The ants have very strong jaws. The wound is stitched by getting the ants to bite on both sides of the gash, and then we break off the body. There is almost no worries about infection because of the acid the ants secrete from their mouths."

"Ingenious. I must put this in my journal."

"Yass. You would like tea now?"

"Only if you will join me, Sister Adah."

The Hausa woman poured two cups. She settled in the chair and remained silent.

"Sister Adah, what is *timbo*?"

The woman laughed. "It is our word for elephant."

"What happens when an elephant becomes rogue?"

Sister Adah sipped her tea. "Mos' bad, Mama Daktor. Mos' bad. The drums say this *timbo* very big. He trampled a village and harmed many people. When a *timbo* goes on a rampage, it must be killed. Lyon and M'pika are fine hunters. They will find this elephant and destroy it before it takes more lives."

A frown drew Margaret's eyebrows together. "How far is the Kikuyu village?"

Sister Adah shrugged. "Ten-day hike. Maybe more

if dey walk slow; maybe less if dey run."

"One hundred miles?"

Sister Adah laughed at the incredulous look on Margaret's face. "In de jungle miles mean nothing. Fast or slow, we get to where we need to be. You will learn, Mama Daktor. You will learn."

Margaret stared at the lush green surrounding the hospital grounds. She had much to discover about her new home.

In a gentle voice, Margaret asked, "How long have you known Lyon?"

Sister Adah was pensive for a moment. "Long time. M'pika, too. They are brothers, you know."

Margaret's quizzical expression brought laughter from the Hausa woman. "The boys had a bad ting happen when they were cubs—about nine. That is when they take a knife and cut"—she made a slashing motion on the pulse area of her wrist—"and let their blood join together. Since that day, they have been brothers."

The two women sat in silence. Margaret's urge to cry grew stronger.

As if she read her thoughts, Sister Adah said, "When the flesh is wounded, we clean it so it can heal. The wounded places in our hearts cannot be reached, so *Yesu* gave us tears. Only Lyon I don't tink has ever cried. The anger in him is as big and dark as the whole Congo."

The question came out in a breathless whoosh. "What happened that was so terrible?"

Sister Adah rose and walked to the open doorway. She was quiet for such a long time that Margaret thought she might ignore the question and leave. Sister Adah returned to the chair, her face a mask of sorrow.

"The telling of it is difficult, and I only tell you because I see the way Lyon looks at you. Maybe you are the one *Yesu* has sent to heal his heart."

Margaret had the sinking feeling that perhaps she did not want to hear the tragic tale of Lyon's life. She braced herself.

Sister Adah Luke began. "His given name is Jeremiah, and his mother and father were missionaries from America, a place called Tex-us. He was a babe in arms when they came to the Kwango-Kwilu. For years life was good, but the Lyons did not know of the secret the Bambala people kept hidden from them. You see, dese people were flesh eaters."

Margaret said, "What is wrong with eating flesh? We all enjoy a little goat or venison."

"Yass, but Mama Daktor, the Bambala were cannibals, you see."

Margaret had this horrible feeling that she was sinking in quicksand. Her hands went to her mouth as she swallowed the bile building in her throat. Hot tears stung her eyes. "Please don't tell me that M'pika is of those people."

"No, M'pika is Hausa, like me. Many Hausa came to live with the missionaries." She continued in a singsong voice. "Jeremiah and M'pika were playing in the jungle when they heard the blood-curdling screams. The village elder always tell the boys when danger comes to climb the highest tree and do not come down until the danger has passed. So as they neared the village and the screams grew louder and the blood scent was overpowering, they did as they had been taught and climbed the highest tree. When darkness hovered over the jungle and all the world was quiet, the boys came down and they ran into the village. The horror they saw that day lives with them still.

"No one knows how long the boys walked before they were found wandering along the river. You see, the magistrate in Nairobi had heard about the massacre and sent a patrol to investigate. Jeremiah and M'pika led the soldiers back to the village. I am told grown men were sickened at the vision they found and could not eat for days.

"As there was no place for them in Nairobi, M'pika and Jeremiah were taken to the orphanage at St. Dominic's in Léopoldville. Many weeks later, a commandant came to see Jeremiah. Among what was left of the village, he had found a brooch that held pictures of Jeremiah's mama and papa and him. It is all that one small boy had left of his family. Papers were found with an address in Tex-us. A letter was written to the names on the paper, telling the fate of Jeremiah's family, and where he could be claimed."

Sister Adah Luke used the hem of her starched white apron to wipe the tears from her eyes. "It is a sad ting when no one from his land in Tex-us wants one small boy."

"You mean no one ever came?"

"I mean no mail ever came to say any ting."

"Maybe the letter got lost. It is a long way from Africa to America."

The Hausa woman simply shrugged her shoulders and shook her head to indicate that she had no answer.

Absolutely nothing could have prepared Margaret for the story this petite woman had shared. Her belly twisted and felt as if it had dropped to her knees. She strove to keep her voice even. "What about M'pika?"

"The commandant told us they had found the human vultures, who were immediately brought to justice. Like Jeremiah, M'pika was, too, left an orphan."

A breeze filtered through the open window. A film of cold perspiration broke out on Margaret's body. Images sprang at her, sickening images. She found it difficult to imagine the horror that marked two little boys and set the course for the men they had become.

"Why does Jeremiah call himself—Lyon?"

Sister Adah wrapped her arms around her body as if giving herself a much-needed hug. "That is a story for another day, Mama Daktor. The telling of this one has wearied my soul. It is time for you to rest, and for me to tend to Doctor Williams. Sister Aganza Mary will bring your supper."

Margaret thanked the woman. She lay back on the pillow. Thoughts ran too fast for her to catch them. At the moment, she couldn't think properly.

How could she ever compare her loss to the horror Jeremiah Lyon had suffered?

Chapter 9

Two days later, the last of the ant heads had fallen away, and Margaret walked about the small cell-like hospital room. After ten days of bed rest, her leg was stiff, and the taut muscles rebelled against the movement. She was eager to stroll about the village, to visit with Dr. Williams, and to meet the people who lived in the mission compound.

A voice scolded her. "Oh, no, Mama Daktor. You should never-never put your bare feet on an African floor, or the ground. Jiggers, you know."

Margaret forgot about the tenderness in her leg and scuttled to sit on the bed, her feet dangling in midair, her eyes darting. "Jiggers! Where?"

Sister Adah Luke's shoulders shook with laughter. "I am sorry to laugh at your plight, but de look on your face." She made every effort to compose herself. "Jiggers are tiny insects that crawl under your toenails and lay eggs. They are nasty creatures, for if de eggs hatch, you have awfully sore feet for weeks and weeks. If you don't pick them out, they eat away your toes."

Margaret leaned across the bed and grabbed her boots from the bedposts. Again, Sister Adah Luke cautioned, "Just because your shoes are turned upside down doesn't mean you shouldn't remember to bang them together and shake them hard, no matter how big a hurry you are in. Snakes and scorpions, you know."

Margaret's dubious smile indicated an easing of anxiety as she held the boots at arm's length and banged them together. "When I leave the hospital, where will I live, Sister Adah?"

"We each have our own *nyumba.*"

"*Nyumba*?"

"Yass, it is Swahili for house." The Hausa woman motioned, "Come, follow me."

Outside, Margaret lifted her face to the sun. The humidity intermingled with the aromas of wood smoke, wild honeysuckle, and delectable foods from the outdoor kitchen.

Sister Adah Luke escorted Margaret through the school. She pointed out the common eating area, which was a large conical building with a thatched roof over a raised wooden floor, open on all sides, and lined with long wooden tables and benches. Nearby was the chapel that resembled a smaller version of the eating area; a small granary, and several *nyumbas*, constructed of sticks and mud, that reminded Margaret of beehives.

The grounds were spotless. The Hausa woman explained that everyone had a job, and that included the daily sweeping of the yards. She also pointed out Dr. Williams' house. "You notice there are no bushes around the *nyumbas*." She smiled. "Can you guess why?"

"Snakes?"

"Yass, you are learning the ways of de jungle. Come, Doctor Williams has invited us to take breakfast with him. He has news to share with us."

Sister Aganza Mary joined the women as they climbed the steps to the dining quad. A much-welcomed cross breeze greeted the three women.

Margaret looked at the frail, ashen man who wobbled when he stood to greet them. He motioned for them to sit. As soon as they were seated, a young woman hurried forward with a kettle of tea. She set the cups before them and poured. Another woman brought bowls of wild raspberries, agave, curd, and a flatbread known as *chapati*.

After a short blessing of the food, Dr. Williams sipped his tea. A coughing spasm left him breathless.

When he dabbed the corner of his mouth, Margaret was certain the hint of pink was from blood-tinged saliva. He quickly tucked away the handkerchief. "Doctor Boynton, are you opposed to healing bodies?"

Margaret gasped. There was an awkward moment of silence. Her protest was more vehement than she intended. "Certainly not. I am a doctor."

He cocked an eyebrow. "Are you opposed to out-clinic treatment—meaning are you willing to travel to villages beyond this compound to treat those who cannot or will not travel to the hospital?"

She shot him a disgruntled look. "I don't understand. Why are you asking me these questions?"

A frown tugged one corner of his thin lip. "Superstition is rampant among the natives. They believe if they leave the security of their villages, they have no protection from all the evil spirits in the jungle. They fear the wrath of the witch doctor. You, Doctor Boynton, will have to prove your medicine is stronger than any witch doctor's."

Silence.

What if she couldn't do this? She gave him a long, considering look. "In England, I was subjected to the prejudices of the male doctors, and the elite populace, and even the commoners who felt that a woman doctor was in some way inferior to her male counterparts. I do not know witchery, Doctor, only what I have learned at the medical university and in private practice. I will use it to the best of my knowledge."

He studied her. Concern etched his face. "Well said, my dear. Use the power of your knowledge and experience. Take a quinine pill every day to fight malaria and, worse, Black Water Fever. Learn to outwit the witch doctors, and perhaps you will survive the jungle, or rethink your decision and return to England."

He seemed to struggle for breath. "I have been in Africa more years than you are old, Doctor Boynton. The jungle has robbed me of my health. Simply put, I am returning to England to live out what few years I have left. I need assurance that you are willing to devote all of yourself to carrying on what has been accomplished by others before my time, and for those who will follow after you."

All three women gasped at the unexpected announcement. His words triggered a flood of tears from Sisters Adah Luke and Aganza Mary.

Margaret gripped her hands together. "I don't know what to say, Doctor Williams. Clearly this is a surprise to all of us." Only a few days ago, she herself had resolved to leave Africa and return home. She didn't want to make a false promise just to pacify a dying man.

He nodded sagely, sadly. "My apologies for springing this on all of you. I had not intended to retire this soon, but Black Water Fever has its own timeline. It has been too long since I celebrated the Yuletide with relatives. By the grace of God, it is time."

Margaret didn't realize she had drifted off into deep thought until a hand touched her arm. Sisters Adah Luke and Aganza Mary looked at her with expectant eyes. Waiting.

Margaret's narrow shoulders straightened. She gave an almost imperceptible nod. "I will do my best to follow in your footsteps."

The answer seemed to satisfy him. "Good. I feel as if a large weight has been lifted from my shoulders. In a fortnight, I will catch the riverboat to Léopoldville and then set sail to my home in Sussex."

Another coughing spasm gripped the elderly physician. "Doctor Boynton, I leave my vast library to you, as well as my *nyumba*. Since the clinic has a lack of patients, there is no need for you to leave the hospital room only to move again in a few days."

"I'm overwhelmed by your generosity, Doctor. A medical library in the midst of the jungle is a rare treasure." Her mouth settled in a resolute line. "Shall I escort you to your bed?"

As if he had no energy left to answer, he merely waved away her offer and signaled one of the boys to help him.

By midday, Margaret had picked jiggers from beneath the toenails of several people who weren't afraid to venture from their villages. One of the men had already lost two toes to the vicious fleas that had burrowed deep into his skin. She had stitched the wounds of two men who had had unfortunate encounters with prickly thorn bushes. She had also diluted iodine and swabbed the sore throat of a child, and then delighted the little girl with a piece of peppermint candy.

Margaret stood and stretched the full length of her lithe frame. Satisfaction washed over her, a feeling she didn't remember experiencing while practicing medicine in London. It had been many hours since breakfast, and she was ready for a cup of chai tea and a bite to eat.

After cleansing her hands, she stepped outside. That's when she spotted him—tall, taller than Lyon, reedy, his face intricately tattooed, a scarf of leopard's skin draped across his shoulder. He created a regal image as he stood in the shadows at the edge of the compound yard. "Sister Adah Luke, who is that young man just there?" She avoided pointing, rather she nodded to indicate his location.

"Oh, Mama Daktor, he is bad *juju*. Much bad *juju*. Turn him away."

"Who is he?"

Sister Adah Luke wrung her hands together. "He is Effion, the only son of Matata. Matata is the mos' powerful of all de *sangomas*. They are leopard people. Fierce warriors, and stealers of cattle."

Margaret's stomach churned. She sent up a quick prayer that she wasn't about to make her first mortal enemy.

She closed her eyes and rubbed her forehead as she recalled Dr. Williams' accusation. She took Sister Adah's hand in hers. "If he is sick and I deny him treatment, then I prove to Doctor Williams that I do not care about healing. Come. I need you to translate for me."

Sister Adah pulled back a little. Margaret scowled as she let the woman's hand fall from hers. "I would never have thought that an educated woman like you believed in *juju*."

Sister Adah Luke returned the frown. "You forget, Mama Daktor, that I am a Hausa woman and have seen what happens when witch doctors cast their spells. Victims have literally closed their eyes, turned their faces to the wall, and died."

The rush of anger Margaret felt was welcomed. It distracted her focus from the fact that she might be walking into a trap. "So be it. I will summon Dr. Williams to translate."

"No. He is sick. Though I am afraid, I will translate."

Margaret reached for Sister Adah's hand and gave it a little squeeze. "I am also afraid."

The two women walked shoulder to shoulder across the yard toward the young man whose solemn expression did not waver.

Margaret inwardly challenged herself to be strong. She was smart, she was educated, she knew medicine, and she was frightened to the point that her knees felt like sodden sponges.

The rapid exchange of words between Sister Adah Luke and the young warrior consisted of many hand gestures and pointing. The words sounded angry, even hostile, and then it was over.

Sister Adah Luke turned to Margaret. "He say his mother is dying. His *baba*'s magic cannot fight the evil that attacks his mother. He say no wait, you come, now."

Margaret's emotions tangled around her, making it difficult to think. "I completely understand why you do not wish to go with me. If you please, find one of the boys who speaks better than average English. My life depends on how well he can translate."

For a considerable moment Margaret watched a myriad of emotions play across the Hausa woman's face before she replied, "You will need a good nurse, Mama Daktor. I will go. Sister Aganza Mary is capable of running the infirmary until we return. I tink Doctor Williams may never leave his bed."

In a show of appreciation, Margaret clasped the Hausa woman's hands and held them. "Thank you." Trying to calm herself, she said, "Ask him if his mother is in pain, and if so, where is the pain."

More rapid exchange of words, and pointing.

"He says her face is swollen the size of a bull elephant's testicles, and the pain is all over. She cannot eat because her mouth refuses to open."

Margaret choked back laughter at the image the young warrior had created with his candid description. "It sounds like an abscessed tooth. At least let us pray that's all it is. Tell Effion we will leave in twenty minutes."

As rapidly as possible, Margaret gathered the medicines and tools she needed, while Sister Adah Luke apprised Sister Aganza Mary of the situation.

With trepidation in her heart, and a throbbing hip, Margaret went silently with Sister Adah Luke, following the young warrior into the jungle.

Chapter 10

Margaret glanced over her shoulder as they left the safety of the mission's compound. She focused on Dr. Williams' advice that her magic had to be stronger than any witch doctor's. Other than healing, what magic did she have?

The scenery grew more lush, and wilder. Trees crowded the land, limb to limb, their crowns entangled into a dense canopy of green that blotted out the sun, leaving the ground below veiled in darkness. The woods were thick with fan-frond palmetto trees and leafy ferns. Vines and bright orange trumpet-like flowers braided together in an intricate embroidery.

Monkeys chattered at the intruders who invaded their paradise. The jungle worked its magic on Margaret, pulling her into another dimension, leaving all her troubles in the distance as she struggled to keep pace with the Hausa woman and the young warrior.

They passed through a shadowy corridor of trees. Birds darted everywhere, flashes of color in the gloom, flitting among the lacework of branches.

Within a few hours, Margaret's face and legs were crisscrossed with scratches. She had slipped and fallen twice. All in all, she was not enjoying her trek through the jungle. She had difficulty seeing what the reference books had described as a beautiful land. She felt the loneliness of this place. By blocking out the sun, the towering trees made getting a sense of direction difficult, which left her with a sense of disorientation. She was drowning in a sea of green.

After what seemed like hours, Margaret and her party emerged from the natural bower into an area where a stream grew wide, looking more like a lake than a stream. The young warrior squatted and scooped a handful of water into his mouth. He spoke, and Sister Adah Luke translated. "He say the water is good. We should drink." The Hausa woman likewise refreshed herself.

Margaret was skeptical. She scooped a handful of water to cool her face. "How much farther? It's getting dark." After a flurry of words and some pointing, Sister Adah shrugged her shoulders. "He say not far."

"What does that mean…an hour, a day, more?" Margaret grumbled as she swatted at a worrisome insect.

"Not far" turned out to be at least another mile. There was an outburst of excitement when the trio entered the village. People emerged from huts like angry ants. A throng of scantily clad men and bare-breasted women crowded around them. Adah Luke whispered, "They won't hurt you, but show no fear. They only are testing your bravery."

Margaret squared her shoulders and pushed through the suffocating heat of bodies. "I don't feel brave."

When someone snatched a strand of her hair, she reacted without considering the consequences, and slapped the offending hand. This brought a yelp and a torrent of harsh grunts, raising of spears, and threatening glares.

The young warrior's tone was harsh and commanding when he lifted his own spear and spoke. The voices ebbed, the crowd parted, and before them stood three men. The lad engaged in what seemed a volatile conversation.

Margaret whispered, "Who are these men?"

"The older man with the pot belly is the chief, the man next to him is an elder, and the tall man wearing the leopard claws on his hands is Matata. Do not trust him, Mama Daktor."

"They are all jumping around like fleas on a hot skillet. This can't be good." Before she could add anything further, Effion grabbed Margaret's arm and dragged her forward. Matata shook his fist at her. He used the tip of his spear to lift her hair, shouting. The only word she understood was *N'Devli.*

Not a woman normally given to violence, this abuse was too much. She drew back her foot and planted a swift kick to the shouting scoundrel's shin. He yowled and hopped around on one foot.

A wave of low voices cooed, and fingers pointed. The chief raised his hand and shouted.

Silence.

Margaret huffed, "Translate, Sister Adah Luke, and say exactly what I say. Do not change one word."

The Hausa woman nodded her understanding.

Margaret's temper flashed as fiery as her red hair. She poked her finger in the witch doctor's chest and in the calmest voice she could muster, said, "My magic is powerful. Touch me again, and I will use my medicine to remove your testicles, and then I will feed them to the hyenas."

She turned and pointed at the witch doctor's son. "I

came because Effion does not want to see his mother die. Either lead me to her or tell your son to escort me and little mama daktor back to the hospital mission."

She placed her hands on her hips, not so much as a show of authority but so no one would see how badly her hands trembled.

Matata's eyes widened until the whites looked like hard-boiled eggs, the pupils dilated with anger. His nostrils flared, and his chest heaved. She knew he was outraged at her threat. Even so, she also did not miss when he crossed his legs and reached down to touch the most sacred part of his body as if checking to make sure he was still intact.

Good. She had won the first round.

The three men stepped aside. Effion motioned the women to follow as he stooped to enter the thatched hut. It took a moment for Margaret's eyes to adjust to the darkened interior. The stench caused her to gag. A moan led her to where a woman lay on a pallet of straw and animal skins.

Effion offered, through their translator, that his mother's name was Hasina and that it meant "good."

Margaret lifted her hands to her nose and inhaled the scent of soap to curtail the hut's vile stench. She didn't know why Lyon slipped into her thoughts at this particular moment, except he would have known exactly what to do in a situation like this.

"Sister Adah Luke, instruct Effion that he is our most important helper, and the first things we need are torches for light and lots of hot water. I need a clean mat on which to lay my instruments, and a table. I cannot perform surgery kneeling in the dirt. Then tell everyone else to get out."

Matata remained in the hut. He rattled bones and began chanting and swaying back and forth. Margaret instructed the Hausa woman, "Matata can stay and watch only if he is quiet. Otherwise, he must get out. Remind him that I will make him a eunuch."

Sister Adah Luke frowned. "What is dis…you-nik?"

Margaret explained.

A mischievous grin lit the Hausa woman's face. "Aah, a *towasi*, yass."

In the torchlit room, Margaret observed the patient's severely swollen face. A turtle shell filled with hot water was brought in, as well as a raised platform.

Effion lifted his mother onto the makeshift operating table. Sister Adah Luke translated as he related that Hasina was his father's first of five wives, and now that she was old and sick he had cast her aside. Effion felt his father did not try to use his medicine to make his mother well again.

Margaret assured Effion that she would do all she could to heal his mother. She washed her hands and asked for more clean water. Using gentle fingers, she opened the woman's mouth. The tooth was black, and multiple pus pockets lined her gums. She dissolved a packet of sleeping powders in a cup of water. Sister Adah Luke propped the woman up while Margaret held the cup for her to drink.

The woman rambled incoherently. "What is she saying, Sister Adah?"

"The pain is bad. She believes Matata has filled her with devils since she is no longer beautiful and says she is useless because she has bore him no more children."

"Assure Hasina that she has a bad tooth, and tell

her that Matata's medicine is weak and he has no power to cast devils into her or anyone else," Margaret said. "By the way, I noticed Matata has a ringworm on his neck. While we are waiting for the sedative to take effect, I will make a paste of salt and vinegar to put on it."

Sister Adah Luke explained to the witch doctor that Mama Daktor had big magic that would cure the *mdudu* on his neck. She told him he must apply the paste for seven days, and then she gave Effion her most serious look. "Mama Daktor has made you an important assistant. You must make sure to apply the paste to your *baba*'s neck for this many days." She held up seven fingers. "When the worm is dead, you will use the talking drums to tell all who listen about Mama Daktor's magic. Understand?"

The young warrior puffed out his chest. The gleam in his ebony eyes was enough of an answer.

Margaret used a ball of cotton to layer on the paste. "Tell Matata the paste will eat the life out of the worm. There may be some pain, but a witch doctor of his power will not cry out like a suckling child."

Effion turned away, but not before Margaret spied the amused twist of his lips. What son wouldn't like to feel more important than his father?

Margaret lifted the eyelids of her patient to check that the woman was in a deep sleep. "She's completely under. Let's begin."

She pulled the woman's head to the edge of the table, then propped her mouth open with wads of cotton. Using a small scalpel, she lanced the pus pockets and drained them of the yellow poison.

Matata stepped forward and mumbled. Margaret

turned, wielding the scalpel, and shushed him.

Once the woman's gums bled clean, Margaret coated them with styptic powder. Sister Adah Luke handed her the forceps. For show, she clacked them together in front of Matata's face. "Sister Adah, let us pray this woman does not die of infection."

"Do not fret yourself, Mama. *Yesu* is in control."

Margaret sucked in a deep breath, gripped the forceps, and tugged. The tooth held tight. She placed a knee on the edge of the table to gain a bit of leverage. "I pray the tooth doesn't break off. If it does, I don't know how I'll ever get it out. You've got to help me, God. I'll do my best, but…"

She tugged, and the tooth came out clean and sharp. She held the incisor high for all to see, and then she placed it in Effion's hand. "This is for your mother."

He took Margaret's hand and held it to his forehead. She didn't know the symbolism but guessed he was paying homage to her. She patted his arm. "Tell him we will spend the night in his mother's house to make sure all is well with her until morning."

Outside, drums and bells and singing drew their attention. "It is for you, Mama Daktor. The leopard people make a feast and sing songs in your honor." Sister Adah Luke cast a wary glance toward the door. "I tink you have made an enemy. He may fear your *juju*, but like the leopard stalks its prey on silent feet, we must be wary of Matata."

Margaret swallowed hard. "I saved his wife's life, and doctored his ringworm. Why would he want to harm me now?"

"Because you have caused him to lose honor in

front of his people. You have stolen his *juju*, and the only way to get it back is to…" The Hausa woman's voice trailed off. "Don't worry. I will stay close to you until we return to the safety of the mission."

Margaret washed her tools in the scalding water, then stowed them in her medical bag. She accepted Effion's invitation for her and Sister Adah to join the celebration, but emotions twisted inside Margaret. She had no desire to spend the rest of her life looking over her shoulder.

She stood bone weary against the wash basin and began slowly and mechanically bathing her hands and forearms.

That night Margaret lay, exhausted, on a mat of fresh palm fibers. She shifted to find a comfortable spot on the hut's dirt floor. She called to mind the noontime conversation with Dr. Williams. It would be a miracle for him to see his homeland, to celebrate a long-awaited Yuletide, to eat figgy pudding, and drink mulled apple cider. She feared he wouldn't live even the fortnight between now and when he would board the riverboat.

She prayed her diagnosis was wrong.

****

The sky was an artist's palette of color when Margaret and Sister Adah Luke left the leopard people's village with a different warrior as their escort. Effion had chosen to stay behind to make sure the village women saw to his mother's care.

Although the humidity tried to suck away her breath, an elation filled Margaret. Hasina had awakened with no ill effects from the sedative. Her gums were clear, the swelling had left her face, and she had consumed a bowl of clear broth.

Margaret left instructions for the woman to rinse her mouth twice a day with warm salty water, and smiled when Hasina held the tooth as if it were a thing of value.

Relieved to leave the village, she turned to give a last look. Matata stood as erect as the spear he gripped in his hand. Evil sparkled in his eyes and curled the corners of his lips. He had washed the salt plaster from his neck. His intent was clear, and his arrogance was astonishing. He'd lifted a hand with a leopard's claw attached and raked the air, emitting a throaty growl. There wasn't anything funny about people being attacked—by leopards or by their own demons.

The day marched on, with one hour drifting into another and without any respite from the heat. At the moment, what Margaret wanted most was a cool bath, a fresh changing of clothes, a cup of chai tea, a decent plate of food, and a few hours of peaceful sleep.

When she thought she couldn't bear the heat much longer, the drums started. Their guide held up his hand to signal for them to stop. She watched Sister Adah Luke's face crumple into anguish and tears. "What is it? What's happened, Sister Adah?"

"The drums say…" The Hausa woman stumbled over the words. "They say…great white daktori is dead."

Margaret's throat clogged as emotion burned her eyes, the tears struggling for release. She battled them back. Destiny had decided her fate.

Part II

"The most painful goodbyes are the ones that are never said and never explained."

~Shakespeare

Chapter 11

Though darkness had not yet fallen, the gas lanterns were lit to ward off predators. Lyon sank into his chair. The ache behind his eyes intensified.

"You are tinking about the Mama Daktor?"

Lyon took a long moment to answer. He leaned his head back. As he let his eyes drift shut he asked, "Have you ever been in love, M'pika?"

"I do not know this feeling. What is love, my brother?"

Lyon searched his mind for an answer. "Have you forgotten? It's the feeling we held for our mothers."

A heavy silence fell between them.

"Why do you ask me dis question, my brother?"

"Do you think about that day…the day the Bambalas came to the mission?"

"Sometimes in my dreams I tink I hear Mama calling my name. I do not wish to remember that day, Lyon."

"Why?"

M'pika shivered as if a cold wind had wrapped around him. "I tink sometimes we love people so much we make the mistake of trying to wrap them in cotton."

Lyon sat up and frowned at his friend. "Your parables confound me."

M'pika flashed a grin. He waited.

Lyon remained silent.

He'd had the dream more times than he could remember. It played through his mind like a buzzing mosquito, wearing on him, weighing on his conscience, ripping at his heart.

Jeremiah, run for help! Hurry! Jeremiah, where are you? And then the pleading, *Please, please...please...don't...*

Always her voice, the frantic pleading, touched nerves. His pulse jumped, his breath came in short, shallow gasps.

He had always felt guilty about his mother's death. To this day he could remember shirking his studies to play with M'pika the afternoon she died. Though twenty-three years had passed and he could now look back on it as an adult, realizing that any boy of nine would rather play than practice handwriting, Lyon couldn't quite forgive himself. It was frightening to think that he'd spent all these years trying to atone for something he could never have prevented.

The word escaped before Lyon could call it back. "No!"

A hand reached out and touched his arm. Lyon pitched himself upright in the chair as the door to his subconscious slammed. The air heaved in and out of his lungs in hot, ragged gasps. He opened his eyes and forced himself to take in his surroundings.

"Drink." M'pika handed him a cup of coffee laced with whiskey. "It has been a long time since the devil dream visited?"

"Yeah."

"Lyon, my brother, you did not say goodbye to the Mama Daktor. We left the mission like hyenas with blazing sticks tied to our tails. Why?"

"I don't know, M'pika. Let it alone. I'm too tired to discuss it."

M'pika heaved a sigh. "You are like the rampaging elephant we will seek tomorrow. Angry. Hurting and wanting to hurt back. I see de way you look at her, and it is not with the eyes a man would use to look upon his mother. Yet the one with hair like fire I tink has set a fire in Lyon's heart. I tink this is why he asks me 'bout love."

Lyon emptied the cup in one gulp. He rubbed his hands hard over his face, then plowed his fingers through sweat-damp hair. "She's married. She has a husband and a son in England."

Using anger to burn away his other emotions, he spat, "What kind of mother abandons her child to trek halfway across the world to maybe never return?"

M'pika's eyes widened. "How do you know this ting?"

"When her fever was high, she kept calling for Seamus and Jonathan, and saying she was sorry. I asked her who they were, and without blinking an eye or showing any remorse, she said they were her husband and son."

M'pika murmured, "I see in your eyes what your heart will not say, my brother."

"Yeah, and what is that?"

"Your heart is still hurting because of that long ago bad ting with our mothers. I tink you hoped the Mama Daktor would heal your heart."

The declaration hardly overjoyed Lyon. With considerable force of will, he shut the door on the subject.

M'pika muttered, "I tell you, she is bad *juju*.

Maybe she is really *N'Devli*."

Lyon gave a snort of disgust. "I'm turning in. We have a long trek tomorrow. You'd better get some rest too."

Twilight had faded into darkness, and the river came alive with the sounds of night creatures who visited to slake their thirst. The moon ducked behind a cloud as Lyon strolled along the water's edge to enter his tent and settle on his cot. He searched inside the hidden pocket of his rucksack and lifted out the small velveteen bag. He removed the locket and opened it. It occurred to him that he no longer knew the woman in the picture, only that she was his mother. He rubbed his knuckles against scruffy chin whiskers. He refused to admit that the redheaded woman doctor with the fiery temper had stirred more than his attention. He snapped the piece of jewelry shut and turned it over to rub his thumb across the inscription. *Always and Forever.* With gentle care, he placed the locket inside its resting place. He lay back, fully clothed, and pulled the mosquito netting around him.

And he dreamed.

He saw himself at nine, small and skinny, barefoot and dirty-faced, running, running through the jungle, holding on tight. Two small hands: one white, one black. Two frightened boys running, their bare feet slapping against the dirt path.

A panicked scream jolted him awake.

Drenched in perspiration, it took a moment to realize he was not the one who cried out.

He flung back the netting and grabbed his rifle. A shriek like that meant one thing—croc or hippo!

Lyon stormed outside. M'pika stood ready, holding

two burning torches. He held them high as he and Lyon scoured the ground until one of the boys yelled, "Here, *Bwana* Lyon."

In the dark, the torchlight showed evidence of heavy drag marks. Lyon knelt. He glanced up at concerned faces. "Croc. Big one."

They followed the fresh swath to the river. Torch lights cast an eerie glow off the dark, still water. There was no sound. It was as if the jungle mourned another lost life.

"Who was it?" Lyon wanted to know.

One of the boys called out, "Ige, *Bwana*. Him Bantu boy."

Lyon commanded the men to search up and down the riverbanks. "There is always a chance the croc let go."

After an hour of searching and calling the man's name, Lyon called off the search. "Try to get some rest. We'll break camp and head out at dawn."

On the way to his tent, Lyon asked, "Did he have family?"

Someone answered, "No. Orphan."

Lyon's stomach churned. "Damn. Damn the crocs. Damn the jungle. Damn it all to hell."

Chapter 12

With the dawn, the noise level in the jungle seemed to increase in volume. Lyon crouched on one knee and frowned, squinting at the wide muddied track that disappeared into the water. His eyes lifted slowly to glance at his friend. "Look at the size of the claw prints. Bigger than my hand, M'pika."

"Dis croc for sure be over fifteen feet. I don't tink we find Ige. Him no more."

Lyon pushed from his squatting position. With one last look at the watery expanse, he shifted the weight of the rifle to the crook of his arm. "Get the boys moving. We'll parallel the river. Tell them to keep a sharp look out. Sometimes crocs leave their spoils on land."

It was a solemn group that set out single file. No matter how gruesome the remains, Lyon knew the Bantu believed that without a burial a man's soul became a ghost and would follow them wherever they went. To keep his boys from running away, he needed to find what was left of Ige and dispose of it appropriately.

The morning air was fresh and cool, but the dark underlayment of the jungle lingered, as always. He had grown up here on the edge of the Lukuga River in the Congo Basin. It was a place of danger. Birth and death was a way of life in Africa for both man and beast. He felt neither compassion or sympathy regarding the subject of death, but he held a great respect for the superstitions that controlled the tribal people.

The jungle was a world unto itself, ancient, mysterious, primal. He had always thought of it as a place with a mind and eyes, and a dark, shadowed soul. A voice snapped his reverie.

A vulture lifted off the branches of a nearby tree, its wide wings beating the air. It lit below to join a squabbling flock.

The boys broke rank, their voices high with hysteria, revulsion, shock. Their arms extended, fingers pointing. "*Bwana* Lyon…come…come!"

He fired his rifle into the air to scatter the scavengers who refused to leave their carrion. A knot formed in the pit of his stomach at the gruesome sight. "M'pika, form a burial detail. Be quick. We need to make the Kikuyu village by nightfall."

Wails lifted in the air. Songs of sorrow were chanted. A hole dug. A body buried. Stones piled. Not to mark the grave, but to keep predators from digging up the remains. No ghost. Now the soul could rest easy.

After two hours of hiking, Lyon felt the vibrations beneath his feet. He called out, "M'pika?"

"I feel it, too, Brother."

Lyon gave the command to halt. Some of the men lay down, some sat with their legs crossed. All listened.

Since leaving the mission, the group had traveled nine days. The drum beats were a long distance away. Too far to hear. A belated tremor of unease rumbled through Lyon. Had something happened at the mission? Was Margaret safe?

Old fears never quite died. They just hid in the dark corners of his mind and waited for the chance to slip out. Lyon lifted the canteen hanging from his shoulder and drank deeply. Part of him wanted to turn around and head back to the mission. He thought about that for a moment. A picture of Margaret swam across his mind's eye. Hell, he'd only known the woman a short time. How had he allowed her to get under his skin? The denial of his feelings built a pressure in his chest that grew like an inflating balloon. It crowded against his lungs and squeezed his heart. A heart that held no room in it for a woman who would abandon her child.

A flurry of splashing drew his attention to the river. Heron and egrets competed for a fish. In a few minutes, the earth's vibrations stopped, and for a few seconds the air around Lyon felt empty. He reconciled his thoughts to the idea that if anything were amiss at the mission, Dr. Williams would send a runner.

Lyon allowed himself a sigh. "Rest time's over. Let's get a move on."

The morning's coveted coolness had disappeared. Heat waves undulated above the river, giving the illusion of water on water. Sweat glistened on M'pika's face. His deep-throated command roused the men to their feet.

Heat still held its heavy hand against the earth; shadows were long and red-tinged by the time Lyon and his safari arrived at what was left of the Kikuyu village. He grimaced at the destruction and puzzled over the reason for the attack. Huts lay like broken broom straw; trees lay uprooted. The trampled remains of bloated goats attracted scavengers. The stench of their rotting flesh assailed Lyon's nostrils.

Caked with dust and sweat, bone-tired and hungry, he spoke irritably. "From the looks of it, this is the work of more than one elephant."

M'pika huffed out a tired breath. "We should not camp in the open, Lyon." He pointed. "Fresh dung, there and there."

"Agreed. Looks like the Kikuyu people have left the area."

"Hiding, mebbe. They never leave their land."

An unexpected sound caused both men to whirl. Lyon and M'pika jacked rifles to their shoulder. Except for a loincloth, a man stood naked. He held no weapon and lifted wide, frightened eyes to M'pika. M'pika handed his rifle to Lyon. He greeted the Kikuyu man with open hands. "*Mutana bawa.*" He added, "Tell the people Lyon has come to hunt the rogue *timbo* who attacked your village."

Lyon understood most of the Kikuyu language, enough to learn that this havoc was caused by two elephants, and they had trampled six people. The villager went on to explain that the elephants ate the crops, and what wasn't eaten had been destroyed as the massive beasts trampled through it.

"*Timbo kubwa…*" The man held his arms wide to indicate the elephants' size.

Lyon glanced around. There was nothing extraordinary about this village. Nothing to indicate why a couple of rogue elephants chose this particular place or why they would return more than once.

"Ask him why he thinks the elephants attacked his village."

M'pika nodded.

The man was convinced that a neighboring witch doctor who coveted the chief's young wife had placed a spell on the elephants and caused them to attack the village. He held up three fingers and said, "This many times they come, and each time they do more harm."

Lyon gave him a further brief study. There was nothing he could say to convince this man or the villagers that their superstitions were unmerited. "Where are your people?"

The man turned toward the forest and pointed. "They are afraid to come out. We are sleeping in the trees at night." He extended his arms as if holding a rifle. "You will shoot and give us the meat. We are hungry. Our grain is gone, our storehouses destroyed. The babies cry because their stomachs hurt."

Those wise in the customs of the clans knew the Kikuyu were farmers. They valued the land and would not leave their homes. The men were eaters of meat. The women ate meat only when offered it by their husbands. Fish and certain birds were considered taboo. This meant making sure the elephants were destroyed away from the village.

Lyon shrugged in a noncommittal way. "I refuse to kill elephants without knowing which ones turned rogue. What was different about these?"

The man gestured as he spoke. "Both were bulls. Leader had broken tusk, and other one, he drag hind leg." He pointed. "Each time they come from there, and return same place."

Lyon rubbed the stubble on his chin. "We will do what we can. The meat is yours."

The three men bowed. Lyon and M'pika bade the villager a good rest.

After the Kikuyu man left, M'pika chafed his hands together. "Two rogues. This is no good. Mos' elephant attacks are the work of those cut off from their herd and driven mad by loneliness or pain."

"Uh-huh. He did say the lead bull had a broken tusk, and the other is a cripple. Maybe pain is the motive, plus being cast out of their herd."

"Mebbe so. I tink we sleep in the trees tonight too. What you tink, Lyon?"

"I think you are a wise man, my brother. Let's have a look around before it's too dark. I'll tell Kobe to make a quick supper while you let the boys know to find a sturdy tree for their beds tonight."

Chapter 13

Lyon nestled against the bole of an acacia tree. Though he preferred a cot, he had slept in worse places. He slung the strap of his rifle across his chest to assure he didn't accidently drop it during the night.

Scurrying sounds of various night creatures whispered in the hazy moonlight, and the occasional barking of zebras was music to his ears. He enjoyed music, and one day hoped to own a phonograph.

He thought about his land on Lake Tsavo, and the house he planned to build in the acacia forest on the floor of the Rift Valley. He wanted a clapboard house with a large wraparound porch overlooking the lake so he could sit and watch the pink flamingos. He dreamed of opening a safari lodge. Yeah, he'd chosen the perfect place. The area teemed with lion, elephant, rhino, crocodiles, and a diverse variety of birds.

A yearning tugged at him. Time was winging away, and by African standards he was an old man.

"You are quiet, my brother. Are you asleep?"

Pushing aside unaccountably abysmal thoughts, Lyon drew in a deep breath of air. "Why are you still awake?"

"Because your thoughts disturb my sleep. What troubles you, brother, de elephants?"

Lyon harrumphed. "Haven't met an elephant yet that scares me."

"Tell me."

"You scare me sometimes, M'pika, with your intuitiveness."

"Brother, I do not know dis big word. You read too many books. What does it mean?"

"It means you know and feel things before they happen."

"Ah, yass! So tell me what disturbs you."

"Lyon's Safari Lodge. I want to build it on the lake. I'm tired of trekking all over Africa. I'm ready to settle down, start a family. I want sons." He envisioned his children… The thought came to a halt.

M'pika's chuckle was soft. "You have de land, you can build de house and start the business, but—" He leaned over in the darkness and whispered, "My brother, you cannot make children without a woman."

Lyon laughed outright. "What about you, M'pika? Aren't you ready to settle down?"

"Yass. My bones are beginning to ache, and I long for a comfortable bed, and a big-breasted woman to make me lots of sons. One ting, though—I have no land for which to build a house, and no goats for which to buy a wife."

"You are my brother forever, M'pika. My land is your land, and I will help you build a house. I guess we are both in a sorrowful spot when it comes to finding wives."

"Yass, my brother. For you, the task is much bigger. Maybe you should go to Nairobi or Léopoldville and stay for a while, or maybe you should go see the flame-haired daktor and ask why she left her husband and child to come to dis land. I tink she has plenty good reason."

"You are addled-pated, M'pika. Get some sleep."

****

The shrill trumpet of an elephant jolted Lyon awake. He tried to orient himself after the rude awakening in the blackness. A shower of drought-parched leaves rained down on him. The tree moaned and cracked its objection as an elephant battered the trunk with its massive head. Pitched sideways, and hanging upside down, Lyon struggled to find a handhold on a branch to keep from plummeting to the ground.

Then M'pika's chilling pleas ripped through him. "Help!…Lyon!…Its trunk is wrapped around my leg…I can't get free…Lyon…help!"

Lyon called on every ounce of strength he could muster to right himself and straddle the branch. He'd seen more than one man who'd been ripped apart by an enraged elephant. The last thing he wanted was to engage in a tug of war with this giant. It was a battle he wouldn't win, and the end result would be the same for his friend.

His brain fired ideas in rapid shots: should he do this…no…should he do that…maybe…what if?

"Hang on, M'pika. Whatever you do, don't let go. I'm going to try for a brain shot."

He inched forward on a branch no bigger around than his arm. He prayed the bough wouldn't break. "I need to get closer. Hang on, my brother. Hang on."

In the Kikuyu language, Lyon shouted, "*Ndeithia*," the cry for help. "*Ndeithia*, bring spears and torches."

The natives arrived shouting, and beating drums. Torchlight outlined the massive monster and the wide frightened eyes of M'pika. Corded muscles in his neck and arms bulged from strain as he fought to keep his grip on the branch. Lyon saw the pain and perspiration that coated his friend's face. He could only imagine how it must feel to have the hip literally ripped out of the joint socket.

He knew his plan would work, but worried that the elephant might not let go of M'pika's leg, and in dying the animal would pull M'pika to the ground and crush him to death.

Lyon righted himself on the branch and scooted forward, thankful he'd had the foresight to sling the rifle strap across his chest to keep from losing it in a possible fall. He hefted the heavy weapon against his shoulder, jacked a cartridge into the breech, then jammed the barrel between the elephant's eyes and without hesitation pulled the trigger. He repeated the action and fired a second time. Then, letting go of the rifle, he leapt forward to grab the gray trunk that imprisoned M'pika's ankle. Wrapping his legs around the tree branch, he used both hands to pry apart the coiled appendage before the elephant crashed to the ground. His fingers ached as he applied more pressure to force the release. He felt the animal's quiver and looked into sightless eyes. Lyon balled his hand into a fist and repeatedly slammed it against the trunk. "Damn you, turn loose!"

Leaves and twigs sprayed in every direction as the mammoth raged against death and reared against the tree. Amid the natives' shouts and the raging trumpets of the second bull elephant, time seemed to move in slow motion.

The moon was behind Lyon, so he could see nothing. A dead calm wrapped around him. And then the tree buckled. He heard M'pika's voice as if it came from a long distance, the world spun, and darkness descended.

****

Dawn crept across the sky as Lyon regained consciousness. He lifted his head and groaned. Gritting his teeth, he tried to sit up. The world around him twirled in a dizzying spectacle before his eyes.

"No, *Bwana*, you must lie still."

A cool cloth touched his forehead. "M'pika?"

A wizened face with a toothless smile rattled bones over him. "You rest, *Bwana*. No talk."

"M'pika… Is he…?" Lyon lay in the cool grass, breathing heavily. Rest. He would just rest a while, then see to M'pika. When he opened his eyes again, the sun was directly overhead. He must have blacked out for several hours, but he didn't even remember losing consciousness.

Chapter 14

Lyon's aching body protested the slightest movement. Chanting, heavy thwacks, the sickening odor of blood, and the smell of death greeted him as he roused from the age-old dream that had him running, running, running from an unseen enemy. He unclenched his fists, and pressed fingers against his aching head.

The two things he wanted most were to find M'pika and to have water to cool his parched throat. Gritting his teeth, he rolled to his knees and pushed to a standing position. A regal man approached, followed by two more. Likely the chief and tribal elders.

The chief lifted his hand in greeting. "*Jambo*. I am Muhoho, chief of dis people. We tank you, *refiki* Lyon. *Muungu* smiled on us when he brought you to kill our enemy and give us meat to fill our bellies. He is a mos' powerful god of all de jungle." The man's smile widened. "You hab broken de curse, for the witch doctor who coveted my new wife is no more. He is dust, trampled by his own conjuring." The chief pointed to the two dead elephants. He poked his finger against Lyon's chest. "*Refiki*."

Honored to be called "friend," Lyon clasped the outstretched arm. He tamped down his impatience to learn about M'pika: How badly was he injured? Did he survive?

"I am honored, Chief Muhoho, that your enemy is no more, and that you have food to give your people strength to rebuild your houses, to plant new crops, and live in peace. May your wives give you many sons."

There, that should be enough protocol to appease the custom of showing good graces. He bowed. "My *refiki*, my friend, M'pika, where is he?"

"He lives. The gods were with him, too. Come, see for yourself."

In the sky above a grove of trees, large black vultures circled. Several of the scavengers landed and squabbled over the spoils. Children had been assigned the task of keeping the birds at bay by swatting them with sturdy poles.

Lyon approached the makeshift hut. His joints objected when he lowered to his knees and entered. A lone woman sat next to M'pika, fanning flies from his face. Wrinkled, breasts sagging to her waist, she was probably not much older than himself, but life was hard in the Dark Continent, where everyone was born old before their time.

M'pika's skin had a gray tinge. His swollen leg equaled the girth of his body. The blood from his nose had dried on his face. His hands were cold, and he did not respond when Lyon spoke his name. He had to get M'pika to the mission hospital. Ten days, one hundred miles. He could trim two days, going by dugout. Eight days of paddling on a river filled with crocs and hippos. Eight days of risking the lives of his men. Eight days to save the life of his friend—the only brother he had ever known. It was a risk he would take.

Lyon patted M'pika's shoulder. "I'll get you home, brother. It's up to you to live until I get you there." He hoped his friend heard the words.

A rolling rumble and dark billowing clouds caused Lyon concern regarding his plan. He pursed his lips and loosed a long shrill whistle to call his men together. They responded, emerging from tree tops and shaded bowers to gather around him.

His first inclination was to wait until the next morning to set out, but the pallor of M'pika's skin caused Lyon to change his mind. He motioned his two fastest runners forward. "I will arrange with Chief Muhoho to give you enough food for two days. Do not stop until you get to a village close enough where the talking drums will reach the Mama Daktor that M'pika is in a bad way. We are coming by river. Understand?"

The tallest of the men said, "No worries, *Bwana*. We good runners. We take message."

Lyon clasped arms with each man. "After you give the message, rest a few days, and then go home to your families." He cast a look at the earnest faces of men who'd been on safari with him many times. Reliable men. "The river is dangerous. Who will volunteer to help me paddle the canoe?"

Three Bantu stepped forward. One spoke for all. "We strong." He poked his finger against Lyon's chest. "You good *Bwana* to us. M'pika good *refiki*. We no 'fraid of de river."

Lyon repeated the gesture of gratitude with each of them. The remaining men he instructed to return to their villages. "Listen for the talking drums to say when I have a new safari. You will come. *Ndiyo*?"

In unison, the men agreed. "*Ndiyo*, *Bwana*, we come."

Another distant rumble caused Lyon to look up. A

rare smile tipped the corner of his mouth. Though the river was dangerous, traveling in the rain had its advantage. High water and cooler weather kept the crocodiles busy mating, and hippos preferred calm, sluggish water. Jagged fingers of lightning streaked across the sky, and gray clouds billowed and bumped into each other. It hadn't rained for weeks, and now it looked like the storm of the century was about to let loose. Wind swirled sand to pelt and sting his face.

He bid his boys good journey and promised to see them soon, then searched until he located his rucksack and rifle beneath a spray of splintered branches. He slung the gear over his shoulder. With the storm's rapid approach, there was no time to fashion a litter to carry M'pika to the canoe. Instead, he searched for skins or cloth, anything to drape over M'pika to shield him from the rain. A chill might be the death of him.

When all was set, Lyon hoisted the injured man into his arms as one would hold a child. He ordered his three Bantu boys to take the supplies, run to the river, and ready the canoe. He followed at a pace hampered by the weight he carried.

One more mile, he challenged himself.

When his lungs felt as if they would burst from the speed and exertion, he labored for breath and was relieved when the hazy outline of the river came into view. His legs threatened to buckle as he struggled with his friend's weight.

A few more paces. He issued another challenge.

Come on, Lyon, you can do this. He took giant gulps of air. Pride kept him from calling out for help.

His feet landed in mud, his boots immediately sinking into the watery mire. Warm air mingled with cooling rain lured swarms of hungry mosquitoes. They sought the unprotected skin of the men, the corners of their mouths, ears, heads, and shoulders. Pinpricks of blood oozed from arms and legs. Each man slapped the biting insects against their bodies.

With the assistance of one of his men, Lyon placed M'pika on the bottom of the canoe and adjusted the antelope skin over his face and body. He did not stir, and Lyon feared the worst.

One Bantu boy said, "You rest, *Bwana*. We paddle."

Lyon's chest heaved in and out. "Get in. I'll shove us off."

He felt as if he were being eaten alive. He swatted, taking out dozens of mosquitoes, only to have more blood-thirsty insects attack. With all his strength, he pushed the canoe from the bank and jumped in. "Put your backs into it. Get to the middle of the river."

Dark water rippled and surged with each stroke of the paddles. Lightning struck dangerously close. Angry skies opened to release a deluge. The past forty-eight hours were taking its toll on Lyon. The adrenalin rush was gone. He longed for a cup of strong coffee laced with brandy, a solid meal, and to slip into the numbness of sleep.

M'pika groaned.

Lyon gritted his teeth against the pain that nagged behind his eyes and the chill that threatened to overtake him. "Stay with me, brother. I'm taking you to Mama Daktor."

Rain settled in on them like a heavy blanket and pressed them deep into the canoe while gluing their clothes to their skin. The river's lazy current picked up speed and helped propel their tippy vessel forward.

Wanumbi, the lead boatman, paddled into a patch of green undergrowth and pulled out lily pads and papyrus plants; enough for each of them. Lyon thanked the man for his quick thinking. By turning them root up, the lily pads became hats offering some relief from the rain. They dined on the sweet, sugary roots of the papyrus.

By the time dusk arrived, only a light mist continued to fall. From the familiar landmarks, Lyon figured they had traveled nearly twenty-five miles. It no longer mattered if the rain persisted. The river's current would continue a rapid flow for several days. He leaned forward to dribble sweet sustenance from the papyrus root between M'pika's lips.

M'pika opened his eyes. His tongue sought the sugary liquid, the words he spoke barely a whisper. "Pain. Bad."

Lyon wiped water from his friend's brow. "Hang on. The current is running fast. We should make the mission in three days."

M'pika's eyes fluttered shut. Lyon figured being unconscious was a good thing. He ordered his three rowers to rest. "I'll take over. Get some sleep."

Wanumbi said, "Current swift. Canoe tip over. I help. Dey sleep. Okay, *Bwana*?"

"Okay. Then we sleep."

Wanumbi nodded and, like a storm unleashed, plowed the paddle into the water.

The memory of Margaret crossed Lyon's mind. She was prim and proper, her manners perfect, blue eyes that lured him, and a temper as fiery as the color of her hair. He smiled at the remembrance, and then he frowned. She had abandoned her child. He knew what it was like to be left alone without a mother. He didn't want Margaret Boynton in his life. He'd lived thirty-two years without any binding ties, and he intended to keep it that way.

Weary to the marrow of his bones, Lyon dipped the broad blade deep into the dark watery depths.

Loretta C. Rogers

Part III

*"You have power over your mind—
not outside events. Realize this, and
you will find strength."*
~Marcus Aurelius
Meditations

Chapter 15

Seated on a bench inside the outdoor common eating area, Margaret flicked a worrisome fly away from her face. She longed for a cross breeze to cool her sweaty body as she continued to write in her journal.

April 1910

We gave Dr. Williams a fine Christian burial. So sad he didn't live long enough to return to England. After crating up his personal belongings and sending them to Léopoldville to ship to his family, I have decided not to move into his house. It is rife with vermin, and the stench of decay still lingers in my nostrils. Sisters Adah Luke and Aganza Mary and I will give the house a proper blessing, and then we will set torches to it to appease the jungle gods. Dr. Williams' untimely demise has left me in a quandary. After three months, I still find Africa an enigma. It is dark and evil, and filled with danger behind every bush. Yet it is like an artist's painting filled with beautiful colors and intricate mysteries. Can I find the peace that I so yearn for in this place? Should I stay...or should I return to England? Do I want to grow old and die in this faraway land? So many questions.

I am ashamed that I deliberately deceived Lyon. Even after all these months, my dear Seamus and darling Jonathan are still very much alive in my mind. A light no longer shines in my soul. I do not wish to love again, the way I loved my husband and child, though at times I yearn for a man's touch, a caress, and comfort. Perhaps Jeremiah—

The truth of her inner voice could not be silenced.

A young mission girl interrupted Margaret's thoughts as she set a tray with tea and biscuits in front of her. "I am learning to read and write, Mama. Someday you will let me read your book?"

A rosy blush crept across Margaret's face. "This is a diary where I record my thoughts and keep a record of things I see and the people I treat. It is a private book, for no one's eyes but my own."

Seeing the girl's disappointment, Margaret hastened on. "The next time I order supplies from Nairobi, I will request a journal. Then you can write your own story."

A delighted smile and clasped hands were all the response Margaret needed. The girl curtsied. "I leave you to your thoughts, Mama Daktor."

Margaret immediately dipped the pen nib into the inkwell. Appalled at the meandering of her feelings, and embarrassed that prying eyes might happen upon her diary, she crossed through any mention of Jeremiah Lyon.

A gabbling of voices drew her attention to Sister Adah Luke walking at a fast pace across the compound. Margaret closed the diary, capped the bottle of ink, and stuffed both into her apron pocket as she hustled down the steps toward the Hausa woman. "What is it, Sister Adah? Is someone hurt?"

Sister Adah Luke waved her hand toward the tree line. "It is a sad case, Mama Daktor. He is a Tani prince. His wives have brought him."

"What is wrong with him?"

"Sad, very sad. His name is Falit. It means *productive*. An evil witch doctor cursed him with the elephant sickness. Now he cannot produce more children. His wives bring Falit to you to break de curse. He cannot make more children with his new wife."

"How many wives does he have, and how many children?" Margaret waited for Adah to translate.

"He has six wives and more children than his fingers and toes."

"Egads, Sister Adah Luke, that is over twenty. Why would he want more children?"

"Because he has a new wife. If he cannot make a baby with her, she can demand to return to her family. This would be very bad for his reputation. If he cannot keep his wife, then the people will tink he is weak. He will lose face. He will lay down and die."

"Surely, you don't mean die in the literal sense as in stone-cold dead?"

"Oh, yass, Mama Daktor. I have seen dis ting happen many times. As you say—stone-cold dead."

Margaret expelled an exasperated sigh. "I don't think I will ever come to understand such primitive customs and beliefs."

Margaret eyed the group of women who stood talking among themselves, casting wary looks toward her at short intervals. She sighed, and waved, motioning the group forward. "I know nothing of this disease. Put Falit in the examination room, and instruct the wives to stay outside."

"*Kuju sasa.* Come now," Sister Adah Luke called. While she instructed the wives, Margaret rushed to Dr. Williams' house. She wrinkled her nose against the musty odor of rot, and the lingering fruity scent of death. The house was much as it was the day Sister Aganza Mary had discovered his body in the bed where he had apparently passed peacefully in his sleep.

Without touching anything, she quickly scanned the vast library of medical journals. None of the titles indicated information about Africa. Dr. Williams had often spoken of writing a book about the diseases he had treated, and how he hoped to someday have it published. A large diary lay on his desk. She reached out to touch it but hesitated. The book surely held pages of personal thoughts. She knew how she would feel if someone were to read her diary. An invasion of privacy. Much like a curious child afraid of getting caught, she opened the book. Neatly penned in fading ink, the title read, "African Diseases, Curses, Cures, and Other Maladies," by Archibald Calvert Williams, Doctor of Exotic Diseases, Oxford, England, late of Mombasa, Africa."

She carefully flipped through the pages, amazed at the intricate drawings with attention to detail of symptoms the patients had described, the treatments that had not worked and the successful treatments. Fascinated, she forgot about the Tani prince who waited for her, until Sister Adah Luke said, "Falit waits. Did you find what you were looking for?"

Absorbed in the diary, Margaret was startled by the voice, and she gasped and clutched her chest. "I think so. Another moment, please."

She flipped rapidly through the alphabetized pages until she came to *Elephantiasis Tropica,* and read, "The natives call it the curse of the elephant."

"Sister Adah, does Falit look like this?" Margaret

pointed to the detailed illustration.

"Yass, Mama, dis is it. 'Cept 'tisn't his legs that be swollen."

The odd smile on the Hausa woman's face piqued Margaret's curiosity. "Then where?"

"Oh, you will see, Mama Daktor…you will see. Come."

Not one for surprises, Margaret simply said, "Brilliant!"

Margaret put a folded sheet of paper between the pages to mark the spot. She continued reading while matching the Hausa woman's rapid pace toward the infirmary and up the steps.

Seated in a chair, his legs splayed apart, the prince was an imposing man. From the length of his legs, she estimated his height at near seven feet. He gripped each end of a leopard skin in his hands. The muscles on his arms bulged from the strain.

Margaret glanced at the page in the book, then at the patient, then toward Sister Adah Luke. She opened her mouth, but the words didn't come out.

"Yass, Mama, what you see is such a sight. Maybe Falit was a bull *timbo* in his other life."

"Poor man. The pain must be unbearable." Margaret once again turned her attention to the journal. She quickly scanned the old doctor's words, hoping to find a plausible treatment. "I truly must learn the Hausa language. Tell Falit to get comfortable…no, that's not quite right, is it? How can he possibly be comfortable, toting that massive thing around all day?" She thought for a moment.

The prince spoke and pointed.

Sister Adah said, "He wants to see the leaves you

hold in your hand."

Margaret tittered. "The book, of course!" She held the page for him to see. "Tell Falit that I must look in my book of magic for a cure. Tell him that I must put him to sleep, and when he wakes, he will be a new man."

"What are you going to do, Mama Daktor?"

"Operate, of course."

Sister Adah's eyes widened. She placed a hand to her mouth. "You don't mean…cut off his baby maker?"

Margaret didn't hesitate. "Summon his wives."

"Mama Daktor, dis is no good."

"It will be all right, Sister Adah Luke. Trust me. Now, do as I ask, and summon Falit's wives, and Sister Aganza Mary."

When all were gathered, Margaret explained that she would use a magic potion to put Falit into a deep sleep. She pointed to his thigh and said she would insert a tube and drain out all of the evil. "Tell them that my magic will only work if his soul is pure."

Sister Adah Luke translated when Falit spoke. "He wants to know if he can pleasure his young wife, and will she bear him a son."

Margaret spoke only to the two nurses. "I will trim away as much fat as possible. He will suffer pain for several days. If all goes well, then yes, he can pleasure his wife. I cannot guarantee conception. Explain it in terms they will understand."

That afternoon, Sister Adah Luke assisted Margaret. In all, five stone jars were filled, emptied, and refilled with the noxious fluid that drained from their patient. Afterward, Margaret began cutting away layers of stone-hard fat. Periodically, Sister Aganza

Mary brought tea for Margaret and Adah to sip.

Hours passed, until Margaret was certain her arms would fall out of their sockets from exhaustion. "I have done all I can do. He will sleep another hour or so."

Sister Aganza Mary brought damp cloths for Margaret and Adah to cool their faces, and a light meal of tea, biscuits, and fruit.

"It is a fine ting you hab done, Mama Daktor. Dr. Williams would say you have strong *juju*."

Margaret smiled at the compliment as she scrubbed tired hands over her face. "We will make a potion of laudanum for his pain. We will observe him for a few days. Then when he is ready to leave, you will tell him how much and when to take it."

"Yass, Mama Daktor."

Sister Aganza Mary said, "You are both tired. Bath water is waiting. Go to sleep. I will sit and watch over Falit."

Margaret stood and rolled her shoulders to ease the exhaustion threatening to wash over her. She looked forward to soaking in a warm tub. At the doorway, she touched Sister Adah Luke on the arm. "Wait. I have a request."

The two Hausa women exchanged wary glances.

Margaret offered a warm smile. "I know you call me Mama Daktor out of respect, and I call you Sisters because I respect you. We are all three equal. I would like very much to dispense with the formality of titles when we are amongst ourselves. Can we just call each other by our first names…Margaret, Adah, and Aganza?"

Sister Adah Luke pulled a dour face. "You are a daktor. We are nurses. We are Hausa. You are—"

The air was stifling, and she longed for the bath that awaited her. Margaret interrupted. "We are women living in semi-primitive conditions. Our goals are the same, to heal people, to give comfort, and to survive whatever life throws at us. It is I who is *not* equal to you. I do not speak the languages, I do not know about jungle medicine." When the women didn't answer, she said, "At least think about it." The women seemed to preen under her flattery. She turned toward the door.

Quiet, almost timid voices stopped her.

"Margaret, I am Adah."

"Please call me Aganza."

Margaret turned back and stretched her hands out to clasp theirs. "I am honored to know you."

Margaret and Adah left the infirmary. They held lanterns to light their way, neither aware of the piercing eyes that watched from a distance.

Chapter 16

Out of respect and for the love that the people at Angel of Mercy Compound held for the late doctor, Margaret decided it was appropriate to celebrate the destruction of the house he had resided in for so many years.

She also wanted to honor the customs of the people. A feast was prepared and *sangomas* were invited, especially Matata from the Leopard Clan and Demissie of the Tani people. She hoped to gain their respect, and perhaps to feel a little safer because of it.

She stood on the hospital's porch and searched through the throng of people. The news of Dr. Williams' death had gone out days ago on the jungle telegraph. Surely Lyon had heard. Surely he would come.

"De one you seek is not here, Margaret."

"You are mistaken, Adah. I'm merely keeping a watchful eye on my two worst enemies." And then Margaret recanted. "I thought Lyon would come."

"He would if he heard de drums. Sometimes the sound does not carry to the ears if the ears are too far away to hear."

When Margaret didn't respond, the Hausa woman laid her hand over Margaret's. "He will come. He is like a moth drawn to the flame. Yass, Lyon will come, for sure. When it is time."

Margaret gazed out across the yard. She trembled with the urge to hide. She trembled with an unspoken fear.

Falit rested on a chair. Two wives held leaves as large as elephant ears to shade him from the sun. Another fanned, while yet another fed him, and two others joined the group of women dancers. Margaret found their movements mesmerizing and erotic. She envied their lack of inhibition. She pulled at the layers of sweat-soaked undergarments that clung to her like a second skin, and she laughed inwardly, visualizing the disapproving expressions of London's elite matrons.

She watched Falit as he stood and swept open his loincloth. Demissie approached the prince. Words were exchanged. Margaret couldn't tell if the loudness of their voices was customary or from anger.

Falit turned, pointing his finger toward Margaret. In spite of the heat, a chill settled over her. Adah hurried up the steps. "What are they saying, Adah?"

"Falit is showing off his baby-maker. He says the Mama Daktor has powerful *juju*, and as soon as he is able, he will mount his new wife like a stallion and ride her to exhaustion."

Peals of laughter and cheers rang out. Despite the pain on his face, Falit made a good showing of strutting like a proud peacock.

A tinge of pride welled in Margaret for the success of a risky and untried surgical procedure. Following Dr. Williams' practice, she had recorded and illustrated each detail in her own journal. She didn't want to think about the consequences had she seriously maimed her patient—or worse, he had died.

Sister Adah Luke clasped her hands to her breasts.

"Oh, dis not be good, Margaret."

Such explicit topics of performing surgery on male sex organs were prohibited in polite society. Margaret yearned for a damp cloth to cool her heated cheeks. "What? Tell me."

"Falit say Mama Daktor's magic is more powerful than Demissie or Matata."

The bravado in Margaret's voice didn't match the tremors she fought to quell. "I am not afraid of two half-naked men who rattle chicken bones and jig around like the bottoms of their feet are on fire."

"Even so, Margaret, I fear for you."

"Then I will keep my rifle handy." She grabbed Adah's hand. "Come with me and translate."

"It worries me when your eyes glint like the cobra about to strike."

Margaret clasped Falit's hand and in a gesture of respect held it to her forehead. He in turn pulled her thumb.

Margaret walked to the center of the compound, bidding the Hausa woman to translate. The drums stopped. Voices quieted. All eyes were on the white witch doctor. She spread her arms. Sister Adah Luke's voice matched Margaret's as she translated: "The spirit of Daktor Williams lives among us. His spirit is restless. He knows there are some who wish to bring harm to Mama Daktor." Margaret drew a breath. "I give Prince Falit, next chief of the Tani people, the honor of offering Daktor Williams' house to the fire gods to protect Angel of Mercy, and all the people who live here, from evil."

When Adah had finished, she whispered, "That is a mos' dangerous challenge, Margaret. It might work. It might not. *Sangomas* have their own gods, like Anansi who can change into a spider and is sneaky and mean."

Margaret pulled a small matchbox from her pocket. She struck the sulfur tip against the coarse striking surface. A spark flashed and the tip flared. She touched the flame to the torch made of straw.

Falit strutted with arrogant pride to stand on the top step of the crumbling house. He offered up an elegant prayer to the god *Muungu* and then touched the torch to the withered and brittle grass of the thatched roof. Like a hungry animal, the flames consumed the easy meal. Smoke billowed and spiraled upward.

The stench of seared flesh permeated the air as rodents fled from the flaming interwoven thatch. A charred python dropped to the ground. Children rushed forward to gather a free meal. The brittle grasses snapped and crackled, and in minutes the flames had burned to the base of the crumbling mud and straw walls, which collapsed into dust and shard.

Margaret longed for the ceremony to end. Her head throbbed from the constant hand clapping, chanting voices, and drumbeats. She was ready to sweep away the debris and have work begin on her new house, one of her own design. One constructed of wood, with an elevated wooden floor, a tightly sealed roof, and high windows. She wanted a solid door with a slide-bolt lock, and she wanted a porch. In the meantime, she would remain in the infirmary.

The noise had escalated to a frenzy. Margaret closed her eyes against the manic mayhem exploding around her. Just when she feared weariness had finally claimed her, Sister Adah Luke screamed, "Margaret, watch out!"

Margaret's heart lurched in her throat, her eyes widened in terror, and her arms and legs refused to move. Surely this wasn't her time to die!

The spear landed between her feet. Merriment was replaced with a deafening hush. Demissie swaggered forward and raised his hand. A long fingernail that resembled the tip of a spear touched her chest. His short cropped hair was beginning to gray, but his manner was still direct, his expression impudent. "*N'Devli—*"

There was no doubt in Margaret's mind that the nail was razor-sharp and could slice as deep as one of her scalpels. She slapped the witch doctor's hand. "You son of a donkey. You braying jackass."

Her tolerance tested, she didn't care if he understood her words. "I am sick to death of these blatant threats! I am not a witch, nor am I a devil."

An instant defense rose up in Margaret and tempered her anger. "Adah, tell this farcical clown that I challenge him to match his chicanery against my medicine, and if I win, the people of his village will know him for the charlatan he really is."

The Hausa woman regarded her with a concerned frown. "Margaret, Demissie will not understand dese big words you use. I am not sure I know de meaning of all dese words. Are dey as bad as they sound?"

"I have indeed insulted the bloody impostor. Say the words with force, Adah, and add whatever you like. Just keep him busy until I return."

Margaret snatched the spear standing embedded in the dirt, threw it to the ground, and to add insult to insult, she gave it a swift kick.

A shock wave of voices rippled through the crowd.

Margaret raced up the steps to the medical supply

room. She collected a small bottle of ether, a bottle of hydrogen peroxide, and other items. Her heart hammered against her ribs. She wanted to be done with this bigotry.

Returning to the porch, she stood on the top step. Demissie waited, his arms across his chest. She wanted to smack the cheeky grin off his face. She pointed to the festering sore on his foot. "Adah, tell everyone that I will use magic water to clean the wound on Demissie's foot. My medicine will eat away the devils that cause him pain."

The Hausa woman barely nodded. She gazed nervously at the witch doctor. No one reacted until he guffawed and slapped his sides. "Margaret, Demissie say he is in no pain."

Margaret's words were crisp. "Ask him why he limps when he walks, and why he stands with the foot propped against his leg. Ask him if he is afraid of my medicine."

Adah's voice was terse. Her breath came out in short pants as she translated. The words had hit home. Demissie's mouth twisted into a snarl. His eyes glowered with malice. Like anyone else, he didn't like to be called chicken-hearted.

Demissie's words were, "Tell the white witch if my medicine is more powerful, then I will cut out her liver and eat it. Then her magic will be mine."

The sun was directly overhead. Margaret could feel the heat beating down on her. She licked her parched lips. She did not doubt his threat.

Adah repeated Margaret's words, "If Mama Daktor's medicine is more powerful than yours, you are to leave her in peace to heal all the people of Africa.

She wishes to learn from you, and you can learn from her. She asks to be *refiki*."

Desmissie spat on the ground. "Bah."

Margaret gazed out over the crowd, and though she trembled inside, she matched the witch doctor's glare as Adah drove home her message. "Prepare to lose face with all the people—the Tani, Hausa, Maasai, and all beyond the Rift Valley. The talking drums will say you are not an honorable man. You are as lowly as the hyena."

With the last statement, Margaret knew she had bested her archenemy. He didn't dare back down from the challenge. She had issued a dangerous ultimatum. Doubt settled over her like a fog. If she failed, her only hope was to escape back to Léopoldville, for she knew Demissie and Matata would kill her.

Prince Falit hobbled to stand between Margaret and Adah. Margaret knew from the beads of sweat on his brow and the slight hunch to his regal poster that he was in pain, but he was wearing it well. He reached for Margaret's hand and pulled her thumb again, a sign of respect and friendship. His words caused tears to well in Margaret's eyes. She willed herself to not cry when he pointed to his chest and said, "Mama Daktor, *refiki*."

Demissie thinned his lips. "Bah!"

His face remained resolute when Margaret ordered him to sit on the step. Adah stood next to her. "Margaret, you must perform a ceremony before doctoring his foot. It is customary to show that your *juju* is strong."

"Oh, balderdash! I am not going to dance around in a circle like a drunken idiot."

"You must, Margaret. If you are to win the

people's trust, you must do something, and the louder the better."

"But I didn't when I pulled the abscessed tooth of Matata's wife."

"That is because wives are considered cattle. They have no importance. Please, Margaret. You must do dis ting."

Margaret expelled an exasperated sigh. She called to Sister Aganza Mary, "Get me a basin and a large spoon."

Overwrought with peevishness, Margaret marched about banging the spoon against the tin tub while she belted out England's national anthem, "God Save the Queen."

Getting into the spirit of things, she marched up to Demissie, set the basin on top of his head, and gave the metal pan a couple of strong whacks. She delighted in the grimace on the witch doctor's face. She removed the pan, held her hands in front of his face, wiggled her fingers, and shouted a magician's word and a line from Macbeth: "Abracadabra. Double, double, toil and trouble, fire burn and cauldron bubble."

Adah gave Margaret a wink. Somewhat gratified, Margaret said, "Enough of this hocus-pocus. Tell him to lift his foot forward."

When he obeyed, she used a scalpel to scrape the festering skin aside to expose a pocket of infection. She pierced the sac and mopped out the yellow, foul-smelling poison, and then she poured peroxide into the wound.

"Adah, tell him my magic in the bottle is killing the evil spirits in his foot." She used a clean bandage to cleanse the putrid area, and then refilled it with peroxide. Observers gathered around to watch the frothing foam. Mumbles of wonderment and pointing fingers greeted her ministrations.

When the bubbling subsided, she cleaned the area again and filled it full of tincture of iodine. She didn't try to hide her smile of gratification when the burning antiseptic brought a wide-eyed yelp from Demissie.

"Adah, it's time for the big finale. Let's hope this wins his and Matata's respect." Margaret rubbed her arms up and down as if she were trying to ward off a chill in hundred-degree heat. She was trying to hold herself together and not shatter like a piece of glass.

She produced the bottle of ether and a handkerchief from her pocket. "Ask Demissie if he is an honest man. Say that if he tells the truth my magic will not work, but if he talks with the split tongue of an adder my magic will put him in a dark place where he will awaken all alone. Tell him that the evil spirits will eat away his foot and he will die."

She offered the Hausa woman a faint smile. The heat settled on them like a heavy blanket. Margaret tried thinking of England's idyllic autumn days. She missed the cool weather. "Margaret?"

Adah's voice intruded into Margaret's momentary escape. She folded the handkerchief into a neat square, then tipped the bottle of ether against it. She did this twice. Demissie was a large man, and she wanted to make sure his slip into a deep sleep was immediate.

She held the bottle high and in her loudest voice recited the children's poem, "Humpty Dumpty."

She made a big show of passing the bottle back and forth in front of the witch doctor's face, and then for good measure, she doused the handkerchief again.

When she sang the verse, "Threescore men and threescore more, cannot place Humpty Dumpty as he was before," she grabbed Demissie's head with one hand and with the other pressed the ether-soaked cloth over his mouth and nose. She hoped the unexpected move would surprise him enough to cause a deep gasp.

Silently she counted. Before she got to ten, his body relaxed, and he slumped into a heap.

Matata rushed forward. He poked Demissie with the tip of his spear. Getting no reaction, he lifted Demissie's hand, then let it fall limp. His eyes widened as he jabbed the sleeping man. He declared that the white witch doctor's magic was most powerful. He worked up a frenzy, saying she had cast an evil spell over Demissie, and that he would call upon the leopard gods to reverse the spell and destroy her.

Margaret sighed heavily. She didn't say anything right away. What was it Lyon had said when they had met?

This is darkest Africa, lady, where life roars by you like a herd of stampeding elephants and you get up the nearest tree and pray it will hold you up.

She instructed Adah to have men from Demissie's village tote him to the edge of the compound and prop him against a tree. She also advised that the ceremony was over and for everyone to return to their villages.

She told Falit she was proud to call him friend. She gave him ten pebbles with the instruction to toss one away each day and when the last one was gone to come see her for a follow-up examination.

Tears filled her eyes. It wasn't fair what life was throwing at her. With blurred vision, she stood for a moment and simply gazed out at the compound.

Aganza Mary placed a hand on Margaret's shoulder. "Come, Mama Daktor. I have prepared soup and bread, and coffee. You are tired, and rightly so. You will rest tonight."

Margaret stared at the spot where Demissie sat sprawled against the tree. She was relieved to see him still there. It seemed ridiculous to fear him, especially tonight. He would sleep. Ether produced nightmares. She hoped the dreams frightened the bejeebers out of him, enough for him to either acquiesce enough to be on neutral terms, or to fear her enough to stay away. Her imagination created all sorts of plausible outcomes. She managed a smile. "What I would like is a tot of whiskey in my coffee."

Tonight she would sleep with the rifle by her side.

Chapter 17

Demissie wasn't sure if he was asleep or awake. One minute he was looking down at his inert body and the next he was cowering behind a tree. He had no idea why he was hiding, until mammoth crocodiles raced toward him with their massive jaws snapping. He tried to climb the tree, only to discover that he had no feet. In desperation, he cried out for *Muungu* to save him.

Much to his surprise, hands reached down and snatched him out of harm's way. He was flung from one tree to another and then another by chimpanzees until he landed on top of a giant ant hill.

Fire ants swarmed over Demissie, injecting him with painful stings until he was certain his body would burst into flames. He rolled back and forth, slapping at the stinging insects, only to discover there were no ants and the pain was from his own hands.

He sat up and reveled in the flood of relief until he looked at the gaping hole in his foot. His eyes widened as the tiny white bubbles grew into white worms that merged into one large cobra that swayed back and forth as though in a drunken dance. When the reptile drew back its head in preparation to strike, Demissie screamed. His eyes flew open, and he fought the giant spider web that cocooned him. He screamed again, not realizing he lay on a hospital bed draped by mosquito netting.

Margaret rushed into the room. Hot on her heels were Sister Adah Luke and Sister Aganza Mary.

Knowing the aftereffects of ether, Margaret and the nurses had prepared for the results the previous evening. Now she said, "You know what to do, ladies."

Aganza grabbed the bucket. In a few seconds everything Demissie had feasted on yesterday was about to come up. Ready to sponge off his sweat-soaked body, Adah brought a basin of cool water and dipped a cloth in it.

Margaret flung back the webbing, then grabbed a syringe filled with a mild sedative. When Demissie leaned over to empty his stomach, Margaret administered the injection.

Adah spoke in a calm voice, commanding the witch doctor to take slow, even breaths. He looked at her, wild-eyed. "Demissie, you will admit that Mama Daktor's medicine is much stronger than your magic?"

He lay back and drew in large gulps of air. She wiped his mouth and forehead with the damp cloth. "Demissie, are you hearing me?"

He glanced about as if trying to absorb his surroundings. He held up his arms. Then he pushed to a sitting position to look at his foot. "Der are no ant bites. Where are de chimpanzees and de crocodiles?"

All three woman looked at each other and, unable to contain themselves, burst into laughter. Adah said, "Mama Daktor's medicine is mos' powerful. She makes you see what is not there, yass?"

Demissie stammered, "I saw them, and de ants were biting me all over, and de worms were eating my foot."

Margaret lifted his foot. "You see, my medicine is

already healing the canker that was eating away your
foot. Eventually, the infection would have killed you."

Adah translated.

Unaware that Margaret had tended him throughout
the night, he said, "What is dis in-fek-shun? I do not
know dis word."

Margaret took a moment to compose her answer in
words the witch doctor would understand, ones Adah
could easily explain. "It is a poison. Many of the people
in your village have this same *sumu* that eats away the
flesh. They will die. You have watched them depart this
life because your magic cannot cure them. Tell the
people to come to the hospital. Let Mama Daktor treat
them."

Aganza Mary whispered the rest of Adah Luke's
words to Demissie, saying first, "Dis is for you,
Margaret." She told Adah to say, "If you continue
trying to do harm to Mama Daktor, the ancestors will
become mos' angry wid you. Do you wish to suffer the
wrath of de old ones?"

Demissie lay back. He scrubbed the heels of his
hands over his face. "I am helpless like de baby. I feel
like a drifting cloud. *N'Devli* has placed a spell on me."

Margaret understood. "Tell him that if he calls me
the devil one more time I will take away all his magic,
shrivel his manhood, and make his voice sound like a
squawking chicken." She pointed to herself. "Mama
Daktor…*Mama Daktor*!"

Listening to Adah Luke's translation, his eyes
wide, he acquiesced as he reached down and cupped
both hands over his genitals. "Mama Daktor."

****

A few days after Demissie left the hospital, people

from his village visited the dispensary. At first only one or two came, and then the numbers slowly grew. There were times when exhaustion rode Margaret to the point she would try to send them away, but they stayed, even after dark.

For weeks Margaret worked hard at the compound. Although her days were full, she wasn't sure how much she accomplished. On an exceptionally hot afternoon, she watched the two native nurses wash each other's hair.

"I envy your short hair." She lifted the heavy coppery tresses from her neck.

"Is there a law in your land that forbids women to cut their hair, Margaret?" Adah cast a curious look toward the doctor.

"I'm not in England." Margaret grabbed a pair of scissors. "Which one of you will do the honors?"

Adah and Aganza exchanged glances. Each shrugged their shoulders. Margaret cocked an eyebrow. "Well?"

Aganza hesitated, then took the scissors. "Promise you will not hate me if you do not like what you see."

Margaret reached up and patted the woman's hand. "Never, Aganza. Start whacking before I lose my courage."

Aganza Mary gathered the long rope of hair in one hand. She snipped, and snipped, and snipped some more, never allowing one strand to fall to the ground. When she was finished, she held the remains forward. "It is very heavy."

Margaret reached up and ran her fingers through the shortened locks. She laughed. "My head feels like it has lost a hundred pounds. How does it look?"

Adah, too, laughed. "You have curls. Not so many as Aganza and me. It makes you look younger. I will get the mirror."

Seconds later, Margaret reacted to the image staring back at her. "I shall never wear my hair long again." She took the long hank of hair from Aganza. "And I shall keep this as a souvenir of sorts."

Amazed at the transition in her image, she again stared into the mirror.

****

On a rainy morning, only two beds held patients. Margaret took advantage of the quiet and sat at her desk reading Dr. Williams' medical journal. She had forgotten about the folded sheet of paper she had found so long ago and had slipped between the pages. She was surprised to find it was a letter that he had written to her.

You are a fine doctor, Margaret Ashton Boynton. A bit naive, a little overly zealous; nonetheless, skilled. I fear I have overstayed my time in Africa and will never see my homeland again. A year from now, no one will remember the many years I have dedicated to Angel of Mercy Mission and Hospital. A word of caution, Margaret—know when enough is enough. Life in the jungle is difficult and perhaps more so for a woman, I fear. Do not forget to take a quinine pill every morning, and never allow the supply to run out. Know this: there is no shame in returning to England when your term ends. It is a lesson I wish I had heeded. Forgive me for my lament.

By now, you have discovered my journal. Another of my regrets is that I procrastinated in sending it to a publisher. I charge you with the responsibility of continuing to record medical information on all the treatments you administer and follow with detailed illustrations. My request is that you send the journal to your connections with the medical board in London. So little is known about African diseases and treatments that I am certain the medical community will consider the publication of this journal an asset. You may claim all rights to any payments earned; just one small conceit: I would like an acknowledgement and a dedication to myself.

A long sigh escaped Margaret. She counted on her fingers. There were days when the passing of six months seemed like a blink of an eye, and on other days it seemed she had been here a lifetime. She opened the locket. Her heart still ached when she looked at the pictures of her husband and son. She brushed away the tears.

Adah approached. "Margaret, you are wearing yourself out. We are all tired. You must set aside a day for rest."

Margaret wiped her eyes. Her father's words drifted into her memory, and she said them aloud. "Be careful what you ask for because it may not be what you want when you get it."

"What is this you say?" Adah questioned, a frown creasing her normally smooth forehead.

"It was something my father said to me before I left England. I hate to admit he was right. I enjoy healing, learning the language, and seeing smiles brighten once-dour faces."

She looked beyond the neatly swept yards of the hospital compound to the vacant space where Dr. Williams' house had stood. She hadn't had time to give much thought to building her own dwelling.

"You are absolutely correct, Adah. We shall work five days and rest on Saturdays and Sundays, unless there is an emergency, of course." Margaret smiled at the radiant expression on the Hausa woman's face. She clasped hands with her friend. "Come, let's give the news to Aganza and the other workers."

While they sat sharing a pot of tea and discussing ideas for her new house, lively drum beats interrupted the quiet respite. Residents of the mission gathered in the yard, and children laughed and clapped their hands.

"The drums say"—Adah listened—"boat comes down the Tani. Mail for the mission, and a large crate."

Margaret sent two strong boys to the river. The arrival of mail and supplies was like opening presents on Christmas Day.

The drums spoke again. "Did they forget something, Adah?"

"No, Margaret. Dese be different drums." She listened. A smile widened, and then was replaced with serious concern. "The Lyon, he is coming."

Margaret's heart thudded with excitement. The distress on Adah's face tamped down any building giddiness. "It's bad, isn't it?"

"Yass, M'pika hurt very bad. Drums say he has a fever. Arrive tomorrow. Send boys to the river with a litter."

Margaret clapped her hands together, and issued orders like a sergeant in charge of troops readying for a battle.

That night after the evening meal, she retired early. Her mind seemed heavy, tired, and haunted by memories. She rolled to her side and punched her pillow, suddenly realizing how long she'd been thinking about Seamus and Lyon, comparing their attributes. Jeremiah Lyon was broad-shouldered compared to Seamus' sparse frame. Lyon was several inches taller, and his posture commanding, whereas Seamus had been relaxed yet regal.

Lyon fired her temper, made her feel alive, and passionate. Seamus had never made her feel lustful, and for that she felt guilty. Lyon was adventurous and daring, and Seamus was—dead. The word hit her like a painful stab to the heart, which only made her feel more guilty.

What was wrong with her? She tried to force back the tears, but they kept coming.

Chapter 18

Three days of unrelenting rainfall finally gave way as the sun inched over the smooth waters which reflected clouds and blue sky.

The pain started in his chest and radiated out to his limbs. Lyon called on every ounce of his fading strength to plow the paddle through the water and toward the shore.

He shivered.

Bloody hell. He hoped it wasn't a shiver.

He shifted just a fraction. Pain shot through every nerve in his body.

He shivered again. Maybe he was just cold from being soaked to the skin both day and night. He felt like the devil, all hot and cold, and oddly out of kilter. He heard something—faint, far away. His name.

Lyon staggered a half-step forward before he realized Margaret was holding him up. He couldn't speak. He coughed. And coughed again. He had difficulty speaking. "M'pika." He tried to point to the canoe.

He didn't remember getting out of the canoe.

"Don't worry, Lyon. We'll take care of M'pika and all of your men." Margaret answered with a reassuring smile. "Come now, let's get you into a bed."

"I'm just tired. I'll be okay by tomorrow."

Margaret looked at him with dubious eyes. His

tawny hair lay plastered to his head, and the level of heat radiating from his body had nothing to do with the glaring sun. Not to mention that he reeked of sickness. It was an offensive odor like that of rotting fruit mingled with the musky scent of sweat.

"You are aware that you have malaria?"

He shrugged, his entire body shaking from the exertion of trying to walk. "Yeah."

"Then why didn't you take quinine?"

"Didn't have any."

He stumbled. She flinched when he grabbed her arm. "You are literally burning up with fever. Lean on me."

He dropped to his knees, panting. Margaret shouted for help.

Someone called his name. A woman's voice. His mother's? Lyon struggled through a quagmire of distorted images to open his eyes. A lone lantern lit the room. How many hours had he slept?

Margaret set a tray of steaming stew and hot coffee on a small table. She felt his forehead, then lifted his wrist to take his pulse. Her hands were cool against his feverish flesh.

He rasped,. "M'pika?"

She helped him sit up. "A dislocated hip, quite inflamed. It took several strong arms to help me pull it back into place. He'll survive, and without a limp. I'm more concerned about the inflammation in his lungs. Tell me what happened."

Between spoonfuls of the chicken vegetable stew that she fed him, he related how the elephant had reared up against the tree and wrapped its trunk around M'pika's leg. "I thought he was a goner for sure. What about my boys, Wanumbi and the others?"

She smiled at him. Her eyes were as gentle as a spring sky when he looked up into her face. She said, "For the days of hard travel without rest, in the pouring rain, and with lack of food, they are none the worse for wear. In fact, with a few good meals and a couple of days' rest, all three of them will be in better health than you and M'pika."

"Is Dr. Williams spending time making his rounds at the villages? Where is my old friend?"

A moment of silence.

"What is it that you're not telling me, Margaret?"

She folded her hands together. "We sent a message by jungle telegraph. You must have been too far away; otherwise, we knew you would have returned to Angel of Mercy as soon as possible."

The air in the sick room seemed to thicken. Margaret spoke against the tightness in her voice. "We buried him weeks ago."

She went on to explain the circumstances of finding his body, and the ceremony of burning down his house, and the feast that followed. She reminded him of a spouting geyser that couldn't be turned off as she related about patients she had treated, about the successful surgery she had performed on Falit, about drugging Demissie with ether—and the hallucinations he thought were real—and Matata's threat.

Lyon's laughter turned into a harsh cough. "You truly threatened to remove the witch doctor's bollocks?"

She offered a smug smile and simply nodded.

"Remind me to stay on your good side."

A series of rattling coughs seemed to take its toll

on him, and as he lay back and closed his eyes, he merely whispered, "Thank you, Margaret."

She reached out and touched his shoulder. "I liked it better when you called me Maggie."

****

Lyon supposed it was too much to try and hide his illness from Margaret. She was a doctor, after all. Although he preferred that she not fret over him, the truth was that he was comforted by her presence. He shouldn't have been, or at least shouldn't have allowed himself to be, but he was. Margaret was beautiful. Her British accent enthralled him, and she always smelled like sunshine.

She was one of the few white women he had known. Maybe she affected him as she did because in all his daydreams, in all his fantasies, he'd never quite pictured anyone like her. He'd only had the small photo of his mother tucked inside the locket as a comparison for most women. From what he could remember, his mother was a virtuous woman. The women he had met on safari were shallow—younger wives married to older aristocrats. Women who openly fawned over him, who slipped into his tent after dark seeking lustful fulfillment that their husband's money couldn't satisfy.

It wasn't Margaret's hair, that rich golden red that reminded him of a setting sun. And it wasn't her eyes, so crystalline blue he wanted to drown in them. Nor was it the shape of her face, or the fine bones that sculpted her nose and defined her cheeks. No, it was something in the way she moved. The way she carried herself. The way she breathed. The respect she commanded without saying a word. It was simply—her. He wanted her in every way a man could want a woman, with the exception that he wanted her for a lifetime.

He didn't know the emotion *love*. It was merely a word he'd heard used from time to time. It was a word often used by the wives who accompanied their husbands on safari. They loved the zebras, they loved the cute monkeys, they loved the flamingos, they loved…

The emotion he felt was foreign to him. It was almost like the effects of malaria. Hot one minute, teeth-chatteringly cold the next, sick to the point it would feel good to die, and when it was all over, happy to see another day. Was this the way love felt?

Sated with nourishment, and seeking more warmth from the chills that still plagued him, he hunkered deeper into the blanket and allowed the solace of sleep to overtake him.

****

After checking on M'pika and heartened that the wheezing in his lungs had lessened and he was resting peacefully, Margaret strolled down the long porch to her own little room. She braced her hands against the railing and leaned forward to catch the night's refreshing breeze. She inhaled the fragrant scent of night-blooming jasmine, and listened. The jungle was alive and making its own music.

She glanced at the trees that crowded around the mission's grounds. Beautiful during the day, ominous at night. Dappled moonlight filtered through the leaves. A low throaty growl followed by a series of chuffs signaled a big cat lurked nearby. Night torches surrounded the complex to dissuade animals from coming too close. She had listened to the varied accounts of leopards pushing through doors or pulling bars from windows to get at their prey. And though she didn't discount the stories, seven months had passed, and she had yet to see any of the big cats. None on her treks to the villages, at the river, or near the hospital.

A shiver wafted over her. Before stepping inside, she glanced over her shoulder and caught sight of a movement. The hairs on the back of her neck and arms prickled. Seeking safety, she pushed against the door. Her hand touched a wet, sticky substance with the distinct coppery scent of fresh blood. Her heart pounded so hard it hurt her chest. She drew a breath to calm herself.

Fleet steps took her back to Lyon's room. Once inside, she secured the night table against the door. She surveyed the room for another heavy object to help create a barricade. Nothing. She pulled the chair close to the foot of the bed where Lyon slept. Facing the door was important. She needed to see the enemy if he broke through the barrier.

She knew the sedative she'd given Lyon would cause him to sleep deeply. A sleeping man was a helpless protector. Nonetheless, being close to him was better than being alone. Perhaps she should call out, sound the alarm? She couldn't seem to draw an adequate breath.

She filled the basin and watched the water turn red as she scrubbed the blood from her hand. This was clearly a warning. From whom—Demissie or Matata? Both were her sworn adversaries.

Every sound put her on alert. Did she hear footsteps or perhaps the padding of paws outside Lyon's door?

Inside her apron pocket, she wrapped her fingers around a pair of scissors. She held herself still as she sat in the room's one chair, determined to stay vigilant.

Chapter 19

The next morning Lyon awakened to soft puttering sounds. Still weak and shaky, he struggled to surface and remain conscious. He needed a few more days to regain his strength. He peered over the blanket and was surprised to see Margaret slumped over, half on the wooden chair and half on the bed. She looked uncomfortable, lying at such an awkward angle. Her right arm supported her head. In her left hand, she held a pair of scissors.

He studied her. She had cut her hair. He liked how the curls feathered around her face. She looked much younger and more approachable in sleep. With an overwhelming need to reach out and touch her, he scooted to a sitting position.

Margaret sighed, and suddenly he was staring into wide-awake blue eyes. He smiled, and she relaxed.

"You cut your hair."

Her fingers fluttered through the curls. "I must look a fright."

"Just the opposite. It becomes you."

Her cheeks flushed pink.

She stretched as if relieving the kinks in her body. "You have malaria."

"Yeah, it's one of the many perils of living in Africa."

"How long have you known?"

"A couple of years, more or less."

"Do you keep quinine with you?" She cocked an eyebrow as if the question was a challenge.

"Usually." He slumped back against the pillow. "We lost most of our supplies on this last trek."

She reached out and touched his forehead. "You are much cooler. A few more days of bed rest won't hurt you."

"I hate feeling helpless."

She smiled, inviting and seductive. "I imagine most men feel the same way."

She was so close to him he could feel her breath against his hair. His hand came up to catch hers. He brought her palm to his lips and kissed the center.

"Don't." Her glance darted toward the barricaded door.

"What's wrong?" He thought of letting go and pretending he'd never touched her.

"Nothing." She gulped down a breath. "I just don't like being startled. If you plan to hug me, I'd like advance notice."

"I didn't mean to frighten you."

She continued to stand near him. "You didn't."

"Maggie," he whispered against her skin. He tugged on her hand, and she looked into his eyes. "Come closer so I can thank you properly." Part of him felt like a fool for moving too fast. He'd not been around proper women enough to know how to act, and he certainly didn't know how to court.

Margaret allowed herself to be pulled forward. She leaned over, and Lyon touched his lips to hers. He made a noise deep in his throat and reached up to draw her to him.

"Jeremiah." The way she said his name sounded like a caress. The heat from her body melted through her sleep-rumpled dress to warm him. He should have been happy just to hug her or hold her hand, but he wanted more.

His voice soft, almost apologetic, he told her, "I don't know how to do this, Maggie. I've never thought about courting a woman. All I know is that I want you near me."

Margaret rested her hands on his shoulders. She was hesitant, almost shy, but she didn't move away, instead letting him kiss her completely. She whispered his name again.

He inhaled the scent of roses that clung to her body. His body responded immediately. In spite of the morning heat, he reveled in the smooth coolness of her skin. Whatever he was about to say was forgotten when a piercing scream rent the air.

Margaret scrambled away from Lyon. She rushed to the door and shoved the small table away from the door and against the wall.

Aganza Mary stood pressed against the porch railing, clutching her hands to her chest. Adah Luke, Y'ro, and Wanumbi came racing across the yard.

Lyon swung his legs off the bed. He wobbled when he stood and stumbled after Margaret as she rushed down the porch. His eyes widened in dismay at the gruesome sight. Claw marks grooved deep into the door of Margaret's room, and there was blood, lots of blood. It glistened in the morning's sunlight. Margaret placed a comforting arm around Aganza Mary's shaking shoulders.

Margaret's words were meant for everyone, but she

looked at Lyon. "Who would do this?"

Wanumbi stepped forward. "I heard de leopard las' night. Him plenty big."

The exertion of scrambling from the bed and hurrying down the long porch had left Lyon exhausted and weak. "No cat did this. I know of only one tribe who worships the leopard and has a witch doctor evil enough to make such a threat."

Wanumbi frowned. "Matata."

A worried Margaret asked, "Will the scent of blood cause leopards or lions to attack the compound?"

As if of one mind, Adah and Aganza both said, "Don't worry, Margaret. By de time we finish scrubbing, dere will be no trace or scent of blood."

Lyon clutched the porch post with both arms as the world spun out of control. Much to his chagrin, his knees buckled. Chills beset him, and everything turned black.

Margaret wrapped her arms around him in an effort to keep him upright. "Wanumbi, Y'ro, help me."

She ran ahead of the men to smooth the sheets and to pour a glass of water and stir in a quinine powder. "Thank you, Wanumbi, for your strong arms."

"Lyon good *bwana*, good *rifiki*. You make better, Mama Daktor."

Margaret noted the command. "It pleases me to know how much all of you value Lyon." A frown wrinkled her brow. "Still, in his weakened state, I fear for his safety…all our safety."

Y'ro said, "I sleep at your door tonight, Mama Daktor." He pointed to Wanumbi. "We stand guard. You keep rifle ready."

"And all of you keep the torches lit." She met their

eyes, and they smiled.

Fury, deep and wild, filled her mind, and Margaret's only desire was to seek the sanctity of her room before she broke down in tears and howled curses.

****

After tending to her round of patients, Margaret returned to check on Lyon. His bare chest and forehead glistened with sweat. She filled a basin with water to cool him with a damp cloth. Jagged scars that resembled claw marks racked across his chest and down his side, the same type of scars that marred one side of his handsome face. Using her index finger, she gently lifted one of the large yellowed teeth than adorned the necklace. Many thoughts raced through her mind. How old was Lyon when attacked? What had provoked the attack? Was it a lion or a leopard that had clawed him? And how had he managed to survive?

She stared at his scars and then at his face. Her heart clamored in her throat, and with an intensity she couldn't control, she realized she wanted to kiss him. Merciful heaven. She wanted him. She wanted Jeremiah Lyon.

The emotion was like a stab in the heart. She was in mourning. She wasn't supposed to want anyone. Decorum was expected. Polite society dictated a full two years of grieving. Sensibility demanded that she walk out of the room and give Lyon's care to either Adah or Aganza. A proper grieving widow should walk away. Instead she stayed seated next to him. She couldn't take her eyes off the thick dark lashes that curled upward, the soft rise and fall of his chest, and the scars that added to his maleness.

She stared at him, licked her lips, and hesitated.

She leaned in just a little. Her lips touched his with the barest, softest hint of a caress. She waited, breath bated, for some small response.

And he did.

His fingers found the small of her back and splayed there. His touch created an intoxicating heat. He didn't exactly pull her toward him, but the pressure was there, and the space between them was barely a whisper's breath.

His voice husky with desire, he murmured her name. His hand slid up her back, leaving a trail of searing desire in its wake. She wanted this. Oh, how she wanted this.

She looked into his eyes—glassy with fever. He was burning up from more than desire. This was too much. Too intimate. Too soon.

"We can't do this," she whispered. "I can't do this. It isn't proper, and...and...I'm not ready. I thought I was...I can't."

She didn't want to look at him, and when she did she was sorry.

He stared at her with such intensity that his gaze seemed to burn right through her. "I never thought of you as a woman who would play coy, Maggie. Apparently, I was wrong."

She pushed from the bed and stepped out of his reach. "You don't know what it's like for me. There's protocol, you know."

"What the hell are you talking about—protocol? We're in the middle of nowhere. In case you haven't noticed, there's not one person or animal in the jungle that gives a damn about the sanctimonious, stiff-necked, hypocritical etiquette of the British."

She stood there, stock still. Her eyes never left his face. "There are things you don't know about me. Things you need to know. Things too painful to divulge."

A shiver wracked over him. He pulled the blanket up to his chin. "Tell me, Maggie, what deep dark secret are you hiding?"

"Maybe tomorrow, when you're better."

Finally, because the silence was simply unbearable, she left his room, pulling the door closed.

It was going to be a long rest of the day, and an even longer night.

Chapter 20

Lyon lifted the folded note that lay on the bedside table, inhaled the soft rose scent, and knew before reading the signature that the missive was from Margaret. Her immediate presence was required due to an emergency, she had written, describing the difficult pregnancy of a young Maasai woman who was unable to travel to the hospital. She assured him that Sister Aganza Mary would take good care of M'pika, and that he wasn't to worry, because Sister Adah Luke and Y'ro were with her.

It was all very convenient, and Lyon wondered if Margaret had used the trek to the semi-nomadic people's village as an excuse to avoid a face-to-face farewell. That's what it was, an escape. Lyon knew the Maasai, knew their resilience. He didn't believe for one minute that there was an emergency in the southern region of Mombasa. If that had been the case, she should have been duty-bound to inform him. After all, the worst of his malaria had passed. He was perfectly capable of accompanying her.

He strolled to where M'pika sat on the porch. "How's the leg?"

M'pika grinned up at him. "Don't tink I can outrun a hippo. Almos' good as new, though."

Both men laughed at the joke.

"What causes de frown on Lyon's face?"

Lyon sat in a chair and propped his long legs on the porch railing. "I'm restless. Lying about like a sated warthog is making me edgy."

"Yass." M'pika patted his hip. "A few more days." He looked long at his friend. "You know, my brother, no matter how many times you wash a goat, it still gonna smell like a goat."

"What does washing a stinkin' goat have to do with going on safari? Didn't you hear the drums about the lion?"

"Mm, yass. But, de Mama Daktor is not here, and the Lyon wears a scowl so fierce it would send *simba* into hiding." M'pika cocked an eyebrow, his smile wide and knowing.

"Okay, so I kissed her."

M'pika's eyes lit with curiosity. "Yass?"

"I shouldn't have."

He had kissed her. *Kissed* her, and he had seen her face afterward. If she could have sprouted wings and flown back to England, he believed she would have done so.

Lyon sat there, on the porch, in the heat, pondering methods of self-punishment.

"And why do you tink kissing was a bad ting?"

Lyon shrugged. "There is something in her past that haunts her. I've known her all these many weeks, yet I don't know *her*, and I've probably ruined any chance of changing that, because of one simple kiss."

Except there hadn't been anything simple about it. How was it that everything about a kiss could exceed his every fantasy?

M'pika interrupted Lyon's thoughts. "I am glad kissing is not so important in my culture. When it is time, I will go to de Tani village to dance in the mating circle. De woman who surrenders to me I will take as my wife."

Lyon gave a grunt and a nod. "I wish it were that simple."

Funny how life could change. He had thought about Margaret every day since he'd first spotted her standing on the riverboat. The day he had commanded she jump into his arms. The day he had inhaled her womanly scent. He had relived that moment, imagining again and again how she'd feel in his arms, and now that it had happened, that he had tasted perfection, he was in more agony than before.

In painful clarity, he now realized the difference between bedding women to satisfy virile animalistic needs and yearning for a woman to permanently share his life.

Sister Aganza Mary approached with a tray. "Time for medicine." She handed Lyon a quinine pill and a cup of hot tea. To M'pika she gave a spoonful of laudanum. "No more of de pain medicine after today. Mama Daktor 's orders."

As she turned to walk away, M'pika called her back. "Sister Aganza Mary, when a man has done a ting to cause bad hurt between him and a special woman, what does dis man do to cure the wound?"

The Hausa woman's forehead crinkled in thought. She cut a keen eye toward Lyon. "Perhaps go on safari, alone, and dis man, he find small gifts from de land to give the woman. He say all that is in his heart. If what he say be true, den the woman will know, and all be good. Yass?"

Lyon was certain she blushed before she excused

herself. "You are an amazing woman, Sister Aganza Mary."

Although the woman's answer intrigued Lyon, he feared things would never be the same between him and Margaret. She'd proven this when she left without telling him of the trek in person. But what the hell, *she* had kissed *him*. She was a married woman who had initiated the intimacy. He didn't want to believe she was an adulteress. Yet he was man enough to know she had not accepted his passion with the expectations of being mauled. Animals mauled, not civilized men.

He stood abruptly and shoved his hands into his pockets. "I'm going for a walk. I need to clear my head."

M'pika admonished, "I tink your head be filled with spider webs when you go into de jungle without your rifle."

"Yeah."

Anger flooding him, Lyon turned away from M'pika.

****

The Maasai had known for days that Margaret was coming, and as she entered the village, a feast was in preparation. Adah explained, "Dis is for you, Margaret, de Mama Daktor."

Margaret removed her pith helmet and wiped sweat from her brow. "I am overwhelmed to be so honored."

She scanned the tall lanky men clad in red. She thought them a beautiful people. The women wore beaded necklaces, and their dresses were adorned with colorful droplets of glass. She marveled at the long, stretched earlobes, and the decorative cuts on the women's faces. "Why do the women and children have shaved heads?"

"Dis is a special time for de young boys. When a Maasai boy comes of age, he enters the *morani*. Dis is when he is old enough to become a warrior. He is expected to be brave enough to spear a lion. If a warrior holds de tail of a lion as it dies, he is awarded with that lion's mane and gains great honor in his tribe."

Margaret edged a bit closer to Adah and Y'ro. She wasn't afraid as much as unsure of what to expect. "How old are the boys when they enter this *morani*?"

Adah offered a reassuring smile. "Every boy who celebrates his seventh year is expected to enter morani."

A fleeting memory of her three-year-old Jonathan caused Margaret to gasp. "Why, they are no more than babies."

"Perhaps in your world, Margaret. In the jungle, it is not so."

"I hesitate to ask what is expected of the little girls."

"Do not fret yourself about tings you cannot change, Margaret. De ways of the African people are as old as de moon." Adah reached for Margaret's hand. "Some day, I would like to hear about the ways of your people."

Margaret smiled, certain Adah would be just as amazed by British traditions. "It will make good campfire conversation."

She looked around, curious at the thick walls of thorn trees that encircled the village. "This is quite a secure fortress. I daresay breaking through a wall of thorns would certainly discourage any enemy from getting inside."

"Yass, Margaret. Dis be called a *boma*. It keeps de

cattle in and de big cats out. Only a lion or leopard too sick to hunt would dare to leap over the top."

"Maybe we should put a *boma* around the hospital compound to keep out certain evil witch doctors."

Adah offered a genuine smile to indicate she understood the cynical remark. "Ah, yass, dat would be good."

After what seemed like the longest walk of her life, Margaret and her party stopped in front of a majestic-looking man seated on a throne of animal skins. To his right sat four bald women. Margaret assumed they were the wives. To his left were three men, one obviously the medicine man. Dressed in tribal regalia, he sat with human skulls at his feet. Adah explained they were the bones of his father and grandfather, who had also been witch doctors, and he received messages from their spirits to help him diagnose his patients' ailments. "His name is Oloiboni."

"Why is he scowling at me? Does he not want me here?"

"Shamans do not smile, Margaret. It is not honorable. To do so might anger the gods."

"Given the threats from Matata and Demissie, I'm a little nervous. I hope the patient isn't the wife of one of the royals."

"Perhaps. I will ask." Adah explained that Mama Daktor did not know the Maasai language. She also related that Y'ro was the friend of the Lyon and was to be treated with respect. When finished, she told Margaret all that she had said.

"Who is the patient?"

"In time, Margaret. First we feast."

"You are not telling me something, Adah. Are we

in danger?"

"Oh, no. Nothing that extreme, except…well… unless the patient dies."

Margaret's stomach dropped. She clutched the handles of her medical bag a little tighter. "Thanks, I think. So what else?"

Adah exchanged glances with Y'ro, who avoided looking at Margaret by gazing over her shoulder.

"Stop it, both of you! I demand to know what you are not telling me—now!"

Adah placed her hands together as if she were praying and touched them against her chin. "Dis be Africa, Margaret. Remember that all tings here are different, including de food."

After a moment's hesitation, the Hausa woman continued, "The Maasai will serve de royal pudding. It is made of cow's milk and cow's blood. And dere will be midge cakes. All dis food be for you as honored guest. It is an insult to not eat."

Margaret was thankful for the warning. She hadn't yet sat down on the feasting mat, and her stomach roiled. "I am almost afraid to ask, but what are midge cakes?"

"Dey are quite good, Margaret. Almost like eating de hazel nut."

Margaret harrumphed. "Except…?"

"Sometimes many questions not be good." Adah heaved a huge sigh. "Midge cakes are made from tiny gnats, you know? De women rake them out of the air by the basketful, press dem into cakes, and dry dem. Then when dey want a few, dey toast de cakes a little to take the mold off. Dey are considered a great delicacy. Mos' delicious."

"Wonderful. First we eat. Then I regurgitate, and then hopefully I will still have enough strength to deliver a baby. Perhaps I should write a book about African cuisine."

"I do not know dis word, kwee-zeen, Margaret." Margaret opened her mouth to explain, but Adah said, "Never mind, we are summoned to sit. As de honored guest, you must take de first bite of everyting offered before anyone else is allowed to eat."

There was a great variety of food, and plenty of it. Calling on her British stoicism, Margaret suffered through the entire meal with as much grace as possible. With each bite, she reminded herself of England's gutter waifs, pallid, malnourished, and starving.

"De monkey and python are delicious, are dey not?" Adah plopped another morsel of roasted meat into her mouth.

Margaret stood. Her legs wobbled as she made her way around and behind a hut. She firmly clutched her forehead in one hand, gathered her skirt in the other, and leaned over to empty her stomach.

Chapter 21

A little unsteady, Margaret was thankful her legs did not crumple and send her to the dirt. Another tremor ran through her. This one was fear. She gazed at the shaman. The words he spoke were gentle. It was the look in his eyes that terrified her.

Margaret swallowed the remaining bile that seared the back of her throat. "I'm sorry, Adah. I tried, truly I did."

"No worries, Margaret."

As always, the Hausa woman translated.

Oloiboni said, "Mama Daktor, the first wife of the chief's youngest son cannot bring forth the child inside her."

He shook his *kayamba,* a rectangular rattle. "I hab chanted the birthing song that contacts the spirits. Dey do not hear my voice. I hab chanted in de morning, and when de sun is high. Never at night," he said, "because the spirits are hard to reach when de shadows cover de moon."

He asked Margaret to help him get his *juju* back. "It is my shame that I am no longer the *juju* mon. Mama Daktor's magic is powerful. You tell de gods to give back my powers."

Margaret considered his request. "Adah, tell Oloiboni in order for me to help him regain his importance as the *juju* man he must do these things:

first, a table must be prepared where I can stand over the girl. It must be scrubbed clean; then he is to say his most powerful prayer to keep evil spirits away and to rattle his *kayamba* this many times." She held up three fingers. "He is to tell the girl's husband, father, mother, and the chief that the girl may die—and if she does, it is because the gods needed her spirit to smile upon them so they may know happiness every day. "Also, after he says his prayer, he is to stay inside the hut, where he is to remain silent. Tell him no one is to enter until I say so."

Anxious to see the patient, Margaret waited until Adah translated.

"Oloiboni say the chief and the girl's husband, father, and mother must come, too."

Frustrated beyond measure, Margaret acquiesced. "Oh, all right, against my better judgment. Now he must take us to the girl, so I can examine her."

Oloiboni gave his attention to Adah, his expression serious as he grunted and nodded.

In a deep and authoritative voice, he issued orders. Women scrambled to immediately obey. Margaret and Adah followed the witch doctor into the elongated mud-and-wood house. Margaret gazed about, satisfied that her requests had been followed. She ordered the shaman to lift the young woman onto the table. In obvious agony, the girl's head lolled from side to side as she clutched her belly.

Margaret spoke soothing words. Upon examining the patient, Margaret scowled at Adah. "Mother of God, someone has mutilated this child."

Adah eyes were sorrowful. "It is the custom to circumcise even de girls." She answered Margaret's unasked question. "Yass, me and Aganza Mary. It is the way of our people."

An anguished cry filled the small space. Margaret checked the patient's eyes. "She's septic, Adah. She will never live long enough to deliver this baby."

Another piercing scream, and then a gasp followed. The girl's arm fell limp and dangled from the table. Margaret knew a crisis was near as she checked the pulse at the girl's neck, and then at the wrist. She listened with the stethoscope. She tried hard not to let her personal sorrow show. "Tell Oloiboni she has gone to meet the spirits. We must work quickly, Adah, if I am to save the baby."

Dismay shone in Adah's eyes. "Save de baby—how? I do not understand."

Margaret offered a strained smile. "Explain that I will cut the baby from the mother. Hurry, Adah, give me a scalpel."

"Have you done this ting before?"

Margaret clasped Adah's hand. "I studied about it in medical school. But no, I have never performed this procedure. We must send up our strongest prayer asking our heavenly father to guide my hands so that this child might live."

"If you fail, our lives will not be worth so much as a tick on a rhino's hind end."

"Understood. Tell Oloiboni, quickly."

The Hausa woman nodded her agreement. She translated as she offered Margaret the surgical knife.

Margaret worked to quell the tremors that threatened to attack her. She looked into the widened eyes of all who stood in the room. Heat seemed to emanate in waves from their bodies. It felt as if all the air had been sucked out of the crowded space. Behind the surgical mask, she was certain she might suffocate. Perspiration pooled in her armpits, and more slid down the bridge of her nose.

Adah blotted sweat from Margaret's forehead.

Margaret drew in a deep breath and let it out slowly. She prayed nothing would go wrong. She looked into the shaman's eyes and saw no malice, only wide-eyed curiosity. Reassured, she leaned over and cut through the wall of the deceased mother's abdomen. She reached in and, with a tug, delivered the tiny baby. She clasped the heels, turned the infant upside down, and swatted its bottom.

Nothing. No lusty cries. No sign of life.

Blinking back tears, Margaret laid the baby on top of its mother's belly and, with gentle fingers, opened the child's mouth, swabbed out the mucus, and then implored, "Come on, baby. Breathe!"

Instinctively, Adah reached out and covered Margaret's hand and gave it a little squeeze.

Again, Margaret turned the child upside down and gave its little bottom a smart smack.

The first sound was a soft mewling much like a kitten, and then a lusty squall. The tiny form looked perfect, and its angry cries and flailing fists were gratifying. Margaret found herself weeping with relief. With infinite care, she wiped the little body clean and wrapped it in a fresh cloth before lifting it into Oloiboni's arms.

"Adah, tell them it's a boy. A healthy baby boy. Tell Oloiboni we will need a wet nurse."

The Hausa woman whispered, her voice hushed with awe and wonder, "You have performed a miracle."

A rumbling of voices filled the hut, with the onlookers pointing and staring in amazement. Adah translated. "Oloiboni say you are truly the Mama Daktor with mos' powerful *juju*. The chief is sorry for the death of his favorite son's wife, but he is truly thankful for this wonderful ting you have done. You see, the chief has seven granddaughters. This is his first grandson. The chief also say you are now honorary member of the Maasai." She smiled. "This is special, Margaret. Very special."

Margaret felt the color rising to her cheeks. She thought this was the best reward she could ever receive. "Tell the chief I am pleased. And tell Oloiboni I hope his *juju* has been restored. What will they name the baby?"

The shaman held the peacefully sleeping infant high and said, "Namunyak."

A chuckle rose from Adah. "The child shall be called Namunyak. It means 'the lucky one.' "

Margaret breathed a sigh of relief. "Indeed, it is a fitting name."

Before the hour was out, jungle drums were giving account of the miracle the great white Mama Daktor had performed.

Unbeknownst to Margaret, not all who heard the news reveled in this supernatural phenomenon.

Chapter 22

One more night of camping before reaching the mission. The long walk from the Maasai village had been both invigorating and exhausting. Margaret rested against a fallen log while Y'ro prepared a meager supper. She valued his friendship, and his hunting skills. She smiled inwardly, recalling how she had caused him to drop a heavy crate on his foot when she'd screamed over a harmless water snake.

He'd not spoken a word of English then, and now he was teaching her Swahili. It seemed so long ago that she had stood on the riverboat anxiously ready to begin her adventure in this wild land.

Y'ro pointed to the flickering flames. "Mama— fire?"

She diligently searched her mind for the correct word. "*Moto*."

"And dis?" Again he pointed, this time at a tuber.

"*Yam*." Margaret joined his and Adah's laughter, for 'yam' was also an English word.

He nodded his approval. "You good learner."

Pleased at his compliment, she gazed up at the broad sky, deepening into indigo. A few stars winked on, along with a thin sliver of moon. "You are a good teacher."

A lovely evening. The kind of evening meant to be shared. And suddenly she missed home, her father, and even her silly sisters, terribly. She'd never really been alone in her life. Besides her immediate family, there had been Seamus, and then baby Jonathan, as well as the servants, her personal maid, and friends and colleagues. She'd had so much company she'd thought she would go mad with it. Surrounded by people, she'd often felt lonely. Now, she suffered a different type of loneliness, a sort of melancholy.

"Margaret, your face is writing a sad story. Perhaps telling me about your home will give you comfort."

Sitting next to the campfire, Margaret met Adah's concerned stare. "That would be lovely." She paused and lifted the cup of coffee to her lips. With a harrumph, she began. "In England, we never have to fear finding poisonous adders in our beds, nor do we have wild beasts that drag people away and eat them, and certainly no witch doctors who threaten to use black magic to harm us."

A sound jerked her attention to the darkness, and she paused to make sure nothing was lurking nearby. She continued. "Like the Maasai, we have cows." She grimaced. "We do not drink cow's blood. Beyond that, there are rabbits, deer and wild boar, sheep and horses."

"Tell me about your customs. Dr. Williams once spoke of grand houses, but he was a private man who seldom talked of his homeland."

Margaret finished her last bite of roasted yam. "Adah, does it never snow in Africa?"

"I do not know this word—'snow'?"

"It is white like sugar, and when it snows, the weather gets exceptionally cold."

"Ah, *theluji*. I have heard of such a thing on top of the mountain Kilimanjaro, but never here in the savanna. Only heat and more heat until the rainy season brings cooler weather and mosquitoes."

A knot of nostalgia fisted in Margaret's gut as she thought about baby Jonathan's first Christmas. She choked back a sob. "In the month of December, we celebrate the Yuletide. A special tree is cut from the forest and set up in the parlor. Popcorn is strung to decorate the boughs, along with colorful ornaments. Stockings are hung over the fireplace to be filled with gifts from old Saint Nick.

"I lived in a grand house with my father and two sisters. Our house is made of brick and mortar. There is a winding staircase to the second story. My bedroom is one of five. We also had two washrooms to bathe in, a kitchen with a huge oven, a modern stove, and wash tubs for the dirty dishes. In the parlor is a vast library filled with books of poetry, history, and fiction.

"There are fireplaces in every room to keep us warm in the winter, and massive windows opening onto balconies to keep us cool during the summer months. My favorite place is the flower and herb garden. It is filled with colorful birds and butterflies, and the loveliest peonies and roses."

Adah sat quietly as Margaret explained about the different foods and desserts, clothing, hobbies, dances, and holidays. She ended by saying, "It is much like Léopoldville. Perhaps a bit more modern."

When Margaret was all talked out, silence except for the crackling fire filled the campsite, until Adah said, "Der is someting else dat is making your soul sad."

Margaret hefted a heavy sigh. In halting words, and through tears, she reminisced about how she'd met

Seamus, related how much she adored their son, told the tale of their tragic deaths. "And now that I've met Lyon, my heart tells me one thing and my conscience tells me something else. I feel as if I am betraying my husband." She used the heels of her hands to wipe away tears.

Adah cocked her head to one side. Her mouth pursed, and her eyes narrowed in thought, and then she leaned forward and pointed toward Margaret's heart. "Your husband and son will live in here, always." She straightened. "In de drought season, de roots of a flower will wither and may die a little until de rain comes, but then it will push through de deep dark dirt and seek de sun so it can once again be beautiful. Sometimes, de flower is stubborn and does not seek de rain. It dies forever. Do you understand what I am saying, my friend?"

Margaret thought about the allegory. "It is time for me to stop mourning and live again, unless I choose to be like the flower that does not seek the rain."

"Yass, but one ting. You mus' tell Lyon what you have told me. De truth always makes strong bedmates."

Margaret suppressed a sudden urge to laugh. An eagerness filled her, an eagerness to see Lyon, to wrap herself in his arms. She stretched and yawned. A spiritual darkness had fallen away, and she was ready for the morning sun.

****

Lyon and M'pika stood in the center of the hospital yard and listened to the drums relaying the message touting Margaret as the great white Mama Daktor.

Lyon pictured Margaret's pretty face, recalled the vivid images of her soft skin. The breath he drew in lodged in his throat. He hadn't realized until this moment how much he missed her. "Well, I'll be damned. All I can say is—I'll be damned."

Wonderment shown on M'pika's face. "Lyon, how is dis ting possible, to pull a living baby from a dead mother's belly?"

After several seconds, Lyon slapped his friend on the back. "It's beyond me. Like the drums say, her *juju* is most powerful, and I believe it."

The memory of the claw marks and the blood on the door to her quarters slammed into his thoughts. He frowned at the apprehension that formed a tight fist around his gut.

He had considered more than once that he might strap on his gear and go after her. Malaria had kept him abed. Besides, Margaret hadn't asked him to come along. She cared about him; Lyon didn't question that. Yet unlike the few women he had known, she had never said she loved him or led him to believe that she wanted anything more than what little time they spent together.

Then there was the small matter of her husband and son. In spite of that, he had come damn near to professing his love for her. He stared out at the jungle again, and a foreboding gripped him. He saw nothing out of the ordinary. The day was as usual—noisy, with all the birds singing their own specific songs that mingled with the myriad voices of crickets.

"What troubles you, my brother?"

Lyon fingered the scars on his face. He shook aside the uneasy feeling. "I'm not sure. Something. I sense it."

"Dis be about de blood and claw marks on Margaret's door?"

Lyon plowed his hands into his pants pockets. "Yep. She's made a couple of powerful enemies. The question is which shaman hates her the most?"

M'pika arched a thick eyebrow. "Demissie or Matata, or another we do not know about?"

The fatigue Lyon had kept at bay suddenly slammed him between the shoulder blades. He fought to keep his knees from buckling. "Both are equally evil."

The expression on M'pika's face was rock hard. "Matata is of de leopard clan. De leopard is eater of flesh. I tink Matata is secret Bambala."

A shudder of revulsion and anger rippled through Lyon. The old childhood vision of his mother's attackers passed quickly behind his eyes. "Cannibalism was outlawed years ago. Still, what you say makes sense." Rage filled him. "If he harms one hair on Maggie's head, I'll rip out his heart with my bare hands and feed it to the vultures."

M'pika laid a hand on Lyon's shoulder. "Y'ro is strong and will guard de women wid his life. But he is no match for cunning *sangomas*. You mus' go to her."

Lyon shifted his gaze in the general direction of the point where he expected Margaret to enter the compound. A coughing jag nearly brought him to his knees. "Don't think I have the strength." He stumbled up the porch steps and to his hospital room, where he collapsed on the cot.

M'pika shouted, "Sister Aganza Mary, come quick!" Leaning heavily on his crutches, he followed Lyon to his room and stood nearby while the Hausa nurse swabbed Lyon's forehead with a cool cloth.

Between raspy hacks, Lyon said, "Damn this

malaria. I'm weak as a newborn cub."

M'pika chuckled as he patted his sore hip. "Soon we be well. Let us travel to Lake Tsavo. I should like to see dis land where I will see my sons born."

Aganza Mary lifted Lyon to a sitting position. She held a glass of whiskey to his lips. "This will calm the cough and help you relax."

The liquor burned a path down his throat and settled like a rock in his stomach.

Lyon uttered a sound of disgust as he closed his eyes. He labored to draw a deep breath. "No wife…no sons."

"Ah, yass. You rest, my brother, and I will tink about de house I will build for when I find a wife."

Finally, sweating and freezing at the same time, Lyon drifted to sleep. His last thought was how to protect Margaret from an invisible enemy.

Chapter 23

The weeks had passed by in a blur. The last dregs of malaria had left Lyon. Refreshed from a bath and a shave, he breathed in a cleansing breath. The drums drew him away from his room, and he walked to the porch.

An emergency had arisen at a nearby village and required the Mama Daktor's immediate attention. They weren't to worry. All was well. She'd return soon.

It was all very neat and easy, and Lyon wondered if Margaret had arranged this emergency as another escape to avoid facing him. She had found one excuse after another not to be alone with him, ever since returning from her triumph in saving the baby of a dead woman.

And it was an escape. He didn't believe for a second that an urgent situation had occurred. If that had been the case, the jungle telegraph would have reported such.

His elbows propped against the porch rail, he leaned forward and looked across the mission yard. It was his fault. He had kissed her. More than that, he had seen her face after he'd kissed her. If it were possible, she would have swum a river of crocodiles to get away from him.

Yes, he had kissed her, and it was the most spectacular kiss of his life. He was in more agony than ever. He now knew what he'd been missing all these years. For the first time in his life, he had tasted perfection. And he vowed it wouldn't happen again.

He understood Margaret's dedication to healing the sick, and her devotion to Angel of Mercy Hospital, but he also knew she was avoiding his presence.

Maybe he should drag his pathetic self to Nairobi and visit one of the brothels. Maybe he should expand his horizons by accepting the Duke of Hamburg's invitation to visit Germany; he could find himself a wealthy wife there. It probably wouldn't cure what ailed him, but it had to be better than gadding about the jungle playing escort to the rich and titled who shot game for sport.

As if the deities had read his mind, the children living on the fringes of the compound raised a bevy of excited voices. "*Bwana* Lyon, *Bwana* Lyon, men come. One wears a funny red hat and a red coat with gold buttons. He say, 'Where is the Lyon?' We say you are here."

Lyon grabbed his rifle. He looped the ammunition belt across his chest. "M'pika?"

M'pika had graduated to one crutch. He met Lyon in the middle of the yard. "Who do you suppose it is?"

Lyon pointed to three men appearing from the jungle. "We're about to find out."

M'pika said, "De one in de red is Algerian. Long way from home."

The men halted. The one in red bowed low. "I am Abu. I speak English. We are here to engage the services of the one called Lyon."

Lyon had no interest in men who projected airs of superiority. Those attitudes usually veiled a good dose of conceit and the morals of stray curs. "I'm Lyon. What services do you seek?"

"We have come from the river at a fast pace. The marquis is an impatient man and will want an answer post haste."

Lyon exchanged an annoyed glance with M'pika, who quirked a shrug. Not bothering with social graces such as offering chairs or refreshments, Lyon said, "I'll ask again—what services do you seek, and secondly, who exactly is your boss?"

The man in the red hat frowned his displeasure. "The Marquis Francois-Henri Charbonneau of France and his party wish to hunt exotic game. He is willing to pay handsomely for your services."

Lyon considered the invitation. He sighed. He really didn't want to go on safari, but a man needed money to build a hunting lodge. Nor could he spend his time mooning over a woman already attached to a husband, even if she had run away from the man.

He placed his hands on his hips. "Take your rest. The well is there for water. Then tell the marquis I accept his offer to pay handsomely for my services."

Within the hour, Lyon had gathered his meager belongings and sent a jungle telegraph summoning his boys to meet him at their usual place below the Tani River Station. They were going on safari. His only concern was if his second in command was up to the long and often rigorous hikes. The question was answered when a grinning M'pika approached with an ammo belt slung across his chest, a rucksack on his back, and a rifle cradled in the crook of his arm. "Time to throw away de crutch."

Lyon peered through concerned eyes. "Are you

sure? You know there are times when we'll need to save our hides by running."

A wide grin lit M'pika's face. "My leg grows lazy wid all dis sitting around. Do not worry yourself 'bout me."

Lyon had one more thing to do. He stomped up the steps to his room. His mood grew stunningly foul as he penned a note to Margaret. They would never be friends again. She was not the kind of woman who took intimacy lightly. It was time for him to leave so she would not feel the need to avoid him.

The note was simple. He hoped she understood his message.

I was wrong. Forgive me.

****

Two days later, Lyon and M'pika stood at the edge of the Tani River Station. Hidden in the shadows of trees and vine entanglements, Lyon assessed the encampment. He harrumphed. "All the comforts of home. My guess is the Marquis Charbonneau is a royal prig."

"Yass. I would not trust a man whose name means black coal. He might speak with the tongue of an adder."

"So you do remember the French that Sister Magdalene taught us."

M'pika held out his hands. "She rapped my knuckles plenty times. Yass, I remember, and you?"

Lyon nodded. "Let's keep this bit of knowledge to ourselves. It may serve us well to play ignorant when they are speaking their language."

"Cunning. Dis be why you are de Lyon."

"How's the leg holding up?"

M'pika patted his hip. "Strong."

Lyon raised his hand and gave the signal to move forward. His faithful men, who had been squatting in silence, rose, lifted their gear, and on catlike feet followed him into the sunlight.

A pair of large, snarling canines raced toward Lyon's group. One particularly aggressive dog lunged at Lyon. Instinctively he raised his rifle and fired.

Abu, the Algerian, called the second animal to obedience. He gripped the dog's collar and struggled to control the frenzied animal.

A woman clad in a pair of khaki jodhpurs, knee-high boots, and a tan safari shirt shouted at Lyon. She cursed in French, and holding a riding crop drew back her arm. "You barbarian, you have killed a prized possession! I shall have you flogged until the flesh is peeled from your body!"

Lyon used the barrel of his rifle to stave off the attack. The crop flipped out of her hand. She rushed him, hands shaped as claws aimed at his face. Lyon tossed his rifle to M'pika just in time to grab the woman's wrists. She cried out in pain as he twisted both arms behind her back.

He ordered, "Settle down, wench."

The Algerian continued his struggle to hold the agitated dog, while an older man of regal stature sprinted from his tent, rifle ready. He too shouted, ordering, "Camille, calm yourself—I command it this second!"

Lyon pushed the harridan with such force that she crashed against the older man's chest.

Trembling with rage, Lyon ordered his men to leave the camp. As he turned to go, the man's voice stopped him. In heavily accented English, he heard, "Monsieur Lyon, forgive this outrageous display. I am most embarrassed by my…" He seemed to search for an appropriate word. "Camille Babineaux is my companion. I assure you that she is a gentle woman, with the soul of an angel."

The Frenchman scowled at the woman as he released her. His voice brooked no argument. "Go to your tent. I wish not to see you until dinner, and then only if you conduct yourself as a lady. If you cannot act as such, I will have Abu escort you back to Léopoldville, where he will arrange passage back to France, and to La Maison Rouge."

Lyon exchanged an amused look with M'pika. Keeping their knowledge of the French language would pay off. So the beautiful woman was no lady but the marquis' mistress.

The man clicked his heels together. "Allow me to introduce myself. I am Francois-Henri Charbonneau, Marquis of France." He extended his arm in the direction of two chairs situated beneath a canvas canopy. "Please, join me in a cognac." He touched his chest and released a deep breath.

Lyon answered in English, "This is my second in command, M'pika. He will always join me at dinner, or any discussions about the hunts." The tone in his voice discouraged any protest.

M'pika nodded. "I will settle the boys."

As he walked next to the marquis, Lyon took notice of the graying hairline and the smudge of black on the otherwise impeccably white collar, the slightly sagging jowls, the red knobs on the knuckles, and the puffy sacs under the eyes. Though straight as an arrow, the marquis used boot black to color his hair, he suffered from joint pain, drank too much, and was well past his prime. Another aging man trying to cling to his youth by killing animals, while hoping to imbibe enough liquor to mount the woman and perform like a stud zebra.

In a split second, Lyon glimpsed his own future. He didn't like the picture.

Settled and with a glass of cognac, he said, "I do not allow dogs on safari. Unless properly trained, they bark at the wrong times, scare the game away, and might cause a herd of elephants to stampede right over the top of us. Muzzle the animal so it can't bark, and leave it at the camp when we go out."

The marquis rolled the goblet between his hands. "You are direct, monsieur. I am not used to receiving orders, only giving them. I do not think I like being ordered." He cocked an eyebrow toward Lyon.

"On safari, there is only one boss—*Bwana* Lyon. Take it or leave it. Up to you." He chugged down the remains of the bittersweet alcohol and stood. He pulled a slip of paper and a pencil nub from his shirt pocket and scribbled a figure on it. "If you decide against my services, this is my fee for being attacked by a dog and an insane woman, and for the two-day trek here. G'night." Lyon turned on his heel, ready to stroll toward where his men had settled.

The marquis called out, "Take me to where the gorillas are, and I will triple this amount."

Lyon did an about-face. "Someone should have told you. There are no gorillas in this part of Africa."

Clearly exasperated, the marquis sputtered, "Then where? I came specifically for gorillas."

Lyon pointed toward the west. "It's a five-hundred-mile hike to Uganda, and just as far to the Congo."

"Damn." The marquis kicked the chair and sent it flying. "Damn! I've come all this way." He grabbed the bottle, refilled his glass, and slogged down the contents.

Wealthy people acting like spoiled brats—Lyon had seen it before. It tested his patience. He decided to join his boys.

The marquis again called him back. "*Mon Dieu*, I've come for gorilla, and gorilla I'll have. We set out for the Congo tomorrow."

Lyon wasn't sure M'pika was up to the long journey. In honesty, he had no desire to play nursemaid to a drunken royal who had more money than good sense. He huffed a sigh. "It's your money, but the price just increased by another two thousand."

Later that night, as he lay on his cot, his mood was stunningly foul. Another cognac and thoughts of Margaret fueled his desire for a woman. He knew this one would come. They always came.

Silhouetted by moonlight, Camille greeted him with warmth. She was a ravishing blonde with a supple body. He reached out his hand, then let it fall. She was too…too what? She wasn't Margaret.

Camille parted the red peignoir. She was curved perfection. Every man's desire. Without a word, she straddled him. He closed his eyes, determined to get it over. Nothing happened. She fondled him until his manroot hardened against his will, and she rode him like an expert horsewoman. He lasted two minutes. With a few choice words spoken in French, she stormed out of his tent.

He was appalled and felt emasculated. He was the

Lyon. He had a reputation for pleasuring women. Hell, he might as well take a knife and turn himself into a eunuch. Damn Margaret! He had tasted her, even if it was only one passionate but fleeting kiss. He was ruined. He let out an incoherent grunt. He felt something tearing at his chest. Probably his heart. He swore under his breath.

Maybe a five-hundred-mile hike was just the medicine to erase the beautiful doctor from his memory.

Chapter 24

Several days and fifty miles later, the tethered Doberman set up a ruckus. Lyon stepped from his tent, rifle in hand. A runner drenched in sweat collapsed in the middle of the camp. Lyon rushed and knelt next to the gasping man. He shouted, "Bring water. Quick!"

M'pika hobbled at a fast pace with a cup in his hand. Lyon lifted the runner's head and placed the rim against lips white with froth. "Y'ro! Easy. Take it easy."

Shock at seeing the man who had become Margaret's self-proclaimed protector caused a cold knot in the pit of Lyon's gut.

Y'ro gulped the water. His chest heaved as he sucked air into his lungs. His eyes fluttered open. "*Bwana* Lyon...you mus' come...fast." The whites of his eyes rolled upward.

M'pika returned with a bucket of water and a cloth to sponge off his friend's overheated body. He placed his hand over Y'ro's heart. "He lives. Just exhausted. No telling how many days he ran without stopping."

Lyon swore under his breath.

Margaret!

Only something drastic could send a runner to seek him, especially her friend. He didn't want to think the worst, not yet. He patted the sweaty cheeks. "Y'ro, talk to me. What has happened?"

The marquis cast a shadow over the inert body as he approached. "*Mon Dieu*, what is the meaning of this? Who is this man? What does he want?"

Lyon ignored the questions. He shouted for several of his boys to lift Y'ro. "Carry him to my tent."

The marquis laid his hand on Lyon's arm. "I demand to know what is going on."

Lyon shrugged off the offending grip. "When I find out, you'll be the first to know." With a severe scowl that caused the Frenchman to take a step backward, Lyon followed after the men.

Once inside the tent, Lyon knelt beside the cot. M'pika stood to one side. Y'ro pulled an object from the leather pouch around his neck and handed it to Lyon. A hollow pit formed in his stomach as he ran a thumb around the object, tracing its filigree oval shape. Jolting pain stabbed his heart when he opened the locket. A miniature photograph of Margaret smiled at him. The second picture was of an aristocratic-looking man and a toddler whose smile mimicked Margaret's. He didn't need to guess who they were.

His pulse thrummed in his ears. He remembered seeing the locket around her neck. He stared at the broken chain. The letters *MAB* erased any doubt the piece of jewelry was hers.

M'pika knitted his brow into worry lines. "Dis be…Margaret's?"

Hammering waves of fear warred for space along with Lyon's mounting anger. "What's happened to Mama Daktor, Y'ro?"

The Tani man propped up on his elbows. He ran a tongue over blistered lips. "Please, more water. My throat is dry."

As eager as he was for information, Lyon handed him a cup. "Take your time."

A splotch of sunlight lit the tent's dim interior as the marquis entered with a swagger. He opened his mouth as if to speak. The impact of Lyon's glare caused the Frenchman to clamp his jaws shut.

Y'ro set the empty cup aside and thanked Lyon for the water as he swung his legs over the cot to sit up. His voice rasped as he strained to talk. "We were one day from the hospital. After supper, Mama Daktor needed to visit de bushes." He dipped his eyes as if embarrassed. Lyon encouraged him to continue.

"Mama Daktor was happy." He gave a brief account of their visit to the second Maasai village, that things went well because the witch doctor had made her an honorary member of the tribe. "She gave Oloiboni back his *juju*. Make him very glad. But den when we leave dis time, he say to Mama dat he see a leopard in his dream, and he tell Mama to be watchful."

Lyon studied the worry lines on Y'ro's face. Clearly the man felt responsible, and perhaps afraid he might be blamed for whatever had happened to her. "Go on. Then what happened?"

Y'ro's shoulders slumped. "When de Mama Daktor did not return, I say to Sister Adah Luke to go see if Mama is okay. I be 'fraid maybe she is snake bit and cannot call out.

"Sister Adah Luke take a torch and go into the bush where Mama went. I hear her scream, and she come running wid dis in her hand. We look and look. It be too dark to see. In de morning, we find leopard tracks. But *Bwana* Lyon, we never heard chuffing of big cat, and Mama, she no cry out."

Clearly beside himself with grief, he continued, "We return to the hospital. Dis when we hear you hab gone on safari, and Sister Aganza Mary remember the direction you took. I run and run, hoping to find you."

The marquis sneered. "How can you trust what this native says? Maybe he harmed this doctor, whoever she is, and is now trying to cover his ass."

Like a flash, Lyon stood and planted his fist against the Frenchman's mouth. Blood spurted. The blow lifted him off his feet and sent him sprawling through the tent flaps.

Lyon followed. He straddled the supine body, reached down, grabbed the man's ascot, and pulled him forward. "You filthy-minded bastard. Y'ro is an honorable man, and if it came to it, he'd lay down his life for Dr. Boynton." He drew back his fist again.

M'pika grabbed Lyon's arm. "No, Lyon. He's not worth it."

Lyon stared at the locket clenched in his fist. He knew his friend was right. He sighed and swallowed down his anger.

"We will find her, my brother. Do not fret yourself so."

"Damn right we'll find her." Lyon stared across the grassy plains and onward to the thick canopy of trees, silhouetted like a dark and gaping mouth in the distance. Guilt settled deep in his soul. The hairs on the back of his neck prickled. Margaret was in terrible danger. He dropped the locket into his pocket.

Lyon's mind raced with a plan. He issued a sharp whistle. His boys came running. "Break camp. We're heading back to the mission hospital."

The marquis dabbed blood from his split lip and

nose with a silk handkerchief. He ignored the mewling attentions from Camille as he pointed a finger at Lyon. "You, sir, are in my employ. I have hired you to escort me to the Congo to hunt gorilla, and *mon Dieu*, not one cent will I pay you until I have bagged as many apes as I desire."

Lyon's gaze flickered over the Frenchman, while he swallowed back a fresh curse. Stupid…stupid man.

He patted his shirt pocket, then laughed out loud. "Imbibing too much cognac does odd things to a man. First, it leaves a foul taste in his mouth. Then it causes him to wake up with a headache, and lastly, it makes him forget that he paid a sizeable amount of cash." He gave a mock salute. "You have two choices. Follow that track, and it will lead you straight to gorilla country, or Abu seems like a capable fella, and he can lead you back to the river, where you can wait for Captain Bachmeir's riverboat to take you back to Léopoldville."

Lyon watched the Frenchman struggle visibly for control, and he found it, lost it again for a second, and looked down at the ground. His shoulders were rigid as he rocked back on the heels of his expensive crocodile-hide boots, and then back again. Sweat trickled down his nose, onto his chin, and farther to dampen his shirt.

"You have a fierce reputation as a tough man, Lyon, and you live up to it. But know this—I am a marquis of France. I have the power and the money to ruin your reputation, to see that no more safari business comes your way. By the time I am finished with you, I will have stripped you of every dignity you possessed. The only thing you will have left to call your own is a sullied reputation."

Lyon smirked. The man really was a royal prig. "I came into this world with nothing. I expect I'll leave it the same way."

"The boys are ready, my brother."

"What about Y'ro?"

The Tani man stepped forward. "No worry 'bout me, *Bwana* Lyon. I will rest tonight."

Lyon offered his hand to show his respect. He squinted up at the glaring sun. "You take the lead, M'pika."

The marquis snorted rudely. He moved with fluid grace as he raised his arm, riding crop held high. "Bastard, I am not yet finished with you!"

The clicks of bolts sliding cartridges into rifle chambers echoed as Lyon's men lifted weapons aimed at the marquis. Those without rifles pointed spears ready to thrust forward.

Lyon continued on as if he hadn't heard the Frenchman, but his words floated back to him. "You can count on it, Charbonneau."

"At least leave your boys to act as bearers and to stretch the ape nets."

"I've given you my answer." Lyon swept his hand toward the line of men, their weapons still at ready. "And they have given theirs."

Taking a deep breath and straightening his shoulders, Lyon gave the signal to move out. He followed his men toward the jungle. To find Margaret.

****

Margaret hated when nature called, especially at night when she had to relieve herself in the bush. She looked for a place to jab the torch into the ground. The primitiveness of the jungle made her appreciate the modern conveniences she had taken for granted at her home in York. She was still adjusting to the onerous tasks of emptying her bladder on a chamber pot, washing her clothes on rocks, and attending to her personal toilette in such primitive conditions.

She had always considered her sisters pampered and spoiled, but never herself. She had prided herself on being the sensible sister. Now, turning in a circle and stomping the ground to shoo away lurking critters, she felt deflated and mildly ashamed. Basic life had certainly reared its ugly head and given her a huge dose of humility.

Finding a suitable area, she scouted for snakes in the torch's halo of light before hiking her skirt. She entertained a smug moment thinking about how the uppity-ups, including her father, would react to squatting behind a tree or a clump of brush.

The shadows were long when she heard the soft, almost inaudible chuff. She quickly finished her task and stood. A vagrant breeze carried a stench that caused her to gag. She listened. There was only silence. She chided herself that this was the jungle, and she was surrounded by unseen creatures who made a variety of different noises. Perhaps she seemed strange to them.

Adjusting her bloomers and smoothing her skirt, she reached for the flickering flame. A throaty cough chilled her blood. Remembering that Lyon had told her big cats didn't like fire, she tightened her hold on the torch—and looked straight into a pair of eyes that glowed like gold nuggets—the eyes of a leopard. The animal rose up on two feet. The light fell from her hand. She opened her mouth to scream, barely issuing a squeak. Shocked, she peered hard at the sly grin and the deep scars that crisscrossed both sides of his cheeks. She lifted her gaze higher. "You!"

She understood the danger but couldn't quite accept it. The animal pounced. Or was it the man? She wasn't sure. She landed hard, her head thumping against a large tree knob. The blow knocked her unconscious for a split second. She fought to scramble away from her attacker. A hand closed over her mouth and nose, shutting off her air. A sickening wave of terror rose in Margaret's stomach.

Unable to breath, her vision grew fuzzy, and the world momentarily darkened. The last thing she remembered was a vision of the saddened expression on Lyon's face when she'd left him standing on the mission porch. She had wanted to tell him she was sorry, to wrap her arms around him, to feel his strength. Instead, she chose to run away, to escape emotions and desires that filled her with guilt. Now she might never get the opportunity to tell him the truth about why she had come to Africa. The world was filled with danger. The Dark Continent seemed to have more than its share, and no matter how brave or careful she was, or how much protection she had, it did not ensure her safety. And if her life were to end tonight, she would always regret not being honest with Lyon about her feelings for him.

She clenched her teeth against the need to scream.

Control. She needed control.

She kicked backward. The heel of her boot connected with his shinbone. He didn't even flinch.

He closed his hand over her mouth. She tried to bite him, but he tightened the grip, painfully pinching her cheeks together. She fought to breathe.

She had learned enough Swahili to understand when he said, "Don't fight me, and don't try to bite me again, or you will regret it."

The rancid animal grease from the offending hand assailed her nose and caused her to gag. Her pulse raced with increasing fear. Sharp claws gouged painfully into her cheeks. Margaret clamped down on the soft flesh between his thumb and forefinger.

A growl rumbled from his throat. She was certain it emulated a leopard.

To Margaret's dismay, he didn't jerk his hand away. Instead, he circled his free arm around her waist, jerking her against his chest. He blew a powder in her face. It stung her nose and eyes. She was aware only vaguely that he lifted her off her feet and carried her into the darkness.

Chapter 25

Single file, the men walked through an open plain of waist-high yellow grass. In the distance a herd of zebra grazed, and nearby stood a group of gazelle. Africa's beauty never ceased to amaze Lyon. Still he kept a watchful eye. Danger could rear its ugly head at any moment. He searched for ripples in the vast field to indicate the presence of a slinking lion. Even the unseen dangers of encountering a cobra or a puff adder concerned him. To their advantage was the sweltering weather. Blood-sucking, disease-carrying ticks didn't like heat.

"Water break."

"In an hour."

"Lyon, de boys need water. You need water. I need water."

"Not yet!"

M'pika's face was resolute. After three hours of hard hiking, his sweat-soaked shirt clung to his body like a second skin. His words were crisp. "Den you go ahead. I will stop and catch up later. My hip needs rest."

Lyon's trousers were drenched. Even his socks squished with each step. He removed his pith helmet and swiped his hands through hair badly in need of a good cutting. His palm came back wet. He squinted at the sun. It was beginning to sink below the horizon. The few scattered acacia trees had begun to cast long shadows. The sun was definitely retreating, but the temperature remained torrid.

After a long moment, Lyon unclipped the canteen from his belt and lifted it to his lips. The water was tepid. He drew a long deep swallow. He heaved a deep sigh.

"You are pushing yourself too hard, my brother."

"We're running out of daylight. We'll stop when it's too dark to see."

M'pika and Lyon silently challenged each other with a staring match. Then, abruptly, M'pika nodded. "So be it." And he hefted his pack.

An hour later, Lyon experienced a painful, squeezing grip in his stomach. He blinked away the little black spots that danced before his eyes. His morning meal was long gone. The heat and dehydration had finally taken its toll. It was his fault they had not stopped for a nooning and needed food, something other than dried salted meat.

He ran his tongue across his lips to moisten them, then loosed a shrill whistle. The line of men ahead of him stopped. Some dropped to their knees. He lumbered forward to meet M'pika. "About a hundred yards to the east is a rivulet, and plenty of shade. Make camp while I get us some fresh game. No tents. We'll sleep in the open."

Lyon pointed to two of the men and motioned for them to follow him. After dusk the group feasted on roasted venison, spider plant, wild onions, and Dwaba berries.

Exhaustion riding him hard, Lyon stretched his long legs toward the fire. He lifted the mug to his lips and welcomed the warm, brandy-laced coffee that slid down his throat, wishing it would hurry up and dull the ache inside him. He took another swallow, then rested the cup on one thigh of his heavy bush trousers. A vast array of stars twinkled overhead. The pale glow of the crescent moon shone against the velvet sky.

A small smile dared to rise over his sadness. He closed his eyes, relishing the sense of Margaret's spirit that hummed in his soul. He knew she was thinking of him. He felt it.

He drew a deep breath, only to have it lodge in his throat. He unbuttoned the flap on his shirt pocket to retrieve the gold locket. Holding it with reverence, he opened the clasp, and by firelight, he stared at the faces looking back at him. He thought about another locket, the one tucked safely away in his rucksack—the only possession he owned from his childhood. The images in it almost mirrored that of Margaret's, images that meant so much to the loved ones left behind.

Damn! He hadn't meant to let Margaret wiggle her way into his heart.

Y'ro coughed to get Lyon's attention.

"Why aren't you resting? We have another hard day ahead of us."

The Tani man handed Lyon a large knife. "*Bwana*, cut me up into little pieces and feed me to the vultures. I am not worthy to die with honor. I did not protect Mama Daktor."

Lyon took the weapon. He stared at it for a moment, then drew back his arm. The desire to avenge Margaret's kidnapping raged strong in him. Y'ro stood stalwart; his eyes focused toward the sky. Lyon heaved from the chair. He pushed all his anger into the throw.

The sharpened point landed with a heavy thwack in a nearby tree. Lyon reached out and gripped the man's shoulder.

Visible relief washed over Y'ro as his chin dipped to touch his chest.

Lyon was certain he'd heard a sob from the man. "This is Africa, where the unexpected happens. Stop faulting yourself and go to sleep."

The Tani man spread his hands wide. "Wid dese hands I will rip out de throat of de one who take Mama." He turned on a heel and disappeared toward the shared campfire.

Tucking his own bedroll beneath his arm, Lyon made the rounds, speaking to each man. He cautioned them to keep close together. "There's no need to remind you that we're in leopard country. Decide who will sit watch first to keep the fires going while the rest of you sleep. You are all good men. I wouldn't want to lose any of you, especially to a man-eater."

He settled among the men. "I'll take the first watch. M'pika, you and Y'ro sleep."

Several others volunteered to sit watch with him and help keep the fires stoked.

He and the remaining sentries made small talk. After a while, conversations ebbed into silence. He jabbed the flames with a long stick as he thought about the incident with Y'ro. He didn't doubt the seriousness of the Tani man's words. He knew Margaret had angered a couple of witch doctors. He was certain her abductor was human. She would have screamed if a big cat had attacked. The question was which enemy had harmed her?

The night still felt hot and heavy, and then the

silence was broken by the distant call of a lion. The low melodic moan of the muscular beast seemed to come straight from the earth before the return growl of his hunting partner shattered back across the silence, as if to confirm their nightly mission. The roar seemed to hit Lyon straight in his soul as it cut through the heart of the African night, alerting all his senses to the beasts' proximity to the camp.

As the hours of darkness wore on, the low calls of the lions seesawed back and forth until they were joined by a sound with a life of its own. There was something about the low whooping of a hyena as it built itself up to a ghostly wail that would have made the hairs on the back of Lyon's neck stand up and salute if he were a stranger to the bush.

Hours later, it seemed as if a silent alarm had sounded to awaken the sleeping men. No words were exchanged. Tired sentries sought positions of comfort to rest their weary bodies. For Lyon, sleep came in fits and starts.

The age-old dream of his childhood was dark and relentless. Images floated through his mind—his mother, his father, the cannibals. He and M'pika were running and running. Lyon snatched half a breath, feeling as if his lungs would burst.

He was gasping now as if he'd run too fast too far. He fought the hands that gripped his arms.

"My brother, it is I, M'pika. Wake up." The voice was a harsh rasp.

A fine sheen of sweat coated Lyon's skin, sticky and cold. "I—I…"

"The dream?"

Lyon raised his fists and pressed them hard against

his temples. A picture of someone familiar flittered before his eyes. He nodded. Pushing the dark visions from his mind, he said, "I could use some coffee."

M'pika sighed. "There are times when I do not want to close my eyes for fear of seeing what I do not wish to see."

Lyon's teeth clenched. "It was a long time ago, but how would you punish the Bambala if they still existed, and we caught them?"

M'pika's voice was soft, the bitterness evident. "I would tie him to the ground, and den I would slit his belly open to expose his guts." He stopped for a second to steady his labored breathing. "I would make de call of de lion, de hyena, and de vultures, and den I would wait for them to come feast, as the Bambala did to our people. And my ears would be deaf to his cries."

Lyon stared out into the morning heat. "One day the dreams will end, and our souls will be at peace."

"I pray dis is so, my brother."

"M'pika, there is a face in my dream. It is always the same. I know this face, and yet I do not. Does this make sense?"

M'pika cocked his head to one side as if giving Lyon's words thought. "What does dis face look like?"

Lyon shrugged his puzzlement. "That's just it. I can't exactly remember. Male, young, but not as young as you and me." He squeezed his eyes shut. "There is something…something…Damn! Just when I think I know what that *something* is, it disappears."

M'pika patted his friend's shoulder. "We were boys of nine, and very frightened. When it is time, *Muungu* will show you dis face."

Lyon wrestled for a moment with the thought.

"Let's get the men moving. With luck, by nightfall we'll be where Y'ro last saw Margaret."

Chapter 26

Her eyes flew open. Sweat trickled between Margaret's breasts as she lay in the dirt. It beaded on her forehead, and one drop rolled down toward her nose. She reached up with a dirty hand to swipe it away. Probably left a grimy smudge, she thought. No one who looked at her now would recognize her as a meticulous doctor.

Stifling odors of layers of decay and rotting flesh permeated the air. These were the menacing smells of death. Margaret compulsively took giant gulps of air, her need for oxygen outweighing her apprehension of the smell. She looked at her hands and was genuinely surprised at how badly they were trembling.

She should be stronger than this. She was a doctor who had assisted in performing autopsies during her internship at the morgue.

"We meet again, Daktor," he said, shrouded in darkness.

Margaret frowned at the vaguely familiar gravelly voice. A lighted torch silhouetted the man against the darkness. She peered hard at his wicked grin and the scars that crisscrossed his cheeks. She lifted her gaze a little higher. He appeared a ghost in the torchlight. A black ghost clad in leopard skins, long nails shaped into claws. Shocked, she stared into his feral eyes. Her heart stopped as the memories of the woman with the abscessed tooth came rushing back to her.

"I see you remember me, Mama Daktor." The sneer in his voice was unmistakable.

With her limited knowledge of Swahili, Margaret focused on each word to understand what he was saying.

"Where am I?" She tried to keep her tone stern.

He touched the torch against several others affixed into the wall. The flames created shadowy specters that seemed to dance in the dim light. Glancing around, she determined that she was in a cave of some sort. The next sight stilled her.

Bones.

Hundreds, perhaps thousands, littered the massive area. She recognized a pelvic, a femur, hands with fingers. All stripped of flesh. These did not belong to animals. Waves of fear pushed through her.

These were—human bones. Bile rose in her throat.

His voice roughened with clear hatred. "Stand up."

She came to her feet, daring not to further agitate him. "Why have you kidnapped me?"

She shivered as he stepped closer. His fetid breath caused her to retch. She didn't want to think about what had happened here.

Murder?

The cold thought came seeping into her, and she shivered again as an image flashed through her head.

Cannibalism!

His lips drew back to reveal teeth sharpened to pointed ends. He emitted a deep, throaty purr. "Leopards need meat to survive. Lots of meat."

She peered at him, trying to sort the logic of what he had said. "But these are h-human bones." The word clogged in her throat, and she had to swallow to continue. "You are a man. Not a leopard. S-surely you didn't do all of this alone."

He leered at her, emitting a throaty purr. "No. There are others like me."

Uncertain if he understood her, she labored over the words. "So…how many people have you eaten?"

To her great surprise, he answered in broken English, "I hab los' count."

She realized her mouth had fallen slack and hurriedly snapped it shut. She clenched her teeth against the farfetched notion that she had been duped by the witch doctor, that he had deceived them all. "You speak English."

He managed a bland smile.

Margaret didn't know if it was the shadows cast against the cave wall from the torches or her imagination or a combination of both that made him seem more ominous by the moment. Flickering amber played upon his face and gave his sharply carved features a sinister look. His kinky hair glistened like polished ebony.

There was no mistaking what that glint in his eyes meant. He planned to make her his next victim. A film of cold sweat broke over her body. Images of other frightened victims and what they had suffered filled her mind.

After a long and torturous minute, he stepped closer and leaned in to sniff her. He lifted a hand to her cropped hair. He plunged his long fingers into the curls and jerked her neck forward. A growl rumbled in his throat.

"Are afraid, Mama Daktor?"

Her mind raced. She fought the building hysteria. "You are insane, Matata. Crazy. Why…why me? Is it because I cured the woman with the abscessed tooth?"

Matata rewarded her with a high-pitched little laugh that sounded more like a braying zebra than amusement. And then he snarled, "You are a mos' powerful *N'Devli*. You make my *juju* weak. Demissie, he tell me 'bout de dream med'cine you gib him. I will take your magic."

She tried to shift away from his tight grip. He said, "I will feast on you piece by piece, and when I am finished, I will be de mos' powerful witch doctor in all de land. No one can kill me. No even my enemy, J'mi Lyon."

She had to get away from him. She had to find Lyon and warn him. It was the name that puzzled her. "How do you know his given name?"

"I do not know dis word *giben*, but when de Lyon is but a boy, I was Bambala den."

Her knees sagged. She recalled what Sister Adah Luke had told her about Lyon's mother, and remembering, she wanted to retch and keep retching. "Cannibalism was outlawed years ago. It is against all human law. The authorities will stand you in front of a firing squad."

"No one can kill me." He leaned forward and touched his lips to the back of her neck. Needle sharp teeth pricked her skin.

Her breath snagged in her throat. A shudder ran through her body, and in desperation she made fists. She twisted around and rewarded him with a sharp jab just above the navel, to his solar plexus. The surprise blow bent him double and caused him to drop the torch.

She pushed around him. He reached out and grabbed her arm, and his sharp claws ripped through her blouse, leaving a painful gash in her side. The fresh scent of blood seemed to excite him. Determined to escape, and fueled by injustice, fury pumping its energy through her veins, she tried to whirl away. She kicked, hoping to land a blow to his gonads. The force glanced off his knee.

She screamed as she clawed at his face, "You son of a donkey, no matter what you do to me, Lyon will hunt you down like the animal you are and kill you!"

Matata slung her against the cavern wall. She slumped in the loamy dirt and curled over in a ball of misery, dry, wrenching sobs tearing at her throat. He glared at her through hooded eyes.

****

The trek to the place where Y'ro had last seen Margaret proved to be the longest in Lyon's memory. A part of him felt he'd let her down. All this time he'd thought she was safe at the mission, and instead she was in trouble. He touched the outline of the locket secured inside his buttoned shirt pocket.

Surveying the resting men, he knew they were all loyal. All had proven many times they would lay down their lives for him. He spoke directly to M'pika and Y'ro. "The mission will surely be short of fresh meat. The two of you take the boys and go hunting. Take all the meat you can carry back to the compound. Tell Sister Adah Luke I will die trying to find Margaret and return her safely."

The two men stood silent. It was M'pika who finally spoke. "Let Y'ro lead the men. I am going with you."

Loretta C. Rogers

Y'ro tamped his spear against the ground. "I, too, am going, and if you order me back, I will follow still. It is I who did not protect Mama Daktor. It is I who will help find her."

The defiance pricked Lyon's patience. He shouted, " Wanumbi?"

A tall lanky man stepped forward. Wanumbi did not question Lyon's orders. He simply replied with a nod of understanding. In a bond of friendship and trust, the two men clasped arms.

None of the men questioned Lyon's orders. They accepted Wanumbi as the leader and followed.

Lyon turned his attention to the two remaining men. "M'pika, you are my brother, but you are as stubborn as a bull Cape Buffalo, and just as dangerous when provoked." He pointed the rifle barrel toward his friend's hip. "I see the pain in your eyes, and the limp grows worse with each mile. If you cannot keep up, you are on your own. I have enough to worry about just finding Margaret and bringing her back safe."

M'pika's black bushy eyebrows bunched together, his face registering a strong aversion to the order.

Lyon directed his attention to Y'ro. "The same goes for you. Keep up. I won't wait for you."

"As you say, *Bwana*."

"Good. Show me where you last saw Mama Daktor."

Y'ro led them to a bushy area with a small clearing. Lyon was thankful for the morning light. More than a week had passed since Margaret's abduction. He knew from experience that finding clues at this late date was close to impossible. He paused for a moment, gazing somberly over the area. "Spread out. Look for anything—broken twig, upturned rock, a scuffed tree knob, animal tracks. This is going to be like looking for a panther in the dark. Whistle if you find something. Stay focused."

"Which direction, my brother?"

Lyon considered M'pika's question. "We're a day from the mission. Whoever took Margaret wouldn't risk the possibility that she'd escape and set the authorities on him." He flicked at a fly. "Either of you know the lands to the north, deep into the Rift Valley?"

Y'ro's eyes widened. "Much evil *juju* der, *bwana*."

"It is unmapped territory, my brother. You hab heard de stories about people who let curiosity get de better of dem, and never returned."

Lyon set his jaw. "I'll understand if you decide to return to the mission."

Y'ro thumped his chest. "I am not a brave warrior, *bwana*, but I will not stay behind."

M'pika patted the butt of his rifle. No words were necessary.

"Sing out if you spot any clues." Lyon added a caution, "Stay in sight. No more than ten yards apart."

The trio separated, each choosing his own direction. There were no maps, no compasses to guide them; only sheer instinct and knowledge of the jungle's hidden secrets. The men pushed ahead in the thick, dark woods. The dense canopy of trees blocked out the sun, making the heat and humidity difficult to escape. Within minutes, Lyon's face was drenched in sweat, and moisture beaded between his shoulder blades, where his rucksack pressed against his shirt.

Lyon stared out at the varied shades of green. Normally he saw beauty. Today was different. He was entering the underbelly of a beast. He settled the hat on his head and squared his shoulders. He would find Margaret, and the bastard who took her had better pray she wasn't harmed.

Following an easy track, they pushed ahead in the dark forest that some referred to as the land of *tabu*. Every so often, Lyon carved a notch in a tree to mark a trail.

The landscape farther away from the mission changed from flat to steep. Rocky ledges and worn tree roots formed a natural staircase. The humidity turned the jungle into an unrelenting enemy. Each step required physical effort. Another week dragged out interminably without locating a clue that would lead them to finding Margaret.

As the sun met the horizon and night spread its veil, Lyon was forced to call a halt to the search. He let out a long breath. Frustrated, he scanned the thick brush. A twig snapped in the distance. He peered through the darkness, looking for movement. For a moment, there was nothing but silence. Then the distant call of a bird broke through the eerie quiet of the jungle.

Lyon shrugged off his rucksack. "We'll rest here for the night." Setting it against a tree, he unbuckled the straps, reached inside, and withdrew a rolled oilcloth that contained a dwindling amount of dried wildebeest *biltong*.

Y'ro set about gathering twigs and small branches for a fire.

A monkey hollered in the distance, in sync with the rest of the night's symphony. While listening to the jungle's background music of humming insects, bird chirps, the haunting roars of big cats, and an occasional growl, the three hunters shared a meager meal.

M'pika lamented, "Water all gone."

Lyon shook his canteen. "Mine's empty, too. Maybe we'll find a stream tomorrow."

Enough was said. Lyon's voice was somber when he spoke, "In the morning, the two of you head back to the mission. I can't ask you to keep pushing without food and water. I'll go on alone."

M'pika scowled. "No, my brother. We are in this together, no matter how long it takes to find Mama Daktor."

Y'ro pointed to his chest. "You can whip me, and shout loud curses at me, *Bwana*, but dis boy will stay too."

Lyon raised an eyebrow. A slight smile quirked the corner of his lips. No other words were needed.

Each man found a spot close to the fire. Lyon lay with his back to the fire, his hand wrapped around the rifle. Exhaustion finally overcame his racing mind, and he drifted into an oppressive, aching, downtrodden feeling of loneliness. He tossed restlessly and could not find any solace for his mind.

He awoke with a start, his body clammy with perspiration. A strange wetness fell on his forehead. He sat up in exasperation at M'pika's riotous laughter. M'pika continued laughing as he pointed toward the treetop. Y'ro, too, covered his mouth as if to shutter his own amusement.

Lyon sniffed. He wiped his hand across his face and wrinkled his nose. "What the bloody hell!"

An adult male baboon stood on a high limb exposing his genitals. Lyon reached down, grabbed a stout piece of burnt wood, and chucked it at the offending primate.

He glared at the two men. "Stop your smirking." He snatched up his rucksack and rifle. "No water for coffee. Let's be on our way."

M'pika and Y'ro, their shoulders shaking in silent laughter, ambled after Lyon. The day broke clear and warm, a sharp edge that promised more heat. Morning passed, and the sun seemed to squat with ominous deliberation, giving no hint of cooling off. Along the way, Y'ro spotted a tamarind tree. Its fruit hung like stuffed bags. "*Bwana*, food."

"Good man, Y'ro." Lyon watched him shinny up the tree to shake a limb, forcing it to drop its fruit.

Each man sighed contentedly as they tore into the long yellow pods to enjoy the sweet pulp and its refreshing nectar. After their short respite, Lyon was eager to get on the way.

After three more hours of diligent searching, he thought he heard the unmistakable sound of running water. He whistled. The men gathered, each sopped with sweat, each heaving for breath.

Lyon cocked his head. "Do you hear that? Either of you know if there is a stream nearby?"

Puzzlement showed on M'pika's face. "De jungle is a mighty land with many hidden secrets. I am not familiar with dis place."

"What about you, Y'ro?" Lyon brushed sweat from the bridge of his nose.

"No, *Bwana*, but dis boy is thirsty."

Lyon nodded his agreement and pointed. "Let's move in that direction. Maybe whoever took Margaret knows this area. Maybe they stopped to get a drink."

There was no clearly marked trail in front of them.

Two hundred yards ahead and in dense overgrowth, the earth opened up, then plummeted down into a tumbling mass of brilliant green ferns by a stream of crystal clear water gurgling over a mass of boulders.

Lyon scoured both directions, looking for clues that would indicate where the abductor might have left the trail to reach the water.

Nothing.

Frustration built like a rock-hard fist that hammered the pit of his stomach. "If there is a trail leading down, it must be well hidden, because I don't see it."

He stepped toward the ledge. The earth gave way, and he immediately lost his footing and slid down the steep slope, butt first, to splash into the shallow depths. He looked up at M'pika and Y'ro's concerned faces, and motioned them to follow.

He removed his pith helmet, filled it with water, and dumped the refreshing liquid over his head. Then, on his knees, he leaned forward to slake his thirst and cool his face. When he raised his eyes, something in his line of vision was out of the ordinary, something that did not belong among the various shades of green. It took a moment for his brain to register.

Splashing across the stream, he hoped and prayed his eyes had not deceived him. As if it were a precious jewel, Lyon looked about until he spied a sturdy twig. Wary of poisonous vipers, he used it to carefully part a mass of shaggy moss, and there it lay, ensnared on a bed of green. He lifted the strip of white, lace-trimmed cloth.

"What is it?" M'pika asked, crossing the stream to Lyon's side.

Lyon heaved a long breath. "A grand prize." He held a strip of material no longer than his little finger. "Whether left by accident or on purpose, this is surely a piece of Margaret's undergarment."

Y'ro peered closely. "For certain it does not belong to a tribal woman."

Lyon surveyed the area. Which way would the abductor go? He looked at the arching trees, the looming shadows, the deep crevices with all their unknown habitants.

Y'ro's bird chirp caused Lyon to look up. The Tani man stood above them and motioned forward, so Lyon and M'pika climbed the slippery bank. Before them lay a narrow trail that was invisible from the opposite bank.

The men spoke in hushed whispers. They all agreed that to go downstream meant traveling in the direction of the mission.

Y'ro's eyes widened. Lyon noted the fear. "What is it? What do you know that scares you?"

His voice hushed, Y'ro said, "In the time of my grandfather, so he told us, de leopard god lived in a sacred place, in a cave. It was said those who worshiped Osebo were eaters of flesh. Chil'ren were cautioned to never speak his name for fear he would come in de night and snatch dem from der beds, never to be seen again."

Lyon and M'pika exchanged looks, a glower of anger in their eyes. Lyon's upper lip curled into a disdainful sneer. "Matata belongs to the leopard clan. He claims he can shift from man to leopard."

M'pika's lean cheeks puffed in and out. His eyes took on a chilling glitter. "You are tinking he is Bambala?"

"Seems preposterous, but yes." An image flashed across Lyon's eyes. He squeezed them shut, concentrating on the face in his dream. The youth attacking his mother had turned to stare up at the trees. He had not given evidence that he saw the two young boys hidden among the leafy boughs. That savage of long ago had a scar above the left eye, a scar that resembled a pitchfork. The sign of the devil.

Matata was not someone Lyon often encountered. There was little reason for him to closely observe the witch doctor. And on a man past fifty and with a face rife with crisscrossed scars on both cheeks and an aged brow grooved with wrinkles, a pitchfork-shaped scar was easy to overlook.

When Lyon finished giving his explanation of what it was that had bothered him about Matata, M'pika massaged his hip. "If it kills me, I will keep up. I see the glint in your eyes, my brother. Your vengeance is my vengeance."

Lyon's mind raced with a plan. His breath came out in short angry pants.

"I am as eager as you to find this cave. We are tired, and we don't know who or what we'll encounter. As difficult as it is, we must eat and rest. I have a few strips of dried gazelle."

"And dere is plenty fish in de stream." Y'ro slid down the embankment to stand in knee-deep water. His spear arched.

****

Margaret watched the fire. The burning wood popped, snapped, and sizzled. The flames writhed and undulated like a fiery serpent. On the one hand her skin burned from the close proximity to the flames. On the

215

other hand, she was chilled. Shivers rippled up her overheated body. Goosebumps raced up and down her arms.

She was going to die. She didn't try to deny the reality. Curled up on the hot surface of the stone floor, she counted the men. Eleven of them, draped in leopard loincloths, their bodies glistening with animal fat, gyrated around the fire. At each pass, they leered at her, snarled and growled, and intimidated her with their leopard claw-covered hands.

She thought about Lyon, and the life they would never share. She was sorry now that she had not allowed him to love her. To feel him inside her. To experience the ecstasy of them climaxing together, and to bask in the glowing aftermath of their lovemaking.

She finally turned her head, looking up at a hole high in the cave's conical ceiling. A patch of blue let her know it was daylight outside, although it seemed to be darkening now, and in her mind's eye she pictured the sun finally sinking from view to darken her prison.

A ceaseless dripping echoed inside her head. She wanted the sound to stop. Searching for the source, her eyes settled on a round pool. White vapor rose from the water's bubbling surface.

The humidity was as stifling as a wet blanket. The stench of unwashed bodies mingled with the acrid odor of burning wood and rotten eggs further sucked away her breath.

Her head fell back. How much longer must she endure this torture before Matata and his maggot-eating cronies decided to end their undulating frenzy to strip the flesh from her bones?

And then that calm, practical, British voice of her

father started talking to her from the back of her head. *You are an Ashton. Ashtons do not cower. We raise our swords and face the enemy. It's time to get tough, Margaret Mary. It's time to spit in the eye of your enemy.*

Her gaze went to Matata.

Don't think. Just do it, Margaret. Be tough. Show the bastard what you're made of. Don't go down without a fight.

She sat up. The world spun. Uncertain of the food Matata had put before her, she had refused to eat and had allowed herself only a few small sips of water. Starving to death or dying of thirst was surely better than being eaten alive.

With a gagging cough, she choked back the bile that rose in her throat. She wanted to scream, long and loud, until she was hoarse.

The grunts and growls and snarls grew louder—deafening. She was afraid, and she hated this. She had never deliberately hurt anyone. She was a doctor, a healer, a giver of life. Oh, God, why had this monster done this to her?

Rotten eggs? Of course! The odious odor of sulphur means we are near a lava tube. The mind is a mysterious thing. Here she was in the bowels of hell, and wondering if Africa had volcanoes. If so, there was little chance of Lyon finding her.

She didn't deserve to be cast into a vat of boiling water.

Hands reached for her. She kicked and slapped and batted them away. Matata's face leered close, and he opened his mouth to show his yellowed, pointed teeth.

Her father's voice came again. *You are my brave*

girl, Margaret. Show no fear.

And then…

There, in the distance. She heard it again. A sound. Footsteps? No…no. Voices. Someone was coming.

She scrambled away from the reaching hands. Her back against the cave's wall, "I'm here," she tried to scream. "I'm here!"

All that came out of her parched throat was a sound like the croaking of a frog. The voices were fading. The footsteps were walking away. She was certain of it.

Desperate for help, she stood, forcing her legs to support her. The voice inside her head shouted, *Run, Margaret. Run.*

Forgetting that her ankles and hands were bound, she landed flat on her stomach. As clawed hands grabbed at her feet and arms, she screamed until she was certain her vocal cords had ruptured.

"I'm here! I'm here! Please, anyone, someone, oh, please don't leave me…"

Chapter 27

Footing grew rough, even for hiking boots. Long, thick grass offered little traction. Twice Lyon lost his footing and nearly tumbled down a steep slope. Rocks and tree roots became stumbling obstacles. M'pika stubbed his toe on a lichen-covered log. He fell, his hands splayed forward. He cursed aloud his aching hip as Lyon offered a hand to help him stand. Within hours, Y'ro's bare legs also wore painful and bloody results of the hike.

Lyon held up a hand to signal a halt. He felt the loneliness of this place, where his companion's footfalls were swallowed up by decades of leaves and other debris. He did not know this region. He felt the disorientation of the towering trees that blocked out the sun and made it difficult to get a sense of direction. They often had to go down into a valley to find a way to continue traveling upward as they crossed it. In a place like this, anything could go wrong. One misstep and any one of them might topple to his death. He was putting their lives at risk. He focused his thoughts on finding Margaret.

This immense ocean of woods was the perfect place for a secret cult of flesh eaters to hide. The thought caused Lyon to shudder as he brought the canteen to his lips for a long, deep swallow. He feared they were running out of daylight.

M'pika rested on a soft mat of grass. He saw it first. As previously agreed, no words were spoken. He made the quibbling sound of a flamingo to get Lyon's attention. He pointed to a tree with a broken branch. The break had not dried enough for the sprig to fall off.

Lyon nodded his understanding, and sprinted to the tree. And then he spotted the crushed fern, brown and brittle. Y'ro raced ahead. He motioned, and pointed to the ground. Blades of long grass lay flat.

Lyon hastened his pace, following the unmistakable signs of human activity as the trail zigzagged through the dense forest and climbed higher until it dead-ended at the base of a wall of stone.

The sun was setting fast. Daylight was slipping through their fingers, to be replaced by a fiery setting sun.

Lyon slammed the palm of his hand against the lichen-covered barricade. He registered two things at once—the jagged bundle of rocks off to his left, and to his right a barely visible path leading upward. He sounded three sharp bird trills. M'pika and Y'ro trotted to his side.

His voice barely a whisper, he said, "The two of you stay here while I follow the path. If I find an entrance, I'll signal. Keep a sharp lookout, and keep your weapons ready."

The men nodded.

Lyon surged ahead, jumping from one rock to another until he entered a heavily wooded area. Thorny bushes and tightly packed trees gave way to a broad clearing. He didn't slow until the ground suddenly flattened and the footing eased up. The acrid scent of rotten eggs teased his nostrils. Placing his hands on his hips, he turned in a complete circle, searching. Nothing, except a massive termite hill.

He eased toward the mound. By his third footstep, the unmistakable growls of many leopards put him on guard. He stopped instantly. Leopards were solitary creatures that only spent time with others when they were mating or raising young. They were also nocturnal and spent their nights hunting instead of sleeping.

Leopards usually spent their time in trees. Lyon was curious to know why these predatory cats were in a cave, and how they found their way in and out. He climbed to the top of the mound and placed his face inside the opening at the top of the cone to get a look.

Margaret came into full view, and any bit of triumph Lyon felt burst like an overly inflated balloon and left him with a cold knot in the pit of his stomach. The white limbs curved into a fetal position, not a woman lying down peacefully to rest, but a bruised body with hands and feet bound, like an animal. Light danced around her bloodless face.

She was dead.

And then, as he watched in the dusky gloom, he swore she moved and looked up at him. Her widening eyes revealed her taut fear. One sleeve of her white blouse had been ripped, exposing the creamy flesh of her upper arm. She moved, and he spotted the brownish red stain. Blood.

The devils had harmed her. It tore his soul to see her tied up and afraid. It grated at his thoughts as it had throughout the entire search, wondering what she had been forced to endure.

The desire to avenge Margaret's suffering raged through Lyon. But given the number of leopard-warriors he counted, and his lack of knowledge as to how many more were inside the cave, he forced down his desire to begin shooting right now, not willing to risk Margaret's exposed position by giving away his presence too soon.

Shock ripped through his veins. He stared at one man's long, thin face, at the shadowy crevices that marred his cheeks. Anger pulsed through Lyon. He would never forget that face, those beady eyes. All the clues clicked into place, all his questions of who had kept appearing in his dream—the question of who had murdered his mother twenty-three years ago was stunningly answered.

Matata!

Lyon glanced again at Margaret's worn, frightened appearance. Guilt tightened his gut. His wrath rose like darkening storm clouds.

The sound hit him all at once: her voice pleading for help. It sounded hoarse and faint, the tone of a woman in desperate need of rescuing.

Frantic to find a way into the cave, Lyon circled around the mound, his gaze sweeping from side to side, fearful of missing any sign of an entrance. The sun shifted. A miracle! It was there, a crevice hidden like a dark thread in a thick layer of vines.

He tore a long strip from his shirt and tied it to mark the opening. He bolted off the first boulder. He bounded downward, one, two, three, four, and then catapulted down the steep path to where M'pika and Y'ro stood guard.

For a moment Lyon just stood there, dazed and angry, and huffing for breath in the heat. Moisture rolled down his face like tears. Maybe he was crying. It was hard to know. He didn't remember the last time he had cried.

Finally, he was able to say, "I found her. She's alive, barely. Matata is there, too. He's preparing her for…" He couldn't say the word. He pointed. "The entrance to the cave is up there."

The sun was well into its evening descent, casting the rough-edged stone walls in gray shadows that stretched into a blanket of greenery.

Lyon narrowed his gaze toward M'pika, eyes burning with the same incredulous concern that rang in his voice. "The climb is steep and dangerous. I need you to stay here, rifle cocked and the trigger ready to pull. I don't care how many you take down, but Matata is mine."

M'pika frowned his displeasure. "It is reasonable that my hip will slow me down. I will stay here, and I will not miss my target."

Lyon motioned for Y'ro to follow.

Caution on high alert, the two men quickly made their way closer, scanning the craggy rocks until Lyon pointed to the strip of cloth that marked the opening to the cave.

Squeezing sideways into the crevice, Lyon and Y'ro exchanged worried grimaces. The pungent stench of blood and death floated heavily on the stale air. The stink nearly gagged them as they stared at the hundreds of bones that littered the cavern's floor.

Certain these were human bones, Lyon's anger roused at the senseless slaughtering of innocent human beings. He pulled a bandana from his pocket and tied it around his mouth and nose. Y'ro tore a strip from his shirt and did the same.

Three quarters of the way into the cave, Lyon spotted a dead man. His heart stopped mid-beat. The haunting sight of the jugular ripped from the man's throat brought hideous thoughts of the past. Lyon's blood pumped faster. Frustrated and angry, he shook his head at the gruesome sight.

Once inside, he quickly scanned the dim interior. His thoughts raced as he calculated how fast he and Y'ro could sneak through the shadows. If his luck held, he would surprise Matata and the other leopard men before they had a chance to grab their weapons. Then he would deal with Matata.

A harsh voice rang out from the cover of darkness.

What the— Confusion pounded in Lyon's chest. He hadn't considered that a guard might be posted.

He cast a glance toward Margaret. Her body jerked. She shifted her position.

The dancing and chanting stopped. Matata brazenly stepped forward. His eyes narrowed in aggravated disbelief.

Lyon watched Margaret awkwardly rise to her knees, saw her catch the heel of her boot in the hem of her skirt, adding more difficulty to her struggle to stand. His heart ached for her at this unexpected development, and his pulse hammered with added concern as he considered how to get her out of this cave.

"So!" Matata curled his thick lips into a lethal grin. "At long last the Lyon has grown from a simpering boy to a man."

Lyon lifted the rifle level with the man's heart.

All hell broke loose.

Matata issued a harsh growl and lunged forward with the swiftness of a cat, leaping for Lyon's throat.

Lyon fired, hitting the witch doctor in the neck and stopping him cold. His body jerked upward slightly, and then he hit the ground full force, his whole body splayed in the dirt. In that same split instant, another leopard-man jumped sideways, grabbing Margaret's arm with one hand as he jerked a torch from the wall and tossed it at Y'ro.

Lyon fired in the same second, and his missed aim slammed into another attacker's chest, the impact staggering the enemy backward. He fired twice more, hitting his targets and sending them sprawling to the ground.

Margaret's struggle was no match for her captor's powerful strength as he dragged her with him, weaving his way around the three dead men.

Anxiety tightened Lyon's stomach into a hard knot. "Move, Margaret."

An unexpected blow, squarely in the ribs, knocked him off balance, and air whooshed from Lyon's lungs as splintering pain radiated through his body. The leopard warrior looked at Lyon and smiled. His victory ended with Y'ro's spear embedded between his shoulder blades. Y'ro leapt forward to yank the spear from the sagging body.

Y'ro whirled and sent the spear flying. The blade found its mark. The impact knocked forward the man dragging Margaret, and he fell into the dirt.

Like rats abandoning a ship, the remaining members of the leopard clan fled the cave. Lyon heard shots and was sure, knowing M'pika's marksmanship was certain, five more cannibals had died.

Lyon's hat slipped off as he dropped to his knees. "Margaret…" His voice was a raspy whisper. The tears leaking from her eyes tore his heart. He wrapped his arms around her, crushing her to his chest, then pulled back, gently gripping her shoulders, moving his hands up to cup her face. "I've been so worried I might not find you."

Pain grimaced her face. His hand came away wet with blood. "Which one hurt you?"

"Matata. He gouged me with his claws." A sigh of relief broke through her trembling lips. "I'm okay now that you are here." She raked her gaze over his handsome face, relishing the sight of him and the euphoric comfort of his presence. She managed a smile. "I knew you would find me."

Trust shimmered in her blue haze. He shouldn't have stormed away from the mission in a huff of anger. He should have protected her. Lyon yanked his knife from its sheath, quickly cut the ropes that bound her wrists and ankles, and then replaced the knife. He rubbed his thumbs across her cheeks, brushing away the tears that moistened her smooth skin.

"Hold me, Jeremiah." She slipped her arms around his waist.

He pulled her up to stand against him, closing his eyes as he drew her into his embrace. "I'm so sorry this happened to you."

"It's not your fault."

Lyon kissed her brow, ran his hand through her shortened locks and along her back, and pulled her closer, wanting to chase away the tremors that shook her body. Through slitted eyes, he glimpsed Matata's inert form lying face down in the dirt. Lyon's body recoiled with relief and aversion.

Margaret touched his face, lightly stroking the

coating of stubble that darkened his bronze skin. "Take me out of this horrible place," she whispered.

He leaned down, intending to kiss her, needing to touch her warmth, to feel the life-pulsing promise of her well-being, to taste her loving sweetness, but a movement caught the corner of his eye and caused him to pause. He glanced past her shoulder and met the glance of M'pika's watchful brown eyes.

Margaret left Lyon's arms to embrace M'pika. "Thank you."

Clearly embarrassed by the show of affection, the Bantu warrior stepped back. "You hab a kind heart and a brave spirit, my sister." He cast a glance at Lyon, and then back at Margaret. He grinned. "And you hab tamed the Lyon."

Lyon arched his brow. He lifted one corner of his mouth into a small smile. "Let's go home."

Outside the cave, Margaret drew a refreshing breath of air. Dark pink and purple streaks coated the edges of the early twilight sky. Night birds chittered, and the jungle came alive with its own particular music.

Lyon cradled her against his side, making sure she didn't slip on the treacherous downhill path. She huffed out a gasp at the sight of dead bodies.

Margaret grimaced. "Should we bury them?"

A pensive sigh slipped from Lyon's lips before he realized he was as tense as a twisted cord. "Let the vultures and other carrion eaters pick their bones clean. It's only fitting."

Her voice was heavily imbued with misery. "Lyon, I'm not sure I can make it to the mission."

Pain furrowed her forehead and glazed her eyes. She staggered forward. Strong arms swung her up and settled her against his chest. Lyon held her tightly. "I'll never let you go, Maggie. Never again."

It began to rain. A gentle misting rain, a cleansing rain to nourish the earth, and to wash away the scent of death.

Part IV

"Life always offers you a second chance. It's called tomorrow."

~Anonymous

Chapter 28

It seemed like yesterday they had all but staggered into the mission's hospital compound, a bedraggled group sorely in need of nourishment and rest. Had it really been a month since her encounter with Matata and the leopard men?

Margaret stood blessedly alone in her small cell-like room. Given the horrors she had survived, she had thought she'd need a good cry. After a week on the trail, the relentless heat, the festering wound in her side, and the newly aroused emotions that revolved around Lyon, she had found herself officially too tired for tears.

She turned her attention to the condition of her body now. The dark purple bruise on her right shoulder had finally disappeared. Her left thigh was no longer yellow and green. The claw marks on her rib cage had produced scars that would forever be a reminder of how close to death she had come and how fortunate she was to have survived.

She peered into the small round mirror that hung above the wash basin. She had definitely lost weight. Her eyes were darkly shadowed, and her cheeks were hollow. She touched the fading bruise on her cheekbone. Like the others, it too would eventually fade.

She was also bruised on the inside.

Margaret's fingers remained on her cheek. She closed her eyes. It was the invisible bruises that took longer to heal.

She turned her thoughts away from the sensitive memories, and in an attempt to stretch her taut muscles, she stretched this way and that several times before bending forward, pressing her palms toward the floor. Upon rising, she repeated the exercise. The long walk across rough terrain, coupled with the abuse from Matata, had left a lingering stiffness that, even now, was still noticeable immediately following her initial departure from bed. Still Margaret considered herself fortunate to be alive.

The sound of voices and footsteps caused her to stride hastily to the bed and grab her robe. Her hands trembled. Her temples throbbed.

Sister Adah Luke called, "Margaret, it's almost time. Are you ready?"

Margaret lifted the latch. She hid behind the door as she eased it open to let Adah and Aganza in. "I can't figure out how to wrap this cloth without it coming undone and leaving me exposed to the world."

Adah laughed as she picked up the long bolt of red material. "No worries. Hold up your arms and allow us to do the wrap and tuck of the wedding *shuka*."

Aganza Mary babbled away, calling Margaret the most beautiful bride. "We are pleased that you honor the old ways of our culture, and the new ways of your people."

For a reason she couldn't explain, Margaret blurted out, "My father spoke to me when I was in the cave."

The Hausa nurses stopped their ministrations. "How can that be, when he is an ocean away?" Aganza

Mary looked at Margaret with widened eyes.

"I don't know, but I am learning that in Africa many unexplained things happen. I heard his voice as clearly as if he were right next to me. He told me to be brave. To fight back." Choking up, Margaret turned aside to hide the tears that promptly sprang forth. "I was never close to my father, always a prickly thorn in his side, yet when I thought I was going to die, he gave me the courage I needed. And now I may never see him again."

"Shh, don't cry, Margaret. It is your wedding day, a day of joy, a new beginning. All will be as it should," Adah Luke murmured consolingly. She laid a gentle hand on Margaret's shoulder.

Aganza Mary carefully lowered the traditional Maasai collar necklace over Margaret's head. Four strands of cowrie shells and colorful beads dangled like bright spots of jewelry against her breasts. Next came the red cape, hand sewn by several Maasai women.

"Why do the Maasai women wear red for their wedding *shukas*?" Margaret longed for a full-length mirror. Red was so unlike the white and pastels she had known for weddings in England.

Adah smiled, something she did often. "Red represents good fortune and prosperity."

"Lovely." Margaret raised and lowered her shoulders to relieve the tension. "I believe I am more nervous today than when I married my first husband."

Adah's dark eyes settled on Margaret. "Have you told Lyon about your husband and child?"

Margaret cast her eyes toward the door. The Maasai were chanting their signal to begin the wedding. She huffed out a nervous breath. "I have not."

Concern darkened Aganza Mary's face. "It is truly none of our business, but he thinks you ran away and left your family. It is not good to start a new life with secrets."

Clasping her hands to her breasts, Margaret's jaw sagged a notch. Chagrined at her negligence, she tried to justify her reasons for not sharing the tragic loss of her family with Lyon. She hugged each one of her friends and thanked them for their honesty. "I will tell him tonight."

Prettily coifed and gowned, she was as nervous as an untouched girl about to share a man's bed for the first time, but she asked Aganza to open the door. She was as ready as she would ever be.

A group of chanting Maasai warriors waited outside to escort Margaret, Adah Luke, and Aganza Mary to the center of the courtyard.

On one side of a fire pit, and in full ceremonial regalia, Oloiboni stood with four tribal elders. On the opposite side, dressed in a black robe, having come all the way from Kenya's capital city, Nairobi, was Magistrate Sir Edgar Godwin, accompanied by Colonel Carl Lockwood of the East African Field Regiment Headquarters.

The courtyard was festooned with colorful flowers and delicate greenery.

Sir Godwin touched his handkerchief to the side of his nose and sniffed. Colonel Lockwood looked dapper in his tan uniform.

The Maasai warriors ushered Margaret to her place next to Lyon and then took their places behind the shaman. Lyon swept her with a teasing look. "Feeling all right, Maggie?"

"Perfectly," she assured him, her smile deepening.

****

M'pika and Y'ro stood next to Lyon, each man handsomely groomed and dressed in tan shorts and matching bush shirts.

Lyon gave a two-finger salute to acknowledge the colonel, and then a courtesy bow toward Margaret. He lifted his head thoughtfully, seeking something appropriate to say.

He was now encumbered by a desire to have her always feel safe and secure as his wife. Realizing how close he had come to losing her had taught him to see beyond the outer shell of this lovely, vibrant woman and read the true depth of her courage hidden within. He realized, with some surprise, there was a deeper, richer emotion taking root in his heart. It had a quality that was outside his realm of experience. As yet, he could not put a name to it. Still, it was very pleasant knowing that she was about to become his alone.

As a show of respect for cultural customs, it had been arranged that the Maasai shaman would begin the ceremony. Oloiboni was dressed in his ceremonial best—his face streaked with white powder, a lion's mane headdress, a complement of colorful beads, and draped in the traditional red cloth. He began the ceremony by waving the fertility horn. He dusted fine powder on Lyon and Margaret's hands and faces. "Bless dis man and woman wid healthy chil'ren."

He produced two amulets, spit on them, and tied them around Lyon and Margaret's necks. "You mus' kiss de charm each morning and each night to protect you from evils," he instructed.

To show his honor and respect toward Margaret, he

spit in the palm of her hand. "Mama Daktor is now our daughter. She is a giver of life, and today I bestow her wid a new name, '*Msai*,' Wise Woman."

A calabash of fresh milk was opened and passed first to Lyon and then to Margaret to sip. Oloiboni spread his arms wide. "We, de Maasai and keepers of de land, are honored to bless dis ceremony."

Each of the elders gave their blessings by coming forth to spit in the palms of Margaret's and Lyon's hands.

Lyon motioned to M'pika and Y'ro, who quickly departed and returned with a Zebu bull and a heifer as payment to Oloiboni for presiding over the wedding.

The bovine were graciously accepted and led away by two Maasai warriors.

Lyon and Margaret then gave their attention to the English magistrate, Sir Edgar Godwin, who harrumphed loudly to clear his voice. He opened his Bible. "Today we are gathered in the name of our Lord and Savior to join this man and this woman in holy matrimony," he pronounced. "Jeremiah Lyon, forsaking all others, do you take this woman as your lawful wedded wife, and pledge to protect and cherish her for all the days of your life?"

Lyon's mind was reeling. A split-second thought of Margaret's husband and child caused him to hesitate. He quickly rationalized that this was Africa, where polygamy was permissible amongst many of the tribes. He gazed into the dark blue pools of Margaret's eyes and was heartened by the loving glow.

"I do."

The magistrate continued, "Margaret Ashton Boynton, forsaking all others, do you take this man—"

He repeated the promise.

She inwardly vowed to put aside her mourning and release Seamus and Jonathan to the heavens. They would always live in her memories, but it was time to move forward, to love again. Today was that day. "I do."

Lifting his voice, Sir Godwin fervently pronounced, "By the powers vested in me, and recognized by the Church of England and the noble state of Kenya, what God has joined together, let no man put asunder. I now pronounce you husband and wife. Jeremiah Lyon, you may kiss your bride."

Feasting and the traditional jumping dances ended the ceremony, with chanting Maasai warriors escorting Lyon and Margaret to their honeymoon site—a flower-adorned tent pitched beneath an acacia tree.

Chapter 29

Inside the tent was a bottle of champagne, two long-stemmed goblets, a tin of scones, and a collection of cheeses, compliments of Colonel Lockwood. A sealed envelope rested against the champagne bottle, addressed to Jeremiah Lyon.

He slid his finger under the flap and joked, "Maybe there's money inside."

Margaret laughed. "Wouldn't that be lovely?"

The serious pucker on Lyon's forehead as he read the contents caused the smile to fade from her face. "What is it?"

"It's from Sir Godwin. He invites you and summons me to his office in a fortnight."

"Whatever for?"

Lyon glanced back at the letter. He shrugged. "To discuss a matter of extreme importance. That's all it says."

He tossed the letter to the table and picked up the bottle of champagne. Waggling his eyebrows, he grinned. "Tonight, the only thing of 'extreme importance' is standing in front of me."

He popped the cork, and Margaret laughed as she caught it with one hand. He filled the glasses with bubbly and offered a toast, "To us."

She smiled. "Forever."

He refilled their glasses, then set his aside to pull a

small round wooden box from his pocket. A lion's head was intricately carved on the lid of the box. "I thought you might like to have this."

Margaret looked at him with curious eyes. "I've never seen such fine workmanship. Did you—"

"No. Y'ro."

She opened it and gasped. Tears sprang to her eyes as she lifted the locket from its nest. "I thought I'd lost it forever. Where did you find it?"

"I didn't." He lifted the necklace from her hands and fastened it around her neck. "The night you were kidnapped, Y'ro searched for you. All he found this, with a broken chain. He was beside himself with guilt for not protecting you."

She touched the gold ornament, clasping it in her hand. "Everything happened so fast that night. I remember struggling with Matata. He blew a powder in my face, and everything went dark. It was hours before I awakened."

She sat in one of the two chairs. "I haven't been honest with you. In fact, I've been downright deceitful."

Lyon opened his mouth to speak. She held up her hand. "Please, let me finish."

She drew a deep breath and slowly released it. "My husband and son are dead."

The pulse in her neck throbbed, and her heart pounded against her chest. Much to her surprise, she didn't cry as she related the incident of their horrific deaths.

"Why did you leave England, your home, and a modern hospital, to come here, of all places?"

"I was devastated. If I were no longer a wife and a

mother, who was I? I thought if I came to Africa to heal the sick, I might also heal myself." She sighed. "And then when I fell in love with you, it felt as if I were betraying Seamus. That's why I pushed you away."

"And now?"

She unclasped the necklace and laid it next to the empty champagne bottle. "There is only you. Today and for the rest of our lives."

He lifted another locket from his pocket and opened it. He laid it next to Margaret's. "This is all I have left of my parents. I barely remember my father. He was a pious man, but my mother was gentle and loved to laugh, and—" His words drifted off. Moisture built in his eyes. "We can both lay our loved ones to rest."

Lyon closed the space between them, his gaze dwelling upon the delicate pink crests teasingly displayed by the loosening red material. His attention was firmly ensnared. Such enticements were too much for a man to ignore, much less for one who found himself hard-pressed by a lengthy abstinence and an ever-goading passion. He tilted his head and smiled at the vivid blush infusing his wife's cheeks.

The corners of his lips twitched with humor as he lifted the ceremonial necklace over Margaret's head. A soft fluttering sigh escaped her as he leaned forward and brushed his lips against her cheek. From there, soft kisses trekked a leisurely descent along the creamy column of her throat. She laid a trembling hand against his steely chest and closed her eyes, accepting the languid caress of his mouth.

Beneath his palm, her heart nearly matched the thumping of his own, attesting to her growing involvement in his game of seduction.

Lyon marveled at her willingness to accept his warming attentions, yet he was wary of being rebuffed. Lifting his head, he searched her face for what emotions might be revealed in that sublime visage and was awed by her unparalleled beauty. Her nose was pert and slender, and her soft mouth winsomely curved and much in need of kissing. In all of that fair countenance, he detected not the slightest hesitancy.

A small gasp escaped Margaret as he loosened the tucked material, widening the placket, allowing the cloth to flutter into a red heap.

"Lyon, please…" Her whispered plea was hardly more than a soft exhalation of a breath.

He settled her on a mattress filled with plush grasses, the blue sheet hand-stitched with intricate designs of lions. He undressed, then blew out the lantern's flame to secure their privacy.

Hovering over her, he claimed her mouth and ravaged its honeyed depths with ravenous greed, searching, demanding, devouring all that was within reach of his tongue. His hand came up to encompass the back of her head as his face slanted across hers, and it became an intoxicating exchange of lips and tongues as he found himself drinking in the sweet nectar of her passionate response.

His mouth blazed a fiery path over her breasts, tantalizing her quivering flesh as he trailed to her thigh. Settled between her parted limbs, he teased her with the heat of his desires, stroking his maleness against the dark veils shrouding the secret place of her womanhood until Margaret began to shudder.

His smoldering eyes roamed her as he continued

his pleasurable assault. Her breath caught at the sensations. It was as if they were both jolted by liquid fire, waves of it pouring through their senses and setting them aflame.

Margaret lifted her hips, inviting him in. "Please, Lyon, oh, please…"

He joined with her in slow, smooth rhythmic thrusts that seemed effortless on his part, a long leisured stroking that rekindled a searing passion and built a burgeoning, exciting, exhilarating, scintillating pleasure that washed through their bodies, senses skimming over billowing currents, quickening movements that drew Margaret up to meet his thudding hardness, waves of pulsating rapture sweeping through their entwined bodies that crashed into unending ecstasy.

A slender arm fell over Lyon's chest; a sleek leg rested against his thigh.

Smiling dreamily, Margaret traced a fingertip across the mat of hair covering her husband's chest and upward to encircle a male nipple. "I think I could sleep an entire week, and all my dreams would be reliving this moment."

A slow grin stretched across his handsome face, displaying the taut depressions of the scar on his cheek as his hand swept down to caress her nakedness. "How 'bout I help make your dreams come alive? Would you be willing to indulge me?"

Her smile was warm and inviting. "Most eagerly, my fierce Lyon, if you, in turn would be amenable to allowing me a few privileges."

His smile brimmed with familiar arrogance. "As many as you want. I do like an adventurous woman."

Scarcely had the words crossed his lips than she

looked into his smoldering eyes with a winsomely mutinous grin. She leaned forward and nipped his nipple, eliciting a surprised chuckle.

Chapter 30

Lyon couldn't help but be content after yesterday's events. He had gotten married. It was almost impossible to believe; Margaret was his wife.

It wasn't until he slid the ivory band on her finger that it had sunk in.

She was his.

Until death do them part.

He recalled holding her in his arms, and how incredibly right it felt, as if her body had been shaped especially for his.

A smile touched his lips. From the first instant he had set eyes on her standing like a haughty princess on the riverboat's deck, he had wanted her. Now, she was his. It was a heady feeling. His pulse quickened as he recalled peeling away her clothes like the delectable skin of a piece of fruit. A breath had snagged in her throat. A shudder had run through her body, and she had arched against him like a bowstring, so taut he feared she might break if he tightened his embrace.

He couldn't hear her breathing, but he could hear her heart—a wild thrumming that eloquently spoke of her elation and passion.

He still wasn't quite certain how it had all come about except that, ever since that fateful day he had rescued Margaret from Matata and the leopard-men, he had known in his heart of hearts that his life would never be the same without her.

When the idea had come to him—to propose to Margaret—it had been like a strange jolt of electricity through his veins. He felt giddy, like a green schoolboy, and he'd barely been able to contain himself.

He gazed out over the veldt and listened to predawn's early morning music—birds trilling, cicadas, the distant hooting of an owl, and the answering call. Somehow he knew that if his mother had lived, she would have loved Maggie as much as he did. For the first time in his life he felt at peace.

A pair of arms hugged him from behind. His heart skipped a beat, and when he turned, he was unable to keep a loopy smile off his face. "Maggie," he whispered. He tucked her beneath his arm. She laid her head against his chest.

"I—" She shook her head. "Never mind."

"What were you going to say?"

"Never mind."

He moved her a little way from him and placed a finger to tip her chin upward. He murmured, "When it's you and me, it's never nothing."

She swallowed, shadows playing across the delicate lines of her throat, and finally she said, "I just…I wanted to say…"

His fingers tightened around hers, lending her encouragement. He wanted her to say it, though he hadn't thought he needed to hear it again. Not after last night. But, dear God, how much he wanted to hear the words again.

"With all my heart, I love you." She stood on tiptoe and brushed her lips against his.

There was a difference in the kiss. It held a promise

of *always*, of togetherness. It gave him a sense of belonging to someone. He returned the kiss, taking the time to explore her, to relish the moment. His hands slid down the length of her chemise, and she moaned as the material bunched under his fingers.

"You are the moon and the stars to me. You are my world, Maggie." And then, deciding there was no use in holding the words to himself any longer, he said, "I love you."

His lips moved across her cheek to her ear, and he nibbled gently on her lobe before moving down her neck to the delectable hollow at the base of her throat.

"Lyon." She swayed against him. "Oh, Lyon."

He cupped her bottom and pressed her to him, a groan slipping from his lips as he held her close and tight against his arousal. He thought he'd wanted her before, but this…this was different.

His voice was husky with passion. "I need you." He lifted her into his arms, carried her inside the tent, and carefully laying her on the mattress of dried grass, said, "I need you so much."

She whispered his name, burying her face against his chest. Her fingers entwined in his hair. "I want you, too."

He lifted on his knees, and her fingers went to his belt and released it from the buckle. Next came the button, and then the zipper.

He struggled out of the bush shorts, his boots, and socks. Lyon pulled Margaret to a sitting position. "Lift your arms."

She obeyed.

****

Margaret wanted to take part, to be adventurous.

She lifted his arms and allowed him to release her from the confines of her undergarments. But all she could do was lie back and revel in his explorations, occasionally reaching out to trail her fingers over whichever parts of his body she could touch.

She closed hers eyes in a rush of shame. For a brief moment she compared Lyon's lovemaking to that of Seamus. The difference was vast. Seamus had been stiff and reserved, almost as if he were performing an obligation. And often she was left unfulfilled. She had made excuses that he was fragile, with a delicate constitution. As a virgin, she hadn't known that the sexual act was beautiful, and sensual, and exquisite.

And now…

She felt loved.

Cherished.

Worshiped.

Humbled.

Emotions all rolled into one that took her breath away.

His lips followed the trail of his hands, sending tingles of desire across her belly and coming to rest in the flattened hollow between her breasts. He murmured her name, kissing his way to her nipple. He teased it first with his tongue, then took it full into his mouth.

The sensation was intense and immediate. Her body convulsed, and her fingers gripped his firm buttocks. She was certain the world had fallen off its axis and she had tumbled into a vortex of bliss.

"Lyon," she gasped, her back arching. His fingers slipped between her legs, not that she needed anything more to ready her for his entry. She wanted this, and she wanted him, and she wanted it to last forever.

He moved then, positioning himself at her entrance. His face was over hers, nose to nose, his eyes glassy with passion. He moved within her, each stroke a wave of intense pleasure. Deep within her a fiery heat built. Lost in a whirlwind of sensation, she clamped her thighs tight and lifted her hips, demanding the length of him. Her breath came in short little pants. His body responded in primal ferocity. She watched his face as he brought her to a climax.

And then he exploded like a randy youth. He cried out her name, and collapsed atop her.

He moved, and she stopped him. "Don't," she said, stilling him with a smile. She whispered, "Don't leave, not just yet."

When she released him, he did not relinquish their closeness as he slid to the mattress. She lay against him, spoon fashion.

She was tired.

She was sated.

In the distance, a lion's roar lifted on the air. Another answered. Margaret was certain it was a lioness answering the mating call. A smile touched her lips.

****

Full dawn streaked the sky with wisps of light filtering through the tent flaps, touching the canvas enclosure with a rosy glow. Margaret lifted her lashes. The rich, earthy aroma of coffee tantalized her senses. Lyon entered the tent, a steaming mug in each hand, a smug smile on his lips. "Maggie, if you keep looking at me like that, this coffee will get mighty cold before we have a chance to drink it."

She stretched and yawned, and purred like a cat. "I

can't believe it's morning. I must have been awfully tired."

Lyon laughed out loud. "You gave me quite a workout. I can't remember when I've slept so well."

She accepted the mug as he sat down beside her. "I've poured a basin of fresh water. After your bath, I have a wedding surprise for you."

Lifting the coffee to her lips, she offered Lyon a seductive smile. She took a deep breath and exhaled on a sigh. "I love surprises."

Except for the melodious song of the jungle beyond the tent, a peaceful silence settled around them. Lyon stepped outside to give Margaret the privacy she needed to complete her toilette.

An hour later, stifling a yawn, she followed dutifully behind Lyon. She couldn't help grinning at the memory of her indignation when, upon their first meeting, he'd ordered her to not walk in front of him. She also recalled the sniggering behind her back as she had marched full steam ahead to the front of the line of men who carried the heavy crates filled with medical supplies on their brawny shoulders.

A cobra had reared its head and hissed. She had been so frightened by the ominous viper she didn't remember hearing the shot, only the blood and bits and pieces of snake that had splattered on her skirt and blouse.

M'pika had trotted forward to scold her. "Mama Daktor, de man always walks in front of de woman so to see de snake first. Den he kill it."

All the men had laughed, and she had choked back indignant tears.

Margaret glanced up at her husband and was struck

by an avalanche of emotions. His manly good looks stirred her. She searched for something to point her wayward thoughts to a different direction. "Lyon, how did you get the claw-mark scars?"

The question seemed to dim the radiance in his eyes a slight degree. "Nothing exciting. I was barely sixteen and on my first safari with another hunter. He was showing me the ropes, so to speak. We were beating a big male lion out of the bush when another male came out of nowhere. I managed to get my rifle up and took him down with the first shot. Then I followed the custom of the Maasai—when a boy kills his first lion, and to show he is extra brave, he grabs the lion by the tail and hopes it's really dead. Mine wasn't. All eight hundred pounds of raging fury, with teeth and claws, attacked. I don't remember unsheathing my knife, or killing the monster, or much else. I'm told I ripped his heart out. The Maasai said the lion's soul became mine.

"I was more dead than alive by the time they got me to Angel of Mercy. M'pika helped carry the litter. He stayed with me all the way. I'd lost a lot of blood. That was when I met Doctor Williams, and Sisters Adah Luke and Aganza Mary. I guess they expected me to die, but Doctor Williams performed a miracle by inserting a tube and transferring M'pika's blood into my body.

"M'pika and I have known each other since we were children. We've always been as close as brothers, but you might say that on that night we truly became blood brothers. Until you, he's been my only family."

Lyon paused. He stared out at the vast green landscape. "Afterward, people stopped calling me

Jeremiah, and I simply became—the Lyon. A symbol, I suppose, of a lion's courage."

Tears stung Margaret's eyes. She flung herself into his arms. "You are indeed blessed to have a brother such as M'pika, and he you."

He held her tight. This woman he loved with all his soul. "Come. My surprise is just a little farther."

Lyon and Margaret continued to follow a game trail no wider than a man's breadth. As streaks of blue collided with puffy clouds, the beauty of Africa still amazed Margaret with its profusion of flowers.

Lyon pointed. "Look there."

Margaret was not prepared for what she saw when they burst into a little glade. There on the banks of a narrow, sluggish stream were a half-dozen trees with gray bark and slender, fine-toothed leaves.

Lyon pointed to one tree that was covered with blossoms in every conceivable color. Two others were just beginning to bloom.

"Oh, they are beautiful! What kind of trees are they?"

"I'm sure there is a scientific name. The natives call them butterfly trees." Lyon looked as if he were trying to curb his grin. He walked over and gave a branch a couple of good shakes.

The blossoms shattered off, but instead of falling, in a burst of color, they fluttered away to another little gray tree.

Margaret squealed and clapped her hands like a happy child. "Butterflies! They are beautiful."

"You try it."

She stepped to a smaller tree and gave it a shake. Once again, the butterflies opened their rainbow-hued wings and flittered to another gray tree.

Tears filled her eyes as she thought of baby Jonathan and how much she would never get to share with him. There was too much inside her. Too many emotions, all desperately pushing to get out. She put her face in her hands and cried. Not from sorrow, and not from joy, but just because she couldn't keep it all inside.

Lyon closed the distance between them. She buried her face against his chest, soaking the front of his shirt with tears. Between hiccups, she managed, "It's the most beautiful wedding gift…so perfect."

He pressed a kiss to the palm of her hand. "Let's return to the mission."

She reached up, touched his cheek, and nodded.

Chapter 31

The humid weather made for a miserable journey to Nairobi. However, they found the living conditions in the city refreshing. When Lyon and Margaret were shown into Sir Godwin's elegant office, with its three ceiling fans to rid the room of stuffiness, he came forward to greet them. His hand wrapped around Margaret's, and he lifted it to his lips and gave it a perfunctory kiss.

"So good of you to come all this way. I trust your rooms at the Fairmont House are favorable?"

Margaret curtsied. "It is quite charming." She offered him a gracious smile. "One could easily become spoiled with such luxury."

Lyon placed a hand at the small of her back and led her to a leather wingback chair. He gave her a knowing smile. "What she didn't say is how much the elegant suite with running water and a bathtub, and the tea service, all make her long for a more civilized environment."

"The room is, indeed, luxurious." She glanced at Lyon, trying to keep her countenance but failing miserably with a peal of laughter. "I felt right at home when a giraffe stuck its head through the bedroom window, although we are on the second story. And at least there was no python in my bed when I pulled back the duvet."

The magistrate's black brows rose. He brushed aside her witty effusions and offered both her and Lyon a glass of ratafia. "Or perhaps a pot of tea with scones?"

Lyon noted with satisfaction the magistrate's surprise at Margaret's humor. He cast a swift, appraising glance over her. There was no denying she looked quite beautiful in her short, coppery, curly locks and the slight flush to her cheeks.

He declined the overly sweet liqueur. "Tea, for both of us." He also didn't want alcohol to cloud his judgment on whatever business it was that had caused the magistrate to summon him all the way to Nairobi. At Godwin's gesture, he sat in the chair next to Margaret, while the man rang the bell on his desk and ordered the refreshments as soon as the houseboy entered.

He harrumphed, adjusted the stiff collar at his neck, and leaned forward, his fingers interlaced. His eyes narrowed as he focused on Lyon.

"Your reputation as a great white hunter precedes you, Lyon. Therefore, I will not beat around the bush but get straight to the point. You were raised in the jungle, you are knowledgeable in the layout of the land, you know the dialects of the different tribes, and you are respected among the native people as well as your colleagues."

Lyon waited as if he were watching a dangerous predator, watching to see when it would attack its victim. He remained silent, wary.

His silence clearly caused Sir Godwin discomfort. "Ah, yes, well. I'd like to offer you a governmental post. Mombasa is turning into a seaport hub. This last ten years, the population has doubled. There are even hints of war building in Europe."

"What does any of this have to do with me?"

"Poaching has increased tenfold. Elephants and rhinos are being slaughtered for their ivory. Gorillas are being killed for their—" He cut his eyes toward Margaret. "I beg your pardon, but you are a doctor. For lack of a more sensitive word, their genitals, to be sold as aphrodisiacs. The council has agreed and voted to hire a game warden—you."

Lyon didn't comment. His time in the veldt had taught him that haste in the face of the enemy makes for a dead man.

"As head game warden, you will receive a handsome yearly stipend. You will be expected to hand pick a deputy warden and also to train wardens. You will set up stations every one hundred miles. These men will also receive stipends and housing, but they must understand they are not above the law, because they are the law. These must be trustworthy and loyal men."

Lyon had to admit that exotic safari life had worn thin, and frankly, he was sick of not having a permanent place to call home. Now that he'd wed Margaret, he needed something more than pandering to pompous nabobs who gleefully delighted in the killing of animals for sport.

He was a brave man. He had proven that countless times in the face of the enemy—both the two-legged and the four-legged kind. But he was also a cautious man.

"What else, Sir Godwin? This offer isn't as straightforward as it sounds."

The magistrate pushed from his chair. He beckoned Lyon to follow him. They stood before a large map that spanned the chamber wall.

Using a long wooden pointer, Goodwin pointed to the boundaries under British protection. "You will survey the area, marking off designated regions for game warden outposts. A new map will be drawn and distributed to the council members, members of parliament, and to all the military outstations. And as this is a new position, if you accept the post, you will write the laws and the suitable punishments for each crime, subject to council approval, of course."

Godwin strolled to his desk and, as if to slake his thirst, drained his cup of tea, then refilled it. "What say you, Lyon?"

Lyon raised his eyebrows. He ran his hand over his jaw. "It's a worthy offer, and one I would like to think on, and discuss with my wife." He looked over at her.

Her lips parted, and for a moment she looked dumbstruck. She sucked in her breath. "How much land is involved in the surveying?"

Sir Godwin didn't circumvent his answer. "As the crow flies, twenty territories, or roughly two million square miles."

The magistrate's answer caused her to stiffen. "Oh, my! Wouldn't it take many years to survey all that land?"

Lyon reached over to clasp her hand. "I'm certain the surveying could be done in increments rather than all at one time." He cocked an eyebrow toward Godwin.

Obviously flustered, the pudgy man removed a handkerchief and wiped his glistening brow. "It would, indeed, take ten years or perhaps more. But, of course, Lyon would use his best judgment of how much time to allot for each phase of establishing boundaries. Perhaps even securing surveyor contractors to assist in this project. With the rumors of war, the council would like the first phase of this project completed within a year, no less than two. We have approved a proposed budget."

Lyon stood and paced back and forth, then stopped, hesitating. "I have often given thought to the idea of establishing game preserves where the animals are protected—no hunting allowed. Poaching on these preserves would bring stiffer penalties."

Godwin slapped a fist to his palm. "By Jove! Splendid! Splendid idea. The council will approve this initiative."

"How can you be so certain?"

"Because I am the magistrate, and I am head of the council."

Lyon nodded. "I get to pick my own men with no interference from the council?"

"You have my word."

"No offense, Sir Godwin, but I'll take your word in writing."

Lyon offered his hand to Margaret, an indication that it was time to make their departure. "You will have my answer in the morning."

As Lyon opened the door, Margaret stopped. She turned and announced, "No!"

Both men looked at her, astonished.

Lyon's heart sank. "Maggie, I—"

Her lips pinched slightly. She held up her hand to silence him. "Jeremiah Lyon, it is written all over your face how much you want this position. I cannot in good conscience allow you to walk away because of how you may think I feel."

She placed her hands on her hips. "Sir Godwin, my husband will accept your offer."

Lyon roared on the inside, roared with an emotion that was beyond his realm of understanding. How had he come to deserve this woman? His smile grew. "You are an extraordinary woman, sweet Maggie," he whispered in her ear.

He reached out to shake hands with the magistrate, who stood gawping like a baboon drunk on marula fruit.

"Yes, yes, of course. Join me over breakfast, and we will begin laying out the details." Godwin cast his gaze toward Margaret. "Of course, you may join us, my dear."

She looped her arm through Lyon's. "Thank you, but a woman never turns down the opportunity to shop. Afterward, I'll visit the hospital to learn what is new in the world of medicine. This is much preferred over listening to 'man talk.' "

****

Neither Lyon nor Margaret spoke until they were alone in their room. She was uncommonly tired, and needed a nap.

"Maggie."

She did not resist, reveling in the feel of his warm, rough palm against hers, making her feel so secure. He led her to their bedchamber, sat her on the edge of the bed, and knelt in front of her. "Maggie, my sweet wife, you astound me always, with your strength, your understanding. Men all over the world would wish for your character, myself included."

Tears made silent silver streaks down her cheeks.

She flung herself into his arms.

"You will come back to me. Promise!"

Lyon wrapped her in his arms and planted a soft kiss on her lips. He buried his face between her breasts and breathed in the sweetness of her womanly scent.

His every thought was focused on how much he treasured his wife. "Always."

Chapter 32

The air was misty and threatened more rain. The arrival of the new doctor and his wife had given Margaret a much-needed reprieve from giving round-the-clock care to the growing number of patients. She gathered her umbrella and crossed the courtyard, trying to avoid slipping on the muddy ground as she hastened down the path that led to the new and modern *nyumba* built to her specific design.

After brewing a pot of chai tea, she gathered her journal and went to sit under the attached *ukumbi*. The gazebo sides were open to the outside, but it had a roof to shield her from the elements, and with the installation of generators for electricity for the entire community, she had a ceiling fan to give her respite from the heat.

The minute she sat down, wracking sobs, huge and unladylike, rolled out of her. She didn't care. Lyon had been gone for five months. She missed him, and with the lack of communication, for all she knew he could be sick with malaria, mauled by a lion, eaten by a crocodile, or trampled by a herd of elephants.

She hated the thought of becoming a widow twice over. The first time had nearly killed her. She didn't know if she was strong enough to survive a second time. Worse, she didn't know if she had the strength to live without him.

She stared out into the rain. She pictured him, saw his face, and his smile. She fingered her wedding band of carved ivory. Wiping away the tears, she sipped her tea, then bent to her journal.

December, 1910

One year seems like a lifetime, and yet I marvel that it passed in the twinkle of an eye. Once a small, almost insignificant outpost tucked away in the jungle, Angel of Mercy is becoming a small metropolis. The hospital is often filled to capacity.

Doctor Myles Gregory (a former military doctor) and his wife Kay arrived from America. They are a welcomed addition to our staff. Kay is a teacher, and a brave woman. The first night in their nyumba, she encountered a cobra in the bathtub. She whacked off the creature's head with a swift stroke of her husband's épeé. In fact, she hit it so hard that she chipped the tub's porcelain. Good-o for her.

I am proud that Lyon accepted the position as Commissioner of Animal Conservation, and even more proud that M'pika is his second in command and Y'ro is helping with the recruiting and training of the new game wardens. It pains me that Lyon has been away for all these months surveying the vast territorial boundaries. It will soon be Christmas, and though holidays of any kind are foreign to him, I yearn to celebrate a little of the Yuletide cheer, and to share a special gift with him.

She loved Lyon. Loved him with an intensity that she had never felt for Seamus. She mused, wondering if her silly sisters held the same affection for their stilted, aristocratic popinjays. A moment of nostalgia swept over her.

She looked out at the rain, which was now thundering down with enough force to strike fear in the hearts of the bravest souls. Lightning struck close enough to prickle the hairs on her arms.

She pushed from her chair to seek the safety of her home's interior. A movement caught her eye. She ambled to the railing. Who would be foolish enough to traverse such a downpour, unless it was a dire emergency?

She leaned out, squinting to see through the gray wall of precipitation.

They appeared like three ghosts. Heads down, they slogged through the deluge.

"Surely not—" She swallowed, focusing her attention on the stick-like figures.

"Lyon," she gasped. She grabbed the umbrella and raced down the steps. "Lyon!" she shouted through the torrential din.

He handed over his rifle, shrugged out of his backpack, opened his arms, and swept her up, with a spoken command to M'pika and Y'ro: "Take care of my gear."

She blinked to clear her eyes as she greeted the two smiling men. "*Nyumbas*, there and there"—she pointed—"are for you."

They nodded and trotted toward the small houses.

She ordered Lyon to put her down. "You can run faster without me in your arms."

And they did.

Once inside their own home, she led him to the washroom and turned on the tap of hot water. She ordered him to undress.

She stared at him as if he were an apparition, a

262

figment of her imagination. He was pale and gaunt and had to lean against the wall for support, but he looked perfect to her.

She unbuttoned his shirt, his belt, and helped strip the sodden clothes from his shivering body. She ordered him into the tub of hot water. It wouldn't do for him to catch pneumonia, or suffer a bout of malaria, or—God forbid—both at the same time.

"I missed you," he said hoarsely.

"Shh, let's get you warmed up and into bed. Then we can talk."

His mouth curved as if he felt like smiling and wasn't sure he could. He exhaled a weary breath. "It isn't talk that's on my mind."

Suddenly she wanted him in bed. She wanted to press her head against his broad chest. She wanted to wrap her arms tightly around his lean waist. She wanted his warmth all around her, his arms holding her close.

He rose from the tub, his manhood jutting forward, throbbing.

She brushed her lips over his, feeling his breath tickle her cheek, feeling the reward of his tremors.

She brusquely dried him off with a towel, led him to the bed, and pulled back the duvet. His trembling hands fumbled with unbuttoning her blouse and pulling it from her skirt. She murmured, "Let me."

She stepped out of her clothing and tossed it to a chair.

When he pulled her down beside him, she fell without protest, feeling his hard arousal against her hip.

He was like a man who had been starved and was now more than ready to indulge his appetite. Her legs parted, giving him access to the soft folds of her womanhood. Wild with need, he buried himself in her in one full thrust, and she gave him more of herself than she'd ever thought possible.

He collapsed on his side, breathing hard. Margaret lay still and quiet in his arms. When he had recovered, he lifted on his elbow and gazed down at her, only to find tears trickling down her cheeks.

"Are you all right? Did I hurt you?"

Gulping back a sob, she nodded. "I-I'm fine, Jeremiah, just very, very happy, and grateful you're home."

"As am I." He kissed away the tears.

He trailed a finger down her throat, between her breasts, and settled his palm over the little mound of her belly. His forehead furrowed into a concerned frown.

"Are you ill, Maggie? I've seen women with tumors the size of melons. They always die. We'll go to England. We'll get you the best medical attention money can buy." He choked as he pulled her into his arms and squeezed her tight.

She tried not to laugh as she pushed from his grip to lie back. She shushed him as she took his hand and guided it back to her stomach. "Shh. Be still and wait."

His eyes widened in astonished wonderment. He stared at her for a brief moment, then grabbed her hands and held them tightly. "Are you—Maggie? Are you with child?"

She laughed. "Merry Christmas. In the spring, I will have another Lyon to tame."

"It's the best gift you could ever give me." He gathered her into his arms and kissed her soundly.

She rested her head against his chest, and knew from the soft puttering of his breath that he'd relinquished himself to exhaustion.

She sighed a smile as she placed her hand on the growing mound and felt the movement of the new life nestled within.

The rain had stopped.

A lion's roar lifted on the wind, and another answered.

This was Africa.

This was home.

Loretta C. Rogers

Glossary of African Words and Translations

Swahili / English
Asante / thank you
Asante sana / thank you very much
Baba / father
Biltong / jerky
Bwana / a term of respect, e.g., brother, boss, master
Chapati / flat bread
Harakisha / hurry up
Hii ni nzuri / This is good.
Jambo / greetings, hello
Juju / medicine
Kuju sasa / come now
Mganga / healer
Marula fruit / a small round fruit that ferments when dried, causing the animals that eat it to get drunk
Mududu / worm
Mutana bawa / a greeting of respect
Muungu / an African god
mzunga / white man's church
Ndeithia / the cry for help
Ndiyo / yes
N'Devli / the devil; satan
Nyumba / house
Rifiki / friend
Sangoma / shaman, witch doctor
Shimbeck / large canoe
Shuka [Maasai] / wedding cloth
Simba / lion
Sumu / poison
Timbo / elephant
Timbo kubwa / How big is the elephant?

Totos / Young or old one who enters servitude
Towasi / eunuch; castrated male
Ukumbi / porch or gazebo
Wajinga / ignorant
Yesu / Jesus

Discussion Questions
for *Taming the Lyon*
a Fiction Romance Novel

1. What was unique about the setting of the book, and how did it enhance or take away from the story?

2. How authentic was the culture or era represented in this book?

3. How does the setting figure as a character in the story?

4. What did you think of the plot line development? How credible did the author make it?

5. What specific themes did the author emphasize throughout the novel? What do you think he or she is trying to get across to the reader?

6. Do the characters seem real and believable to the reader? Can you relate to their predicaments? To what extent do they remind you of yourself or someone you know?

7. What moral/ethical choices did the characters have to make? What do you think of those choices? How would you have chosen?

8. Are the character's actions a result of freedom of choice, or of destiny?

9. How do the characters change or evolve throughout the course of the story? What events trigger such change?

10. What effects do events, time, nationality,

physicality have on the character's self or personality?

11. In what ways do the events in the book reveal evidence of the author's world view?

12. Did certain parts of the book make you feel uncomfortable? If so, why did you feel that way? Did this lead to a new awareness or understanding of some aspect of your life that you had not thought about before?

13. Did you like the book? If you have read any of the author's other books, how does this book compare?

14. What is the book's message?

15. How did you feel about the characters? Whom did you like or not like and why?

16. In a movie version, who would play the hero, the heroine, and major secondary characters?

17. How did you feel when the characters did or said…?

18. How do you think the character felt when she/he said…?

19. Are there any symbols that may have cultural, political, or religious reference?

20. What type of vision does the author use in word choices? Is it optimistic, pessimistic, prophetic, cautionary, humorous, satirical, venomous, cathartic?

21. What did you think of the ending?

Book clubs have been such great champions for my novels. Thank you for reading *TAMING THE LYON*.

Asanta sana,
Loretta C. Rogers

A word about the author…

Romance with a Twist…Expect the Unexpected is the promise award-winning author Loretta C. Rogers gives to readers. Once an avid horsewoman, she now travels with her husband on their motorcycle.

She enjoys hearing from readers and encourages them to contact her at:

Author, Loretta C. Rogers | Facebook

https://www.facebook.com/Author-Loretta-C-Rogers

www.ingramcontent.com/pod-product-compliance
Lightning Source LLC
Chambersburg PA
CBHW071234260626
47161CB00003BA/780